W9-AAV-532

THE
TENDERNESS
OF
THIEVES

DONNA FREITAS

PHILOMEL BOOKS
An Imprint of Penguin Group (USA)

PHILOMEL BOOKS
Published by the Penguin Group | Penguin Group (USA) LLC
375 Hudson Street, New York, NY 10014

USA | Canada | UK | Ireland | Australia | New Zealand | India | South Africa | China
penguin.com
A Penguin Random House Company

Copyright © 2015 by Donna Freitas.
Penguin supports copyright. Copyright fuels creativity, encourages diverse voices, promotes
free speech, and creates a vibrant culture. Thank you for buying an authorized edition of this
book and for complying with copyright laws by not reproducing, scanning, or distributing
any part of it in any form without permission. You are supporting writers and allowing
Penguin to continue to publish books for every reader.

Library of Congress Cataloging-in-Publication Data
Freitas, Donna.   The tenderness of thieves / Donna Freitas.   pages cm
Summary: After witnessing a robbery which ended with the death of her father,
seventeen-year-old Jane Calvetti falls in love with town bad boy Handel Davies.
[1. Love—Fiction. 2. Criminal investigation—Fiction.] I. Title.
PZ7.F8844Te 2015
[Fic]—dc23
2014017359

Printed in the United States of America.
ISBN 978-0-399-17136-9

10 9 8 7 6 5 4 3 2 1

Edited by Jill Santopolo.   Design by Semadar Megged.
Text set in 12-point Bembo Book MT Std.

To Carlene Bauer,
who convinced me I should keep writing.
For this, for giving me courage, and for so many other reasons.

The blade pressed into the tender skin of my throat.

I held still, frozen in fear, but frozen, too, because I knew even the slightest movement would send the knife cutting deep into my neck. My captor held it there, steady, standing behind me, his body against my back. I couldn't see him, not his face or really anything else, nothing except for the tip of the heavy-soled boot he wore on his right foot. There was a band of metal along the toe, and it was caked with dirty snow and ice.

"Please," I whispered to him. "Let me go."

But he ignored me—at least at first. The man—maybe he was older, maybe he was younger than I'd originally thought—was barking orders at the others, his ugly voice rising above the din of chairs being smashed to splinters and books tumbling to the floor.

The snow was coming down harder now, the view out the window so peaceful, like the picture on a postcard for some winter wonderland, and so utterly unlike the situation inside the house.

My situation.

A vase shattered, the noise high and startling, and I jumped.

I couldn't help it.

I was lucky, though—well, as lucky as a girl can be when there's a knife at her throat—because I was spared. The blade didn't sink into my skin, not right then, but it provoked another response, one that sent me to the edge of something I feared even more.

My captor turned to me again, chuckling. "What's that?" he whispered in my ear, his breath hot, his tone mocking. There was a faint smell coming off him. Sweetness and rot. Sweetness covering the rot. Cologne masking fish. "Is there something else you need from me?"

I tried not to flinch.

He started fumbling around, I wasn't sure with what, maybe his glove, but then I realized it was my sweater, his hand searching for the hem, trying to reach up under it. I thought I might die, that now was the time to scream, to end this before the worst could happen, when one of the others called out something—I didn't quite catch what, but it sounded like a question—a question for him.

A distraction from me.

Before he answered, he whispered one more thing. "Now be a good girl," he said. "And nothing bad will happen."

But of course, the bad was already here, wasn't it?

My captor didn't let go, kept the knife tight at my neck, but his other hand was now occupied elsewhere, gesturing at the various things they should take. He shifted—just a little—and the knife sliced the chain of my necklace in two. The tiny mosaic heart slid softly down my chest, all the way to the floor with a soft *chink*. I closed my eyes, wishing I could melt away like the snowflakes hitting the warm glass of the window, all that delicacy transformed into something so elemental, so basic, but most important, so difficult to hold on to.

ONE

IT WAS A DAY LIKE ANY other when he first spoke to me.

That boy.

The one who would change everything I thought about life and love and right and wrong.

The one *I* would change.

At the time it didn't seem so out of the ordinary. It even seemed right: the good girl who gets to go out with the bad boy. Everyone knows that story. It was mid-June, and summer had just started. We were fairly rich with boys by then—me and my girls. They were always crowding around us at school, teasing, talking, inviting us to go somewhere in their cars, trying to kiss us in the rain. It was almost like we deserved it, *I* deserved it, after a winter that threatened to shatter everything I knew, everything I was and am. I was holding things together as best I could, leaning into my new visibility like it might prop me up. But it's dangerous when we let the boys fix the broken parts within us. It makes us vulnerable. It scars us for life.

"Jane," he said, just like that, like we'd already been introduced, like he knew me and I knew him.

And we did, sort of.

I was walking by, strutting really. I was happy the school year had ended, relieved to be on the other side of those four walls, walls that used to feel like a welcome shelter but lately felt like a prison. The air was hot and humid, the signs of a heat wave on its way. I wore a string bikini, not ostentatious, not bright pink or dotted with flowers or a shiny silver, but a dark plain blue. Then again, when is wearing a string bikini not ostentatious? A beach towel was draped over my right arm, lush green, so when I set it down on the sand it was like lying on a patch of grass.

He laughed. "Jane."

My name a second time.

I stopped and turned. Looked at him. The ocean breeze whispered across my bare skin.

"Handel," I said as though I knew him, too, his strange black eyes holding me there. I'd seen him before at school. He played hockey. Graduated last year. Worked on the docks. The bad boy all the girls whispered about. Lusted after. Not me, though. Not until that very moment, my name poised on his lips. "See you around," I said then, my skin hot, flushed, tingling.

"See you," he said as I walked away, hips swaying, the ties of my bathing suit bouncing against the tops of my legs and back.

"Hi, ladies," I said, Cheshire cat grin on my face, just five minutes later.

Tammy, long blond hair to her waist, turned to me, the ends of it swinging over her left shoulder. "Ooh, Jane has something to report!" Her big eyes were wide.

Tammy, short for Tamra, was the daughter of Russian immigrants, the bossy one among us, bossy and loyal. The boys loved her but didn't quite know how to make their approach. She could be intimidating if you didn't know her well.

I plopped down on Tammy's towel, wedging myself between her and Bridget, another of my girls, the sweet one, the one the boys fawned over easily and who would kiss anybody. She was lathering sunblock all over her fair Irish skin. The smell of cocoa butter and summer wafted everywhere.

"I do have a story," I said. "But it's a short one."

Bridget handed me the lotion. "I'll take any distraction from this heat. Since when does it reach ninety in June?"

"Don't be so melodramatic, B." This from Michaela, lifting the sunglasses from her eyes a bit and her head from the rolled-up T-shirt underneath it. Her knees pointed toward the hazy blue sky, her body parallel to us. Michaela was the down-to-earth one, practical to her very center. Always the mediator. Protective. "It's not that bad out today."

"Spoken like an Irish who got her Italian mother's skin," Bridget said to Michaela, rubbing sunblock into places she'd just put it a minute ago.

Our New England town was a regular melting pot of immigrant families. I came in on the Italian side. One hundred percent. There were the fishermen and their sons, passing along the livelihood to the next generation, and the neighbors, nosy with their gossip, sunning themselves on front porches, looking out toward the wharf. There were summer residents, too. The folks who came year after year, renting the same house, dragging the same chairs and umbrellas down to the sand and their favorite spots. But mostly it was just us, the year-rounders, long ago in love with the beach even when it was raining or blurred by snow, streaked with the kind of cold that runs through you like a ghost; a place so remote that the paraphernalia of the now was useless and we liked it that way. The summer was sacred to all of us.

"Can we focus, please?" Tammy demanded. "Distract us, Jane."

I stood. Took my time setting up my towel, dropped my bag at one end of it and a single flip-flop on each corner at the other. Enjoying the suspense, I put my sunglasses on, propped myself up on my elbows, and, finally, said his name. "Handel Davies."

It was all that needed saying.

Bridget squealed. "No way."

I nodded. My grin reappeared.

"Well?" from Tammy, still impatient for more information.

Michaela didn't react. Not at all.

"I was walking down the beach to meet up with my girls," I said, savoring the words as they came out of my mouth like they were candy. Looked at each one of them individually, Tammy, Bridget, Michaela. "I didn't even see him there, not at first. Then I heard my name. I heard him say, 'Jane.'"

"Handel Davies knows your name?!" Bridget's tone was all exclamation points and question marks. That's how she always spoke.

"I know," I said. "Crazy, right?"

"I have dreams about that boy." Her voice turned woozy.

"Keep them to yourself, please," Michaela said. Michaela had dated a lot of boys, but none of them seriously, or not that we knew. She didn't kiss and tell like Tammy and Bridget. Tammy and Bridget were always bubbling over with the details if they'd made out with someone in the janitor's closet during American History (Bridget) or while skinny-dipping the first day of June (Tammy) or in the back of a truck in the school parking lot during free period (Bridget again). I, on the other hand, didn't have details to share. Not lately at least.

Tammy was watching me. "And then?"

"I bet I'll have dreams about Handel tonight," I said, looking at Bridget, appreciative of her Handel appreciation, unwilling to let Tammy rush this. Then to everyone, "So I hear my name once, twice, then I stop and turn to see who it is, and there he is." Bridget cupped her mouth with her hand to stop from squealing again. Tammy's eyes were glued to my face. Michaela was silent. I couldn't read her. "He's looking at me like he knows me, like we've known each other forever. Like we share a secret," I added, at first for dramatic effect, but then, I realized, because it was true. I'd felt it in his stare. "And I say back to him, 'Handel,' just like that, all even toned, like we really do know each other, like, *of course* he knows my name."

"Good for you," Tammy said, proud of my cool in the face of gorgeous and bad and boy. Tammy probably would have glared at him without saying anything, but the rest of us lack that level of restraint.

Now it was Bridget's turn to push. "And *then* what?"

"Then nothing. Then I walked away. Walked here."

"Smart," Tammy said.

Michaela watched me, unsmiling.

Bridget was outraged. "Jane! That's *it*?"

If it had been Bridget, not me, she would have sat down next to Handel, sat down in his lap if he'd let her, and chatted for an hour. "I told you it was a short story, B," I said. "You said you didn't mind."

Michaela finally spoke. "I don't like it. There are so many other boys you could pick. But *him*?"

"Don't mother her," Tammy said. Ironic, since Michaela's not the bossy one.

Michaela got her defenses ready. Looked at Tammy, then Bridget. "Handel hangs out with the Quinn brothers. And the Sweeneys. He's a Davies, for Christ's sake." She turned her attention directly on me after naming the most infamous three families in our town. "Jane, he's bad news."

But Bridget's eyes were still dreamy. "Isn't that why they call them bad boys?"

"Spoken like a cop's daughter," I said to Michaela with a laugh, trying to cover the unease suddenly threatening like a rain cloud.

"Takes one to know one," she shot back.

I bristled. Retreated.

I don't talk about my father.

Michaela recognized her mistake. Looked like she wanted to disappear.

"Nothing happened, M," I told her. "Handel and I barely acknowledged each other. Besides, he doesn't seem anything like his brothers."

"You don't know that, and you really don't need any more drama," Michaela said quietly. "Not after everything."

Even in the hot sun, my blood turned to ice.

She had to go and push things.

"Michaela!" Tammy snapped.

Bridget reached for my hand, squeezed it. "How *are* you lately about . . . *that*?" she asked in a whisper.

Carefully, so as not to hurt Bridget for the kind gesture, I slipped my hand from hers and lay back on my towel, body flat against all that green, hoping the sun would burn away the feeling creeping over me with Michaela's reminder. I was silent a long time, while my friends held their breath.

"Fine," I said eventually, expelling mine with this lie. "Absolutely fine."

"Mom? You home?" I called out later on.

No response. The house was silent. She was still at the beach.

The old floorboards creaked with every step, and I left a faint trail of sand behind me. A fine layer of it covered the floor of every one of our four tiny rooms, with thicker lines along the edges. Feeling the rough grains underfoot was a sign of summer, so it was something Mom and I welcomed rather than tried to sweep away.

I dropped my beach bag onto the beat-up seaweed-green couch in the living room and headed another three feet into the kitchen to pour myself some water. Our house was cramped, the kitchen open to the living room with everything else jutting out like four short legs. My mother's bedroom, my room, the sewing room where my mother worked, and the screened-in porch. I'd just settled in with a novel, feet on the coffee table, when I heard someone coming up the front steps.

Seamus McCormick was peering through the open window next to the door, his hand over his eyes like a visor, blocking out the sun. We were the same year in school, and we saw each other constantly in classes because we were both in the honors program. Seamus was a devoted admirer of me and my girlfriends even before we showed up on the radar of the other boys. We'd always loved him for it.

"Seamus, what on earth are you doing?" I cried out when I saw his face through the screen. "I could be naked!" I laughed. "Or, worse, my mother could be!"

"Hey, Jane—"

"Why can't you knock like a normal person? Are you planning on stealing something?" I went on, teasing him, but as soon as my words were out, I regretted them. I'd hit right smack in the center of the place where I'd been hurting. Pushed my finger into my own wound and opened it up in front of Seamus.

He started, horrified at the accusation, at the association I'd just made, and with him of all people. "Sorry, Jane, really sorry. I was just trying to see if someone was home. I didn't mean to scare you. I would never."

I took a deep breath, pushed the pain off to the side. "No, of course not. I'm the one who should be sorry. Now that you've seen me, come on in, all right?"

The screen door groaned as it opened. Soon Seamus was standing there, all tall and lanky, watching me with those shy blue eyes of his, the freckles on his face and arms trying to hide the flush staining his skin. Hands in his jeans pockets, Seamus shook the hair away from his face.

I patted the space next to me. "Sit down."

The couch cushions sagged with his weight, and I felt myself lift a little, like we were on a seesaw. Seamus stared straight ahead at the wood-paneled wall. "I didn't see you and your friends at the beach today."

"You didn't look hard enough." I stared at Seamus while he watched the wall like it was showing a movie. "We were there."

"Michaela?"

"Yup."

"Bridget?"

"Yes."

A pause. A breath. Then, "Tammy, too?"

I patted his knee. "Of course."

He didn't say a word, but he didn't have to.

"She's not with Devin anymore," I said. Devin was Tammy's fellow skinny-dipper. The basketball player she'd dated off and on during the winter and spring, then decided she was bored with the last week of school. "Are you ever going to ask Tammy out?"

"Why would you want to know that?"

"Okay, fine," I said. "Don't talk to me about it."

Seamus's knee was bobbing up and down like the needle on my mother's sewing machine. "I tell you everything, Jane." The note of accusation in his voice was faint, but I'd heard it, clear. Seamus told me his secrets, but I didn't tell him all of mine.

"I don't think so," I said.

"I do, you know. And if I needed to confess something about Tammy, I would. But I've got nothing for you."

I smirked. "When you're ready, I'm here." I sang those words to him, trying to make everything light and sunny.

Seamus turned to me then, with those shy-boy eyes. Deadly serious. "Same goes for you, Jane. I mean it."

Words piled up in my throat, but none of them made it out of my mouth. Seamus and I sat there, silent, our unspoken questions flitting around the room like anxious moths. The sounds of the neighborhood boys playing street hockey sifted through the screens, filling the empty air.

"I gotta go," Seamus said eventually, when it was clear I wasn't talking. He got up and hovered in the doorway about to head out, giving me one last wide-eyed look, one more look that said *you can trust me, Jane,* before he was gone.

But I couldn't trust anyone. Not anymore.

TWO

HIYA, MRS. LEVINSON," I said, and began emptying my basket at the register in Levinson's, the corner grocery closest to my house, just a half block up from the wharf. It was right before lunchtime on our second official day of summer, and it was hot—hotter even than yesterday. The soft bump of boats against the dock played a faint and steady sound track. Lettuce. Thump. Onions. Thump. Potatoes. Thump.

"Hello, Jane, sweetheart," she replied. Mrs. Levinson called everybody "sweetheart." "Roasting a chicken in this hot weather, are you?"

"I was thinking about it, you know, for the leftovers." I glanced at the plastic-wrapped plucked and skinned bird sweating on the counter. "Maybe it's not such a good idea after all."

Mrs. Levinson eyed my items. "The heat from the oven is going to turn your house into a sauna." She picked the chicken up and set it to the side. "Larry! You got any of those roasters left from the bridal luncheon?" Silence. "Larry, you hear me?"

"Gimme a minute," he yelled from the storeroom in the gravelly voice of a man who'd spent the majority of his life smoking cigarettes.

"You don't have to do that—" I began.

Mrs. Levinson shushed me. "It's not a problem, sweetheart. I'll be right back." She ambled off, everything about her rustling.

The only sound left after a while was the talk in Russian coming from the radio she kept on the counter.

The bell over the door jangled as it swung open and shut, and my heart swooped and dipped. Handel Davies walked in and made an immediate left down the first aisle. Talk between the Levinsons floated out of the storeroom and mingled with the Russian words swirling around up front. The potatoes and onions I'd set next to the register were staring at me. My entire body had gone still, as though it were waiting for something to happen. Goose bumps covered my bare arms and legs, and I longed for something more substantial than a tiny sundress to hide my skin. A shiver traveled up my spine, and my body shook off the unease creeping over it.

Footsteps behind me—slow, sure—tapped their way from the wall-sized fridge holding milk and yogurt and soda at the back of the store. I wished for Mrs. Levinson's reappearance, or maybe I wished it away.

There was the faintest sound of breathing.

"Jane," Handel said with that laugh of his.

My name from his mouth a third time.

I turned a little, but only just. Enough so there was the sway of long dark hair and the display of my profile. "I saw you come in," I said.

Bold, I know.

Handel stepped to the side so he could better see my face. "I saw you, too."

I looked at him, all six feet of him, Irish skin and blond hair, thick and long. His eyes, too dark on someone with such fair coloring. I smiled then, just a small one. Didn't say anything, though.

There came the sound of rustling again. Mrs. Levinson ambling along, returning to the register to break the strange spell that had fallen over the front of her store, and with a roast chicken of all things. "Here you go, sweetheart," she was saying, the tip of the kerchief tied over her hair flapping with every step. "Saves you the trouble of cooking it yourself, all right?" The chicken thunked onto the counter. "It's too hot today."

"Thanks, Mrs. Levinson. Really, thanks so much," I said. She rang everything up. Money exchanged hands. A bag was passed over the counter, and I took it. In a flash I was saying, "See you later," about to head out the door, a quick "Bye," to Handel, like it wasn't a big deal we'd been exchanging words when of course it was.

Before the door closed behind me, I caught another few of those Handel words.

"A pack of Marlboros, Mrs. Levinson."

I set the bag of groceries on a bench outside and found a ponytail holder to tie up my hair. Get it off my neck.

Was I stalling? Waiting?

Maybe.

Fishermen congregated on the docks, taking a break, some of the Sweeney boys among them. Old Mr. O'Connell and his sons. The smell of salt and seaweed and ocean pressed into the heat, pressed into all of us. We were tender with the newness of summer. Raw.

Mr. O'Connell put up his hand in a wave.

I waved back. Slipped the bag over my arm again.

"You headed home?" Handel appeared next to me, cigarette dangling from his lips. He took it out of his mouth, and a stream of smoke followed.

"How can you smoke in this weather?" I asked.

"Habit." He took another drag. "I'll walk you partway."

I nodded toward the docks. "You don't have to work?"

"They'll live without me awhile."

"All right," I agreed, and suddenly there I was, walking down the street, Handel Davies at my side, like he already knew where I lived and maybe he did. We passed the neighborhood gossips sitting on their front stoops along the way. Old Irish ladies and old Italian ladies. Old Eastern European ladies, too. Their mouths grew hushed as they watched us go by. Then they went to work again afterward. Clocked some overtime.

There's Jane Calvetti with the youngest Davies boy, I heard one of them say. *I thought she was going out with that nice Seamus McCormick. The smart one.* People were always guessing I was dating Seamus, but they were always wrong. *That Davies family is bad news. Always in trouble.*

"Is that your dinner?" Handel asked after a long silence, still puffing on his cigarette. He nodded at the bag in my hand.

"It is," I said, blinking in the bright light. Tossed my ponytail.

"For your family?"

"My mom and me," I said. "Just my mom and me," I added.

A pause. Then, "Yeah, I read about that."

"Yeah, I bet," I said. It was in all the papers.

Another long pause.

"I should probably get back," Handel said next.

What he didn't say was *sorry about your father,* and this was a relief.

I stopped—we both did. We'd gone five blocks, and I only had another two left. Handel had walked me more than partway. "Okay. See you around," I said without ceremony. Tried not to stare at him but failed. I suddenly wanted to get up on my toes, lean closer, and kiss Handel's lips. It was the way he watched me that made me want this, I think.

Handel took another drag of that cigarette. Those black eyes of his holding me there for the second time in my life. So many firsts, seconds, and thirds for Handel and me in such a short period of time.

Then, a question from Handel. "Can I see you tomorrow? On purpose?"

"Okay," I said. Bit back a smile. "Yes."

He watched my face. Smiled a little, too. "I'll come by your house."

Something in me resisted this. "I could meet you at the docks."

"I'd rather pick you up."

I laughed, nervous. "All right. If you insist. My house is—"

"I know where your house is."

"You do," I stated. Somehow I'd already known this. Accepted it without question or concern.

He nodded. "Eight?"

"Eight."

"See you tomorrow, Jane," Handel said.

My name a fourth time.

I would have to stop counting soon. Not yet, though.

"See you tomorrow, Handel," I said.

Then he was turning and walking back the way he came, and I was continuing on the way we'd been going, my mind a whirl.

Tammy and Bridget were going to die.

I had a *date* with Handel Davies.

Michaela, well, she was going to disapprove.

But I didn't care.

Ever since that night in February, I'd wanted my luck to change, and my luck was going to change with Handel Davies. I knew it would be with him. I knew even then. I just didn't know how, and at the time, it didn't cross my mind that sometimes luck could be bad.

THREE

There came a loud knock on the door.

I startled awake, my novel draped across my stomach.

"Jane?" my mother was calling out. "Can you get that? I'm at the machine."

"Sure, Mom." I set the novel on the wobbly metal coffee table, facedown to keep my place, and got up. Mrs. McIntyre watched me from the other side of the screen, a big brown leather purse clutched to her side like someone might run up and steal it. Then again, in our neighborhood, someone might.

"Hi, Jane, dear," she said in a strong Irish brogue. "I've got an appointment with your mum. Sara's wedding's coming up in no time."

"Hi, Mrs. M.," I said, letting her in. "When's the date?"

"The last weekend in July," she sighed. "The twenty-ninth. We're tearing our hair out with the arrangements."

"I'm sure. Hang on a sec, and I'll tell my mother you're here."

"Thanks, dear." She took a seat on our beat-up couch, purse still clutched tight.

I poked my head into the sewing room. Hot-pink satin was speeding through my mother's old Singer—she swore the antique machines worked better than the electric ones—her bun sticking into the air as she bent over her work. "Mom?"

Everything came to a stop.

My mother took the pins from her mouth. "Tell her I'll be just five more minutes, would you, please?"

"Sure."

The corners of her brown eyes crinkled. "Come give your old ma a hug."

"You're not old," I protested, and went to her.

She found me from beneath the yards of satin and drew me into a sea of pink. "I love you, you know."

"I do know," I said, wanting to stay in her arms and leave at the same time. Eventually I pulled back. "Finish up so you don't keep Mrs. M. waiting. She seems stressed."

My mother rolled her eyes. "She's always stressed. It's not just the wedding. The stress runs in her veins."

I laughed. Gave my mother a quick peck on the forehead just before she got that pedal going again, the needle moving up and down so quick it was a blur.

"Stop your fidgeting," my mother was saying a while later.

"What?" I'd been daydreaming about Handel. Lost in my head. It was so good to be lost in wishful thinking, in romantic possibility. It pushed away the bad, the dark, the fear that's had me lost ever since winter, alone in a tiny, rickety boat in the middle of the sea.

My mother shifted the heavy, ruffled train of Sara McIntyre's wedding dress, and I could feel its strong tug on my lower back.

Sometimes my job in the dressmaking business is to be the mannequin of the house. Today it definitely was. Mrs. McIntyre needed to get an idea of how her daughter's wedding dress was coming along, and I was to help her with the vision. Mrs. McIntyre seemed happy, with all that *ooh*ing and *aah*ing, but I thought the dress was hideous. Spangles and sequins and pearls everywhere and enough ruffles for a princess. I kept silent, of course, since this meant my mother was going to make a mint with the kind of work it took to sew all that beading. I knew my mother wouldn't be offended, either, if I gave her my opinion later. *I just make what the customer wants, not what I think is pretty,* she'd say.

My mother shifted the train a little more to the left. "If you keep moving, Jane, I'm never going to get this right and we'll be here all afternoon."

"Sorry," I said, and tried to stand still.

"Well now," Mrs. McIntyre said. There was a hidden smile in her voice. "We wouldn't want that! Jane's doing me a favor, standing in for my Sara while she's away." She glanced up at me, then again at my mother. She smirked. "Did your daughter tell you? She's been taking walks through town with Handel Davies."

My skin burned at this, bright against the bleeding white of the dress.

"Is that right, Jane?" my mother said absently, but I could tell she was interested.

"We were just talking. And it was just one walk." God, I hated this neighborhood sometimes. People talked too much, and unfortunately a lot of this talk went on while my mother was pinning up fabric and pinning on fabric and the ladies she was pinning it up and onto were yapping about every damn thing that happened around here, gossip-worthy or not.

Mrs. McIntyre looked at me, and I knew she wasn't seeing her daughter's wedding dress now. "That Davies boy runs with a rough crowd."

Whether she was informing my mother or me of this was unclear. Like I didn't know this already. Like *everyone* didn't know this already.

"All right," my mother said, unperturbed. There was the short rip of a zipper. "This gown is all set for today."

I wanted to kiss her. "Can I go, then?"

"Yes, but you need to change first," she said.

"Obviously." I lifted up the giant skirt and gathered the train over one arm. Did my best to fit through the narrow doorway and cross the hall to my room without tripping and killing myself. I stepped out of the dress, trying not to shift any of the pins. Hushed conversation floated through the house from the sewing room as I slipped a tank top over my head and shimmied on a pair of jean shorts. Heaping the gown into my arms, I tiptoed back to my mother and Mrs. McIntyre, trying to catch them mid-gossip.

"—there hasn't been another one since," Mrs. McIntyre was saying.

I halted just outside the sewing room. Listened. Watched them through the crack in the open door.

My mother shifted in her sewing chair. "I just never thought—I couldn't have imagined my daughter caught in the middle of something like that. And her father . . ."

"How are *you* feeling, dear? What a loss. And poor Jane."

"Oh, you know. It's hard," my mother said. "I wish they'd catch whoever did it."

My breath caught, a tiny, sharp intake. A dart to my throat.

Sometimes I wished the police would catch who did *it*, but honestly, sometimes I wished everyone would forget all about *it*.

That I would forget, too. If they caught the *who,* then *it* would become real again. I would have to relive *it.*

Mrs. McIntyre was tsk-tsking. "All those robberies and nobody home and then . . . what are the chances Jane would get caught in the middle of all that? What if she's still in danger? Aren't you just terrified for her?"

The wedding dress turned into a sack of stones. It threatened to sink me. I didn't want to hear any more about danger and break-ins, about *my* break-in, as I'd come to think about it. I wasn't sure what was worse: gossip about Handel Davies and me, or the town tragedy, which was also *my* tragedy; ours, I guess, if you counted the fact that my mother used to be married, once, to my dad. I nudged the sewing room door open with my knee. The hinges creaked; the gossip stopped. Worried eyes, guilty eyes turned on me. I held up the gown in my shaky arms. "What should I do with this?"

My mother blinked. "Let me take that."

I gave it to her, gently, carefully. If only all the weight in my life could be shifted to someone else this simply, this literally.

"Oh, it's really lovely, Molly," Mrs. McIntyre said, sounding relieved to go back to the real reason she'd come to my house, speaking my mother's nickname, Molly, short for Amalia, like an Irish song from her mouth. She took some of the fabric into her hands and leaned close, inspecting the beading. "What gorgeous work. Sara is going to look beautiful on her wedding day."

"I'm off to see the girls at Slovenska's," I said to my mother.

"Bye, Jane," she said with raised eyebrows.

She was waiting to see what I'd heard. Checking to see if I was okay.

I nodded, one slight bob of my head.

Then, after a quick peck on her cheek, I headed out, just in time to hear Mrs. McIntyre whisper, "She's such a lovely girl, Molly, but her eyes—they're so sad."

The screen door shut with a loud bang as I left the house, left my mother and Mrs. McIntyre to continue their gossip. Their words, though, trailed behind me as I walked, like the tail of a kite or the train of that ugly wedding dress. Pulling on me. Holding me down.

February 19

The night of the break-in I'd been out working, later than usual.

Before everything happened, I house-sat for some of the wealthier folks in town. Took care of the dog or the cat when they were away. Watered the plants. Whatever they needed. I had no reason to worry about the darkness, not back then. Life was safe and secure, and everyone seemed like a potential friend, even the people I didn't know very well. Or at all.

This time, I'd been house-sitting for a professor and his doctor wife. The O'Connors. They were an older couple, one of my regular customers. They'd always been nice to me, the professor in particular. He knew I was college-bound, which was unusual for a town like ours, and that I studied hard and nearly always had my nose in a book. We'd talk about my latest read when we exchanged keys or met up for him to pass me a check.

Their place was big, mansion-like really, with its three stories and tall columns that stretched across the porch. They lived in the nicest neighborhood in town, where all the houses had that majestic look, sturdy and graceful, with manicured lawns and tasteful architecture and New England charm.

It was cold and rainy that day, and dark by half past five. The snow was melting, little piles of it like icebergs scattered across the lawn and dotting the tops of the bushes. Occasionally I glanced out the window from the third-floor reading nook of the professor's library, watched the harbor far off in the distance, bleak and gray and lonely as the fishermen shut down for the night and headed off to the bars, the light bleeding from the sky. Sometimes I stayed there for hours, lost in one of the leather-bound novels the professor kept on the shelf by his desk. The O'Connors didn't mind if I spent time there. The professor usually left out a stack of books for me with a sticky note attached to the one on top that would say something like FOR JANE CALVETTI'S PERUSAL AND EDIFICATION.

It always made me smile.

"Have a good time," I'd said to Professor O'Connor as he and his wife were heading off on their winter vacation that same day. Their bags were packed, and they'd left their keys on the kitchen counter, right alongside the to-do list and instructions they'd written up for me. It was only six, but a single lamp by the fridge provided the only light in the grand, ghostly space.

Professor O'Connor glanced at the list, checking its contents. "If you need anything, don't hesitate to call us. All our numbers are right here."

"Don't worry. Everything will be fine," I said to him.

"I left you some novels upstairs," he said. "There's one in particular I think you'll like. It's on top."

I looked up at his weathered face. I smiled. "Thank you."

He rapped his knuckles on the counter. "Not a minute past nine p.m. this week, Miss Jane," he said in his best fatherly-sounding voice, returning the smile. "You need your rest."

"Yes," said Dr. O'Connor, his wife. "I don't want your mother at home worried about you being here."

"Absolutely," I agreed. "Not even a minute."

They hovered. Checked a few more things before they said their good-byes, and I locked the door behind them. Their footsteps echoed on the front walk, first loud, then more distant, until they disappeared altogether and I was alone in the house.

I should have listened to them. Left before nine. Left when it was still safe.

But I didn't.

By eight that night, the rain had turned to snow.

I pulled on a thick gray sweater, the one I kept in my bag during winter. Tried not to shiver. The O'Connors had turned down the heat before they left, and I hadn't bothered to turn it up. Soon I'd be able to see my breath in the lamplight. A thin layer of white covered the grass and floated over the wet of the street out front. The temperature was dropping fast. Everything would turn to ice during the night, and the world would have a thick coat of it by morning, the roads slick like glass and the trees turned crystal. The view out to the wharf was magical, the lights brightening the snowflakes as they fell across the ocean, where they disappeared into nothing.

The book open across my lap had so occupied my attention that I didn't notice the moment the rain became a snowfall, not until it was already coming down. The forecast hadn't predicted a storm, but then, it was never right around here. When you lived next to the water, all kinds of weather blew in unexpectedly.

I went to the kitchen and made myself some tea. Carried the steaming mug to the reading nook carefully. Set it next to the stack of books the professor had left me. Stared out the window some more at the snow and tugged my sweater tighter around my body. The tea warmed me as I sipped it, so much so that I had to stifle a yawn. Leaned my head against the wall for a minute, no, just for a second, to rest. Closed my eyes. Opened them to see the swirl of white. Closed them again. They felt so heavy. Sleep kept coming for me, tugging on me. It wouldn't let me go.

I don't know when it was that I drifted off.

All I know is that I did.

FOUR

I COULD SEE THE McCallen brothers hanging out on the corner of Maple just a half a block ahead of me, beers sweating in their hands, cigarettes pinched between their lips. Joey McCallen, the oldest, was as ugly as ugly gets. Thick square head, thick square neck, everything about him sharp edges and ninety-degree angles. He was covered in freckles so dense they were like spilled coffee across skin. Brendan, one of the middle brothers, had gotten luckier in the looks department with his sky-blue eyes and lanky build, but all five McCallens had menace permanently stamped into their expressions, even the youngest one. Seeing them made you want to cross the street, like they could hurt you with their stares, but of course, you didn't. You were more likely to catch their attention that way. Not something anyone in this neighborhood coveted by a long shot.

The hairs on the back of my neck stood on end as I neared their corner. Slovenska's Diner, the place I was headed, was just on the other side, so there was no avoiding those boys. I made a show of hefting my purse from one shoulder to the other, an excuse to cover up part of my body. I tilted my head to the side so my hair would cover up some more.

"Hiya, Calvetti," Joey said to me, his voice rough and deep. His brothers' eyes kept darting my way in between long gulps of beer. Patrick, the youngest one, stared boldly.

"Hi, Joey," I returned with a nod, still on my way.

The cigarette dropped from his mouth to the ground. He crushed the cinders under his foot. Watched me. "You being careful around town, aren't you?"

I stopped. There went the ice in my veins. I could almost hear the slushy rush of blood. "Yeah, sure. Of course."

"I don't know, Calvetti. Gotta watch yourself, all right?"

My next breath lodged in my throat. A perfectly smooth pebble. "What are you trying to tell me, Joey?"

"Nuthin. Nuthin, really." The menace in his eyes disappeared, traded for something more serious. Concern. "Just thinkin' your father would want someone looking out for you."

I nearly laughed, despite the mention of my father. That *my* father, the *cop,* would ever want Joey McCallen worrying himself about me, was as unlikely as the Atlantic freezing over. "Why, Joey? Are you volunteering for the job?" I asked him, full of skepticism. For a second, it crossed my mind that maybe he was fishing for information, that maybe he knew something he wasn't telling me. Maybe Joey McCallen was trying to trick me into talking. I filed this away to think on later.

Joey was silent, as if a debate was raging in his head. Patrick leaned toward him, used his beer can to block their whispers. Then Joey looked at me. Shrugged. "I watch out for all the neighborhood girls," he said with a sudden laugh, the worry disappearing as quickly as it had showed up. The rest of his brothers heh-heh'd.

I rolled my eyes. "'Course you do." I started on my way again. "See you later." I threw those words over my shoulder, glancing back at the McCallens one last time before moving on, relieved to be putting some distance between us.

It was right then that my attention landed on Patrick, snagged on the tiniest of details really, the black, heavy-soled boots he was wearing—boots that were not unusual in and of themselves. Plenty of boys around here wore them daily, even in summer when they worked on the docks. It was the quick flash of metal along the toes that caught my notice, momentarily blinding in the glare of the sun. My heart started running a race and the world seemed to spin. I put my hand out, pressed my palm against the white clapboard house next to me that served as the town post office. I waited a moment, steadied myself, decided it was just a coincidence. The entire night was such a blur in my memory that my imagination was playing tricks. But even as I told myself these things over and over, the pit in my stomach, the one that rooted itself there months ago and wouldn't go away, had already grown a little bit bigger.

I knew those boots.

The air-conditioning in Slovenska's Diner did nothing to smooth the gooseflesh bumping across my arms and legs. The sign advertising this cool relief was three times as big as the information about the food. Tammy and Bridget were already occupying our favorite booth. Bridget had on a simple tank top and jean skirt, but with her fair skin and long hair, she managed to be gorgeous without even trying. Tammy had on the pale yellow sundress she bought the other day, and with the color she'd already gotten from the sun this spring, she was looking a whole other kind of pretty. Seamus and his friends Roger and Anthony were sitting nearby. Seamus had positioned himself so he had a nice view of Tammy; Roger and Anthony were angled so they could admire

Bridget. Seamus waved when he saw me, and I waved at him but didn't stop and chat. Bridget and Tammy were fixing me with stares that said something was up.

"Hi, girls," I said, determined to act normal. I slid into the booth next to Bridget. She always seemed a safer bet than Tammy.

Bridget immediately launched into conversation. "Did you see the Mc—"

Tammy halted her with a look. "Slow down, B."

"Yes, I saw the McCallens." I shrugged. "What of it?"

Tammy played with the spoon in her iced coffee, swirling it around and around. A milky storm. "They were just in a talkative mood, is all."

Bridget pressed her lips together, locking them shut.

The waitress came toward us. I stopped her by gesturing at Tammy's iced coffee. She turned and made her way toward the fridge. "How so?" I asked, trying not to sound too interested.

"Can I talk now, Tammy?" Bridget said, all prim and sarcastic. She took Tammy's silence as a yes. "We were passing the corner, and the boys said hi, and we said hi back, of course, but then suddenly they wanted a conversation. Guess what about?"

Before I could guess, Tammy leaned in. "Our friend Jane Calvetti."

The waitress plunked the iced coffee in front of me and headed off to another table. My heart sped up again, that flash of light from Patrick's boot a glaring memory in my brain. "Why would they be talking about me?"

"I don't know, J," Bridget said. "But they started asking us questions, like about where you were and how much we saw you and what you were up to these days. We didn't say much, just answered as best as we could with as little information. I mean, we had to say *something* because it was the McCallens."

Tammy gave Bridget a sideways glance. "Mainly it was me doing the answering, Jane, because Bridget was too busy ogling one of the middle brothers. Jimmy, I think. Or maybe his name is Brendan. I get them all confused."

Bridget's mouth was wide with protest. "I was not ogling!"

"You were too," she said. "You were giving him those sexy eyes you get when you think a boy is cute."

"I don't give anybody sexy eyes."

Tammy cocked her head. Batted her eyelashes in imitation of Bridget. "Sure, Marcus!" she mimicked, her voice high and sweet. "I'd *love* to meet you in the janitor's closet during fifth. As luck would have it, I've got a key!"

Two rosy dots appeared on Bridget's cheeks. "Tamra Komarov, you are *not* going to deny that it's a good place for making out. You've spent plenty of time there yourself, courtesy of me." She pouted. "I only go there because it's private."

I nudged Bridget, grateful for the turn in conversation. Happy to help it along. "Calm down, B, it's not a bad thing that boys fall all over you."

"Whatever." Bridget sank farther down into the booth, arms crossed. The universal sign for *this topic of conversation is over*.

Tammy's attention shifted from Bridget to me. "Back to the McCallens."

"Joey talked to me, too," I said with a sigh. "It was like he was being protective. I'm not going to worry much about it." Even as I said this, I knew it was a lie.

Tammy did, too. "What's going on that you're not telling us? Did something else . . . *happen?*"

A chill spread over my skin, tiny peaks of unease. The diner was freezing. Hot coffee would have been a better order on my part. I pushed my glass toward Bridget, who'd drained her own before I arrived. "Have this, B," I said, both a peace offering and a way to avoid answering.

Bridget sat up again. Elbows on the table, hands around the frosty glass. She looked at me. "Did you know there hasn't been, you know, another one since? There was an article in the paper about how, um, *yours* was the last."

Apparently my friends thought of the break-in as "mine," too.

Tammy leaned closer and whispered, "You don't think the McCallens had anything to do with it, do you? Everyone's always wanting to know what you remember about that night . . ." She trailed off.

There it was. The opening to tell my friends everything running through my mind. An invitation from Tammy to confide my fears and suspicions. And I was close, I was nearly there, but then I couldn't do it. "Nah," I said quickly. Too quickly. I got up from the table. "I've got to go to the ladies'. Be right back."

The bathroom at Slovenska's was like something out of the fifties. A mirror with big bulbed lights framing it. Chipped Formica made to look like marble surrounding the sink. Old tiled floor that used to be a deep red but had faded to a dull brown. A tall, overly green plastic plant sat in its matching brown plastic pot on the floor. I splashed warm water on my face. Patted my cheeks with a rough paper towel. If I only glanced at myself quickly, a familiar girl looked back, but if I stopped to stare too long, I saw someone I no longer recognized. A girl who kept things from her friends, things that mattered. But then, what if I told them about Patrick McCallen? What if I put them in danger by doing so? What if I made things more dangerous for myself? With a deep breath, I turned around and pushed my way through the ladies' room door into the chilly diner again.

Michaela had arrived while I was gone and was sitting in the booth next to Tammy. She sipped what remained of my iced coffee. Tammy and Bridget were probably telling her tales already.

I put a big smile on my face as I approached. "So I have another story today, and it's not as short as last time," I said a bit too brightly as I slid into the booth. Before anyone could respond, I kept going. "Earlier, I was at the market picking up dinner and who should walk in but Handel Davies."

There was a short pause, then Bridget perked up. "Did you talk to him?"

I could always count on B. "Yup. And this time, we exchanged more than names. He asked me out. He'll be at my house to pick me up tomorrow at eight."

This got Tammy, too. "You. Have a date. With Handel Davies," she said, all staccato and surprise.

I nodded. Waited for Michaela's critical commentary, but all I got was the angry sound of bubbling air as the last of the coffee was sucked up her straw. She shrugged. Looked at me with lidded eyes over the top of the glass.

Bridget was nudging me. "Where is he taking you?"

"I have no idea," I said. "I hadn't gotten far enough to wonder."

"You should wear something sexy," Bridget said.

Tammy was nodding. "Maybe that green slinky tank you wore to Spring Fling."

I gave Tammy a disapproving glance. "Well, I would, dear Tamra, however you borrowed it for your night that ended in the infamous skinny-dipping episode, and I haven't seen it since."

Her mouth opened to protest, then she closed it. A pause. "You might be right about that. Sorry." She smiled, closing her eyes. "I really did put it to good use that evening, Jane. Hmmm."

I shook my head and laughed. Tammy loved to dish about her boy escapades.

Bridget giggled. Tossed a balled-up straw wrapper that hit Tammy in the chest. "Yes, we remember. In excruciating detail." She nudged me gently with her elbow. "Now back to Handel and possible sexy outfits. Let's discuss."

But I was focused on Michaela. She'd been staring at the wreckage on our table this whole time, as though crumpled napkins, coffee spoons, and scattered grains of sugar were more interesting. Her silence was driving me crazy. "Will you just say your judgments out loud, please? I know you're thinking I shouldn't be going out with him."

Michaela's face remained blank; her olive skin—the same color as mine—wasn't even flushed from the chill of the air-conditioning like everyone else's. "I have nothing to say about this, Jane. *Really.*" She slid her glass of iced coffee to the side. "I'll save my comments until you report how it went. Maybe Handel will turn out to be a sweetheart."

"Who wants a sweetheart?" Bridget asked with a laugh. "Jane, I hope he turns out to be as bad as bad boys get. I want *that* report tomorrow."

Tammy's hand went up. "Me too. If you wanted a nice boy, you could go out with Seamus." She nodded in his direction, and when their eyes met, his face lit up.

The four of us gave him a wave, and his smile got bigger.

"I don't think Seamus is into *me*," I said, watching Tammy.

"Well, who is he into, then?" she asked.

"Are you *seriously* asking?" Bridget, Michaela, and I responded at once.

Tammy's brow furrowed like she really didn't know. "What? Seamus and *me*?" When we didn't answer, she rolled her eyes. "He's *way* too nice. Like, kindhearted and all that. Not my style."

Bridget sighed. "For a girl who claims to know everything there is to know about the boy species, sometimes you are oblivious, Tammy." Before Tammy could protest, Bridget turned to me again. "Let's talk about what we think Handel Davies has planned for you tomorrow," she said dramatically. Put her elbow on the table and rested her head in her hand, all dreamy-eyed. "Maybe he'll take you out on his father's fishing boat. He'll take you out on the water, and then he'll ravish you!"

"Carried away much, B?" Michaela said as we all laughed. Michaela gave me a knowing look. "Maybe he'll take you to an extra-special street corner for Natty Lights and cigs as the sun sets."

"You're a bitch," I said, but I was smiling. Her joke meant she was coming around.

"I still don't understand why you think Seamus likes me," Tammy said, as though the rest of us hadn't already moved on, which lightened the mood even more.

As we joked and gossiped, our previous conversation about the McCallens faded far into the background, almost too far to remember. But after the waitress cleared our empty glasses and we paid the check, Michaela stopped me before I could head off on my way home.

"My father wants you to come down to the station again. See if you remember anything new." Her voice was low, like she meant this to be soothing. This request was anything but. "Jane?"

I shrugged. Then nodded. Even with all the other break-ins before mine, I was the only one the thieves had held hostage. Not the way a girl wants to be singled out. But I agreed, because the timing of the request was eerie. For the first time since that night in February, maybe I had something real to report.

"Okay, I'll go," I told her. "Not until the day after tomorrow, though," I added, before saying my good-byes. I didn't want anything to spoil my night with Handel, and seeing Michaela's father, well, it would. Of course it would.

FIVE

WHEN I GOT HOME from the beach the next day, my mother was sitting at the kitchen counter eating some of the leftover chicken. Pulling at the meat of a drumstick. She smiled at me. "Did you go for a swim?"

"More than one." I pulled out a stool and joined her on the other side of the counter. Glanced at the clock by the sink. Six fifteen. "What's up with you?"

"Sewing. Beading. Bustling. The usual." She licked a finger. "Mrs. Levinson's a saint."

"I know. It's good even the next day. I had some for lunch."

My mother swallowed another bite. "Saint of Roasted Chickens."

I laughed. "Yeah."

"So." Her eyebrows arched. "Anything you want to tell me?"

I took a deep breath. "Yes. So. I'm hanging out with Handel Davies tonight."

My mother offered me the wing of the chicken. "Interesting."

I shook my head. She shrugged and took a bite of it herself. "Apparently, more than I realized," I said.

She wiped her mouth with a napkin. "Well, you know the people around here."

"Yup. Lived here my whole life and all."

Another smile from my mother. "Raised you the entire time, too."

"Raised me to be a smart girl," I said, looking at her directly so she knew I meant what I said.

"That's what I like to hear."

"He'll be here at eight, Mom."

She looked me up and down. Took in my tank top and short-shorts. "You're going like that?"

"Nah. I'll change," I said. "I should, right?"

"You should." She got up. Washed her hands in the sink. Dried them. "I've got something you could wear."

"Really?"

"Of course. Follow me."

My mother's room was small. Compact, but tidy. Bed made perfectly. Italian lace curtains flowing alongside the windows. Not a piece of clothing peeking out from a drawer or draped over the chair in the corner. Order was essential when you lived in a tiny house, she always said. Order was important for a good life.

She opened the closet, searching. I sat down on the bed, careful not to muss it. Watched her go from one dress to the next. Noticed the way her dark hair flowed long and thick over her shoulders while she moved, Italian curves from head to toe. My mother was thirty-five, had me when she was eighteen, was married by nineteen and divorced by the time she was twenty-one. I took after both my parents—my mother's nose and eyes, the color and style of her hair, but I got my father's tall, thin build. My mother shifted, and I saw a slice of profile. Suddenly tears were pushing into my eyes. I'd lately become aware of how things could change from one minute to the next, how I could lose something precious in a single moment, and I drank in the sight of my mother like I might never see her again. Like I needed to remember her every detail, just in case.

Details.

Michaela's father. Wanting more details.

Like the metal plate on the toe of Patrick McCallen's boot?

But that was for tomorrow. Tonight was still mine.

"Found it," my mother said, the sound of her voice breaking into my thoughts. She pulled out a skinny silk tank the color of a cloudless sky. Something she'd sewn herself. "Casual yet pretty, and you can wear it with your jeans." She held it up to me. "It will look better on you, anyway. You have the right body. It's a little slutty on me."

"Mom!" I laughed.

She started laughing, too. "It's the truth."

I took it from her. Leaned in and gave her a hug.

"What was that for?" she asked, tilting her head. Taking me in.

"I just love you," I said. "Thanks for your help."

"You're welcome. Now go shower. I'll stay out of sight when he shows, all right?"

"You're the best," I told her, and took off to my room, thinking about how strange it is to feel so lucky and so unlucky all at once.

My heart pounded. It wouldn't stop. I put a fist over it.

Handel Davies and I were walking toward town. He hadn't said a word about where we were headed. Either Bridget or Michaela might be right about our destination. At any moment we could stop on a corner for the night or end up on a fishing boat. I was hoping for something more interesting.

43

"So it's only you and your mother in that house?" Handel asked.

I watched him light a cigarette. Take a puff. "Do you think we could hide anybody else in there?"

The left side of his mouth turned up in a smile. "I guess not."

"It's just us. My mom didn't have any more kids after she got divorced."

Handel gestured left, and we turned down Chestnut. "My ma knows her."

"Really?"

"I think every woman around here has been to your mother for some reason or another. Wedding. Christening. Funeral."

We were passing Mrs. O'Brian's house, and she was in her front yard, watering some plants. She stared hard at Handel and me. I gave her a wave and a look that said *mind your own business,* and she went back to her watering.

"Which one brought your mother to mine?" I asked.

"My sister needed her prom dress fitted," he said. "That, and my uncle Billy's funeral."

"Oh. Sorry to hear that."

He shrugged. Took one last drag of his cigarette, then stubbed it out on the edge of a trash can at the street corner and tipped it inside. "That's business as usual in my family."

I didn't say anything. I didn't know what to say, and I was a little surprised Handel spoke so easily about it. I remembered reading about how Billy Nolan had gotten shot in the middle of the street one day, but I hadn't thought he might be related to Handel. Then again, it was well known across town that Handel's family—extended family at least—was deep into shady dealings. Sometimes living in this town seemed like being on a movie set. Nolan must be Handel's mother's maiden name. I wasn't sure how much more I wanted to know on the subject of Handel's family and their, well, business.

Handel hooked a finger into the belt loop of his jeans. "So, some friends are hanging out over in the dunes tonight." We reached the end of Chestnut, and Handel stopped. "I thought we could head there."

"Yeah?" I asked, trying to seem casual. I knew about the parties in the dunes. They'd been going on for years. It was the place people went to drink and have sex and get into all sorts of trouble during the summer, and therefore a place I'd always avoided. "Sounds good."

Handel's eyes flickered over my bare arms and the low cut of my tank top. "You going to be warm enough? It's cooling off now that the sun's going down."

The way his stare slid across my skin simultaneously gave me chills and made me nervous. I shrugged. "I'll be fine," I said, but as we cut right, then left, and I could see the wharf in the distance, I wasn't so sure, and I didn't mean about the cold. I could practically see my mother purse her lips in a tight line if she found out I was going to the dunes with Handel Davies. My friends would be divided. Michaela would cross her arms and get judge-y. Tammy would say I should go see what it's like, and Bridget would probably celebrate the idea, and make some comment about how Handel could just ravish me on the beach instead of his boat.

But then there was me.

What did I think?

For so long, I'd always done what I was told. I'd gotten good grades, been a good friend, been a good daughter to both my parents. Been a teacher's pet, worked hard for my spending money, crushed on nice boys who didn't notice me. After the break-in I'd tried to go on like before, as though nothing had changed, doing the same things as always—studying, working, helping, listening. But for some reason those things had become much harder lately, as though they were just out of reach. This spring there were days when I felt like skipping school, when I wished for a party instead of studying, and when I found myself wanting to kiss someone—no, *more* than kiss someone—who wasn't good for me, who might break my heart in such a way that the pain would overcome the agony from that night that still permeated my every cell. The good in me had started to peel away like skin, as though all along it had been a mask I'd worn that, with the slightest touch, would fall apart, revealing this other Jane below.

A Jane who wasn't as good.

I glanced at the boy next to me, his blond hair pulled back from his face, his eyes, beautiful and dangerous, a demeanor that said *come here* and *beware* at once.

Handel was perfect for her.

This new Jane.

The briny tang of the beach got stronger as we got closer, and my lungs expanded to take it in, my heart calming as the scent made its way into my body. When you grow up alongside the ocean, there's nothing better than that seaweed smell, potent and constant, the surest sign that you are where you belong. I paused, closed my eyes, and felt Handel slow his pace. I let the feeling of home steady me. This place, this town. What it meant. How it meant everything. But then another feeling worked its way inside, hooked into me sharply: the sense that Handel already knew who I was, that I was a girl on the verge of tipping one way or the other, and that he wanted to be around to see which way I went.

When I opened my eyes again, there he was, waiting.

Stare steady. Piercing.

I nodded. I was ready.

"This way," he said quietly, and led me down some wooden steps along the wharf. They creaked under our weight. The sound of water lapping against the boats mingled with the talk of nearby fishermen as they smoked and remembered the business of the day. There was Mr. Johansen and his sons, Mr. Lorry, Old Man Boyd—who everyone actually referred to as Old Man Boyd—a few guys too hidden behind the others to recognize, and a couple of the Sweeney brothers. They were staring full-on and hard at Handel, then at me, puffing their cigs in unison like an ugly chorus line.

When we reached the beach, I slipped off my flip-flops, careful not to step on the sharp shells littered underneath the tall wooden pilings. The sand was cool between my toes in the evening air.

"You hungry?" Handel asked.

"A little," I admitted.

"We could grab a bite at Aunt Carrie's before we head to the dunes."

"Sure," I said. Aunt Carrie's was a lobster shack built on the beach. There was a counter where you ordered and a few picnic tables in the sand and that was it. My mom and I went there twice every summer, once over Memorial Day weekend when it officially opened for the season, and again on Labor Day before it closed.

When we got there, a few families were scattered about, eating out of red plastic baskets lined with red-and-white-checkered wax paper, and more than a few people were unself-consciously munching corn on the cob, stray kernels and butter dripping down their chins. Handel and I went to the window. I asked for clam cakes and red chowder and a lemonade, and Handel asked for a basket of fried shrimp and a Coke. I dug in my pocket and came up with a few crumpled bills, but he waved the money away.

"I've got it," he said, and paid for us both.

I bit my lip to hide my smile. Handel paying made it feel like a real date. While he waited for our order to come up, I went and chose a picnic table, the one farthest to the side, just under an old, majestic tree with branches that hung out over the beach. I debated whether to sit on the end of the bench facing the ocean, which would be an invitation for Handel to sit next to me—maybe a little weird, but then we'd both have a view—or take the very center of it, which would signal that he should sit facing me on the other side of the table. I settled on the second option, deciding it was more casual.

It wasn't long before Handel was heading my way, a tray full of food, napkins, and drinks, balanced across his arms. He set it on the battered gray wood, then placed the Styrofoam bowl in front of me and the brown bag already stained with grease next to it. Then he sat down facing me, just where I thought he would.

For a while, we ate in silence.

Handel popped shrimp after shrimp into his mouth, occasionally glancing my way. I did my best not to slurp or get too much food all over me, which was difficult when dipping clam cakes into chowder. In between sips of lemonade, I tried to think of something to talk about and ended up on a subject that had me curious since Handel had first spoken to me on the beach two days ago.

"Handel," I said, watching as he wiped his hands with a napkin. "What's up?"

"Your name. Handel. I was just wondering, you know, why Handel?"

His face colored a little. "It was my mother's idea."

I scraped my spoon along the bottom of the bowl. "Parents usually *are* the ones who decide their children's names."

"Yeah, well. Mine's embarrassing. I've always felt that way, ever since I was a kid."

I finished up the last crunchy bite of clam cake. "You? Embarrassed?"

Handel dragged one of his shrimp through a plastic cup of cocktail sauce. "What? You think I'm immune?"

"I don't know. Kind of," I admitted. "You're . . . *you* after all."

He chewed slowly. Then swallowed. "What does that mean?"

"You're Handel Davies, Town Bad Boy," I said, before I could stuff the words back in with the rest of my dinner.

Hurt—or maybe it was worry—flashed across his eyes. But then Handel chuckled. "I'm not really that bad."

"No," I said slowly, looking at him. "You're not."

This got a grin from him. The first one of the night. "You're not so bad, either, Jane."

I laid my spoon down. This time I didn't try to hide my smile. "Thank you, but we've gotten off-topic."

"I like this topic," he said, still grinning.

"We were talking about your name."

He pushed his basket to the side and leaned his elbow on the table, eyes on me. "It's not something I talk about with just anyone."

I pushed the remains of my dinner next to his and mimicked his position. "I'm not just anyone."

"No," he said, the way I had before. And added, "You're not," just like I'd done.

"You can't flirt your way out of answering," I said.

He furrowed his brow. "Was I flirting?"

I felt the blood rush to my cheeks. "Um, yeah."

"Only because you started it," he countered.

"Just tell me," I demanded, my face flushing even deeper. "Or there shall be no more conversation this evening." I tried for a jokey tone, but it came out more vulnerable and nervous than kidding.

Handel didn't move. Just stayed there, propped on one elbow, watching me with that beautiful, strong face, skin tanned from so much sun, long stray locks of hair falling across his forehead, and those strange dark eyes with their halo of blond lashes. "All right," he said finally.

I took a big gulp of my lemonade. "Whenever you're ready."

"So, when my mother got pregnant," he began with a bit of resignation, "she started thinking about how she'd always wanted some other life. To get out of here and do something big and important and how she never did it. Instead she got married young and had my three older brothers, and worried all the time that they would have the same fate as her, especially since they were boys. They would become fishermen like our father and all the other men in this town and settle into the life before they'd chosen it." Handel paused to take a sip of his Coke. "With me, she wanted to do everything differently from the beginning, and for my mother, everything began with the name you gave your kid."

"That sounds reasonable," I said.

Handel reached over and tapped the table in front of me. "Like Jane, for example. Do you know why your parents called you Jane?"

The mention of my parents, plural, made me flinch the slightest bit. I shook my head.

"You should ask your mom," Handel said. "I'm sure there's a story there." He hesitated a moment, seemed like he wanted to say something else about this, about my name or my mother or my parents. But he didn't. "My father was the one who named my older brothers. Aidan, Colin, and Finn." Handel watched me with some curiosity, as though he wasn't sure how much I already knew about his family. Or even wished that maybe I didn't know much at all.

I nodded to tell him I did know. Because of course I did. Everybody around here knew about the McCallens, the Sweeneys, the Quinns, and, lastly, the Davies boys. We knew their names, the parents, the brothers and sisters, even the grandparents if the family was second generation, and sometimes the cousins and uncles, too.

"With me," Handel went on, "my mother decided she was

doing the naming and put her foot down about it with my father. I was due around Christmas, and every year my mother goes with my dad to the holiday sing with the symphony up in the city. She loves it, and he takes her to make her happy. Do you see where I'm headed with this?" He looked at me again, like maybe I could finish the story for him.

A lightbulb had gone on. "I have an idea," I told him. "Maybe." I wasn't going to let him off the hook that easily.

He sighed. "Well, my mother's favorite part of the symphony is at the end when they ask everyone to stand up and join in for the 'Hallelujah' chorus—"

"By Handel."

"Yes. George Frideric Handel, to be exact. And that particular year, with my mother in her ninth month and nearing her due date, she was belting out the words next to my father, and apparently, I was kicking along to the music." Handel's skin flushed deep red underneath his tan. "This is getting too graphic. I'm sorry. I'm also mortified."

I burst out laughing. "You shouldn't be. I'm enjoying this. I'm just surprised."

"Surprised? By too much information?"

"No," I said, trying to suppress the laughter that still wanted out. "I just thought you'd be different."

Handel's eyes danced. "You've given me some thought? Before coming out tonight?"

"I'm not letting you flirt your way out of finishing this story." I fought the blush that threatened to compete with Handel's own. "I want to hear it to its very end, even if it turns out to be more graphic."

"Fine," he said, wiping a hand across his face like this might erase the flush in his cheeks. "The graphic part is over, though; don't worry." He took another long sip of his Coke and swallowed. "So my mother decided this was a sign, and that was the moment she decided to name me Handel. She figured if she named me after a famous German composer, then maybe I would be destined for great things."

"That's sweet."

Handel stared at the remains of our dinner. "I hate the thought of disappointing her since it looks like I'm turning out just like every other Davies in the family."

"Don't say that."

"Can't help thinking it, though, you know? Now I'm just another townie turned fisherman—just one with a fancy name." Before I could respond, Handel turned away, glancing at the water and the sky, which had turned the bright blue of evening, except for a rose-pink streak along the horizon. The stars were starting to come out. "You about ready to head?" he asked.

I nodded.

We got rid of our trash and began making our way farther down the sand toward the place where the beach got wider and the dunes got higher.

"Thanks for telling me that story," I said. "I thoroughly enjoyed it."

"I think you owe me one now," Handel said with a laugh.

A piece of clear blue sea glass caught my eye in the fading light. I bent down to pick it up. Inspected it, then put it in my pocket. Continued down the beach. "I don't know that I have any stories quite that good."

He glanced at me quickly. "I know that's not true."

The playful look in Handel's eyes disappeared, swapped out for something more intense, and I wondered if the story he was sure I could tell him had to do with the night I didn't remember as clearly as everyone wished, the same night I wanted to forget altogether. I forced a laugh. "You think you already know me that well?"

He shrugged. "Maybe not. But I'd like to," he added.

My heart swooped.

Handel stopped this time. Bent down to retrieve a flat object like a mushroom cap that seemed to glow. Held his hand out to me, palm open. Sitting at its center was a sand dollar. It was perfect. Fragile. Delicate. "Take it," Handel said, everything about him soft, vulnerable, beckoning me like the open hand he offered.

I picked it up, my index finger grazing his skin. "It's beautiful." I brought it close, admired the star that marked its back, the tiny hole meant for breath. Felt how light it was, an airy meringue from the sea. I pocketed it, nestling it next to the sea glass. "Thank you."

"Jane," Handel said.

I waited for him to go on. He didn't. The evening light had reached that point where it seemed to make everything shimmer, turn the world to a mirage. "What?" I asked.

"I'm glad you're here," he said.

I drew an arc in the sand with my toe. Then drew another. Looked up at him. "Me too."

Handel's brow furrowed. "No—I mean, yes, I'm glad you're

here, now, but I'm glad nothing bad happened to you that night . . . when . . ." He trailed off.

I swallowed. "Let's walk. It's getting late." I started off again.

Handel followed. "You don't like remembering it, do you," he said. "Or talking about it."

I glanced at him. Saw how every one of his steps left an impression in the sand. "Would you?"

"Sometimes remembering things can help," he said.

"Not for me."

Handel's eyes were on me. "What do you remember, if you don't mind my asking?"

"Not much." I stumbled. Caught myself. "Can we change the subject?"

"Of course. Sorry." Handel hesitated. "If you ever do want to talk about it, you can," he offered.

"Okay." I concentrated on putting one foot in front of the other. The air had a chill to it, and a shiver passed through me.

"Jane," Handel said as the dunes took shape ahead of us. "I really am glad you're here. The world is better with you in it."

SIX

GROUPS OF SHADOWS TOOK shape in the moonlight. Figures rose up from the dunes, shifting, appearing, and disappearing again. Handel and I started along the sloping sand, tall grasses on either side of us, forming a path.

"You ever been here to hang out?" he asked. "I don't remember seeing you around."

"No," I admitted, slightly pleased Handel had memories about me, even if they were memories about my absence.

"Sometimes it's fun," Handel said, turning slightly left so we could start our climb up the dunes. "And sometimes it's not. We'll see what it is tonight, and if it's not so great we can leave."

"Okay," I said.

He dropped his flip-flops to the ground and slipped his feet into them. Glanced down at mine. "You should put your shoes on," he said. "Sometimes there's broken glass."

So I did.

We arrived at a big round clearing between the hills of sand, the sea grass at the center long ago stamped away by the feet of crowds partying constantly during the nights of summer. There were people everywhere, more than I'd expected, a lot of them guys, and all of them with big cups in their hands or cans or bottles. Laughter scattered across the dunes, along with high-pitched giggling. A group of girls stared our way and whispered to one another. I looked around for someone I knew, and I recognized a few faces, but pretty immediately realized this was an older crowd. Girls and guys who'd graduated at the very least last year, if not a few years before.

Handel looked at me, hesitant. "There are a few people I should say hi to. There's a cooler with beers over there." He pointed toward a place off to the side where there was still enough grass to hide everything. "If anyone gives you a hard time, just say you're with me. I'll be right back."

I nodded. Watched him walk off toward a series of shadows on the periphery. On the one hand, I liked that Handel wanted me to tell people I was here with him if they asked, but on the other, I was dismayed he didn't seem interested in introducing me to his friends. I headed to the cooler, not so much because I wanted a beer but because I needed something to do. A few guys stood around it like guards, and it occurred to me I might not be able to just grab one, that I might have to pay. But the second I got close, one of them gestured at me and opened the lid.

"What's your pleasure?" he asked.

There was a smile on his face, but not one that put me at ease. Even in the darkness, I could see his eyes running all over me, my arms, my legs, where the tank top I wore dipped low across my chest, the same place Handel's stare had gone. With Handel I'd liked the attention; it made me feel bold and wanted, his gaze on my skin an invitation to become something more than I already was, to experiment with new versions of myself. But this guy just made me uncomfortable. For a split second, I wondered if he could have been one of the guys from the break-in. I shook off the feeling as quickly as I could.

"I don't know," I said stupidly, wishing I had a sweater I could close over my neck.

His eyes returned to my face. "Why don't I help you find out?"

"That's all right." I bent down to grab the first beer on top—a can of what, I didn't know—careful not to let my top fall open, clutching it with my free hand. I didn't need him looking down my shirt. "I can help myself."

He fit the lid back onto the cooler. "That's too bad."

I popped the top of my beer, and it responded with a loud *shhhhh*. "No, really. It's not." I turned to leave, to find Handel, or really anyone else who seemed safer to talk to than this guy, but then he grabbed me, his fingers wrapped around my arm.

"Don't go," he said. "You haven't even told me your name."

"Get off me," I said through clenched teeth. I yanked my arm away hard—so hard that his hand went flying into the air.

"Jesus," he said, shocked and annoyed.

I didn't care. I was already stumbling toward the other side of the dunes, trying to ignore the stares of the people who'd witnessed what just happened. I glanced behind me to make sure he wasn't following me, when I bumped into someone else.

"Sorry," I said automatically, only to look up and find myself staring into the eyes of Patrick McCallen.

"Jane Calvetti," he said.

I swallowed. Why had Handel left me alone like this?

"Hi."

"What are you doing here?" He sounded surprised to see me. "Are those friends of yours around somewhere?"

I kept my eyes level, refusing to check out his shoes, to see if he was wearing those boots with the metal toes. I couldn't handle it right now if he wás. "No."

"Did you come alone?"

From his lips, the question seemed ominous, though his tone was friendly. "No." I tried to remember to breathe. It occurred to me I should be listening to his voice, trying to see whether it was familiar, but it was so hard to concentrate. The world sounded like the inside of a conch shell.

But Patrick was smiling at me—smiling kindly. "Aw, they went off and left you by yourself in this place?"

He sounded so *nice*.

I nodded slightly. Studied his eyes, so open, even sweet. He suddenly reminded me of Seamus. Then I let my gaze drop to the ground, and there they were.

Those boots.

My heart contracted. Squeezed tight, refusing to expand. Patrick's demeanor together with the boots didn't add up. "I should go find the person who brought me," I said. "Handel Davies. He's probably wondering where I've gone off to."

Before Patrick could respond, I walked around him and then kept on going, needing to be away from him as quickly as possible. I searched the shadows for Handel. I'd been having a good time earlier tonight, but now I wasn't. Not at all. Everywhere around me I saw unfamiliar faces. Any of them could have been part of the break-in. My hands curled into fists.

I forced my breath to slow. Tried to get ahold of myself.

If I could just calm down, think straight, maybe everything would be okay again. After all, technically, nothing bad had happened. A guy flirted with me at the cooler, and I ran into Patrick

McCallen, who—aside from what were ultimately unfounded suspicions at this point—had tried to be nice to me.

I went to a place in the clearing where no one else was standing, one at the crest of the dune with a view to the ocean. I studied the waves awhile, focused on the sound of them crashing, and even took a long gulp of my beer. It was terrible, but at the moment, I didn't really care.

I was starting to feel better.

But then a girl, familiar, but I couldn't think of her name, older by a few years, was staggering around in the dark, a big cup of beer in her hand—or maybe it was something else—sloshing this way and that with her movements, liquid spilling over the lip down her arm and onto the beach. I stepped aside so we wouldn't crash, but she followed and stopped in front of me, standing way too close—closer than a person who was sober would.

"Who are you?" she asked, her words slurred. She fumbled in her pocket and pulled out a lighter. She flicked it and held it up to my face, a tall orange flame burning between us. Her eyes were glassy in the glow, a splash of freckles bright across her nose and cheeks. "Wait—I've seen you before. You're that girl that was in the wrong place at the wrong time. The one whose father—"

Before she could finish, before she could say that word I knew came next, and before I could think better of it—I raised my arm high, and it came down fast, smacking away her cup. The unexpected swipe had stolen the rest of her speech. In her other hand she still held the lighter, but now her jaw was hanging open. "You bitch," she slurred. "That was my beer!"

Like I didn't know this.

Once again, I turned around and started walking the other way. There was nowhere safe for me to be.

"That's right," she yelled after me. "Leave! You don't belong here!"

Despite being drunk, the girl was right. I didn't belong here—I never would. It wasn't my scene. Why had I come? Why had I allowed Handel to bring me? And why had he wanted to? I longed for the familiarity of my friends. Bridget's easy laughter. Tammy's sarcasm. Michaela's protectiveness. Finally, *finally*, after what had seemed like hours but was probably only the span of a few minutes, I saw Handel. He was standing by himself, smoking a cigarette. He seemed lost in thought.

I went straight up to him, and before he could say anything, I spoke. "I want to go," I said. "Now."

He blinked, startled. "Is something the matter?"

Yes. Everything.

"Are you okay?" he asked. He sounded so concerned.

I shook my head. "I just want to go."

"All right," he said. "Give me a sec. I need to tell the guys we're leaving."

I watched as Handel went to his friends, a series of shadowy figures, notable only by the occasional orange burn of their cigarettes, tiny fiery lights in the darkness. But I didn't want to wait, not even a minute. I started to walk, not with any particular direction, not at first, but then I was up and over the dunes on my way toward the water. The sound of the waves was so close, so constant. They drowned out the doubt and unease threatening me, carrying it away with the tide.

A little ways ahead I saw a blanket set out on the sand, an abandoned towel forgotten by some beachgoer. It was an invitation, and I went to it, kicked my flip-flops to the side, sat down, legs outstretched, and leaned back on my elbows as though it was daylight and I was sunning myself. The night and the starlight and the familiar crash of the ocean in the dark knit themselves around me like a protective shield. After a while, I lay down completely, giving in to the way the beach called me to relax, my eyes on the sky, following the black shapes moving across it, summer storm clouds on a trip toward the moon. At some point soon, it was going to rain.

"Jane," I heard Handel call out from down the beach.

I lifted my head slightly. Handel was a tall, moving silhouette.

Soon, he stood over me, looking down at my stretched-out form. "Did I do something to upset you?"

"I just . . . I just don't belong there," I said, then rested my head against the towel again.

He was silent a moment, digesting this. "Did someone do something to you?"

"No. Yes. I don't know." I gripped the blanket tight in my fist. Then let it go. I looked up at Handel. "You know how you said that sometimes that place is really fun, and sometimes it really isn't? Tonight, it wasn't. And then, you left me all alone."

"I'm sorry," he said. "I shouldn't have taken you there. I should have known better."

I stayed silent. Waited for him to explain.

"And I shouldn't have left you even for a minute," he went on. "I just . . . had to get something out of the way with my friends, and I didn't want you to be around for it. I wish we could go back to the beginning and start the night over. I would do everything differently." Handel sounded so yearning as he said

62

these words. He stared at me lying there. Seemed like he was debating something. Then he spoke. "Can I join you?"

At first, I didn't answer. I was thinking maybe we should just call it a night.

But then I reminded myself how our evening began. How much I'd been enjoying it. I shifted as far as I could to the towel's edge to make room. "Okay," I said.

And just like that, our night was saved.

When Handel asked if he could join me, I didn't think he would lie down, but that was what he did, and now we were stretched out, side by side, on a blanket meant for one, staring up at the stars as they disappeared behind the clouds. For the first time since dinner, I began to feel good again. My breaths came slow and full, the warm ocean breeze a soothing whisper all around. There was something so childlike and innocent about lying here with Handel. It was the kind of thing Bridget and I did when we were small and still sat with our mothers under their umbrellas and dug for crabs in the sand. Handel and I managed not to touch, not in a single place, not our shoulders or our hands or our feet, but I was so aware of him, his skin in the places it was exposed and his clothing in the places where it wasn't, the curve of his jaw and the rise of his chest as he breathed. I wondered if he was thinking the same about me.

It's amazing how much was said without saying a thing.

After another while, Handel shifted positions. He rolled onto his side, facing me, propping himself up on his elbow like at dinner. I could feel his eyes on me.

"You won't tell anyone about the story of my name, will you?" he asked.

I laughed softly, my eyes still on the clouds above. They were about to eclipse the moon. "No, I won't," I said. "I promise."

He let out a big breath, a long sigh of relief. "Good."

"Were you really that worried?"

I could almost feel the smile cross Handel's face even though I wasn't looking at him. "I've got an image to maintain."

"Oh yeah?" I rolled onto my side, too, so we were facing each other. I propped myself up in the same position, happy to note that the smile I'd imagined on Handel's face was real. "And what image is that?"

"You said it yourself earlier. I'm the town bad boy. One of them at least. That story about my name would kill my reputation."

I reached out and flicked him on the arm. "You're leaving out the other half of what I told you. The part about how you're not so bad."

"Yeah. Well. I have my days." He combed his fingers through his hair. Glanced toward the ocean. "Sometimes it's hard to look my mother in the face. Knowing that every time I go off to work on the docks, she's wishing things turned out differently."

Thunder rumbled far off in the distance. The air around us was growing thick with humidity, like you could slice it. "Maybe it's a sign," I said.

"A sign of what?" Handel asked.

I was so tempted to reach out and touch him, but I settled for a look. "A sign from the heavens that your mother was right," I said. "You are destined for great things."

"Oh, of course I am." He laughed. "What things exactly?"

More thunder sounded. "Meteorology?"

"In this town? No way."

"Right," I agreed as a bolt of lightning cracked and lit up the ocean, flickering, then going out. "Firefighter, then?"

"I don't know. Maybe the storm is a sign I should be a fisherman after all."

In other circumstances I might have laughed at this, but Handel's voice was so even, so steady. Like he really believed this was what he was meant to do. Or that it would be a relief to just let himself be this and only this. So all I said was, "Probably, that's what it is," and we turned our talk to other things.

"Why are you doing this, anyway?" I asked Handel eventually.

"Doing what?"

"Hanging out with me."

Handel looked out over the ocean at the lightning again before turning, ever so slightly, in my direction. "I just," he said, and paused. "I just . . . wanted to get to know you."

"Okay," I said, because I felt like he'd told me the truth, and because it *was* okay. I wanted to get to know him, too, so much, more now than ever, and this seemed fine. More than fine. Like something I deserved.

Just before the rain came, we agreed we'd better get going or risk getting stuck in the storm. All I could think about was whether Handel would try to kiss me. Or if the right moment arrived, whether I would try to kiss him.

"I'll walk you home," he said.

"You don't have to—"

"Of course I do."

"It's not like it isn't safe," I said with a laugh, one that died in my mouth as the word "safe" strangled me a little, because I wasn't sure if that was true anymore. Especially not with Patrick McCallen just down the other end of the beach.

"I picked you up and I'll drop you back," Handel insisted, his voice light, a smile on his face that made me forget those dark thoughts, that made me swoon really.

We made our way up the beach toward the wharf and the parking lot. We reached the sidewalk and I stopped under the light of a streetlamp to slip my feet into my flip-flops. When I looked up again, Handel's eyes were on my waist. There was a sliver of exposed skin along my hips, between the hem of my top and the start of my jeans. A thin line of sand clung to it. Handel reached over and brushed it away, his fingertips sliding along my navel so quickly it was a whisper.

Right then, big fat drops of rain plopped one by one on the ground around us.

"We'd better hurry," Handel said.

We made our way down the street toward my house, dodging raindrops in the dark, neither of us with an umbrella. Thoughts of leaning just a little closer to Handel, close enough that our lips would touch, darted in and around me as we walked, a game of hide-and-seek among trees. I wondered if this crossed his mind, too, as the rain picked up, becoming a torrent, and we started to run, the two of us racing until we reached my yard.

"This way," I shouted over the din, going around to the porch at the back of my house, grabbing for the tiny metal knob of the screen door and opening it so we could rush inside.

The two of us were soaked and panting from the run, my long hair wet and tangled, just like his. I started to laugh between big heaving breaths and so did Handel, the earlier, unpleasant part of the evening erased by all that intimate talk on the beach. I switched on a lamp. It was a murky dark green, made from an old jug, and the light from it was weak but enough to see the expression on Handel's face. His eyes were different, bright and easy. Everything about him was different now, less weary and cautious. He looked younger.

Then he noticed the picture frame on the table.

My dad and me, just a year ago. He wore his uniform and was standing next to his police car. I was perched on the hood of it, knees up to my chin, a smile on my face, dark hair falling all around. A camera catching that split second when a girl suddenly becomes someone worth seeing.

Handel picked it up. Studied it.

I watched as the weariness in him returned.

"You were close with your father," he stated, the memory of my family gripped tight in his strong hand. "You must miss him. You must want the police to catch whoever killed him."

My mouth opened. Shut. Handel had startled me. Such boldness. Cut right to the heart of things. Of me. "I, um," I stuttered. Stopped.

He put the frame down, a soft *click* against the wood. "Sorry. I shouldn't have pried."

I watched Handel. He wouldn't look at me anymore. Looked everywhere but. Tension radiated off him, his shoulders, his neck. There was silence, things grown awkward and strange after so much ease. I wanted to fix it. I wanted the connection back. "I don't know," I said quickly. "Sometimes I hope they don't catch anyone."

His eyes found me again. Slowly. There was something in them, but it was something I couldn't quite read.

"No?"

I shook my head. The rain pounded harder on the roof of the porch, filling the gaps between words.

Handel blinked. "It's late. I should probably go."

"Okay," I said. He was right. It was late. But I didn't want him to leave. I didn't want our night to end like this. I wanted that kiss.

"Yeah," he said, like he was torn. Caught between two things, maybe to stay or to go. Maybe.

"See you around," I said then, just like that first day at the beach, before I'd walked away from him. No, I'd strutted. Definitely. Acted like I didn't care. Like Handel and I talking didn't matter.

He already mattered, though. A lot.

"See you," he said, just like that day, too, but this time it was Handel leaving me behind, and me, watching him slip through the screen door of the porch into the pouring rain, listening as the door banged shut, closing him out or maybe it was me in, the sound of his footsteps pounding through the wet and the darkness of the night.

SEVEN

THE MORNING AFTER THE rainstorm was heavy with mist. The whole world smelled like the ocean. I could hear the seagulls crying overhead, flying farther inland because they couldn't tell where the beach ended and where the rest of the town began. The storm had taken with it the oppressive heat, and there was a crispness to the air. I lay there in bed, the quilt pulled tight around me. The sun had come up, but the world was still gray. Its light hadn't made its way through the cloud cover yet. I loved days like this. They were lonely, but not in a bad way. The beach would be nearly empty, free of the tourists who wanted their day in the sun. It made me want to walk along the ocean and stare into its depths because it was suddenly all mine. At least it always seemed that way to me.

After last night I had some interesting topics for reflection, despite how my night with Handel had ended. The better part of it had been good, and this was the part that held my focus. I started to get dressed, my body already humming with the need to get down to the water while it was still early morning.

Then I remembered.

Michaela. Her dad. His request that I go down to the station today. Patrick and his metal-toed boots. My motivation evaporated, and I crawled back under the covers, jeans and all, and closed my eyes.

. . .

I woke later to the sound of the telephone. The landline my mother still kept in the house because cell service was spotty at best in our town, and nonexistent in most of it. She held on to it just in case we needed it someday, she always said. By the fourth piercing ring, I figured she must not be home to answer it, so I stumbled out of bed and went to the kitchen. Grabbed the phone after two more rings threatened to split my eardrums. "Hello?"

"Jane," said the voice on the other end. Male. Deep and older and one I knew well.

My hand went to my head in an attempt to ward off the headache I didn't have but was coming. "Hi, Professor O'Connor." I held my breath.

"Jane," he said again. Quietly. Worried. "I've been trying to reach you for a couple of weeks. You haven't returned my calls."

A mixture of guilt and resistance swirled my insides. "I know. I'm sorry."

"You don't have to apologize. It's not easy what you've been through. What you and your mother have been through," he corrected.

I didn't say anything. Just stared at the phone on the table. The number pad with its big raised buttons, like a strange plastic toy from another era. My mother had left the newspaper out, and the headlines caught my attention, glaring at me.

RASH OF BURGLARIES OVER? RESIDENTS HOPEFUL; NO SUSPECTS IN SIGHT, POLICE SAY

I flipped it over, blotting out the words, but Professor O'Connor was still waiting for me to speak. Dealing with the headlines was easy, but it's not like I could treat him in the same way and hang up.

I guess he got tired of waiting for me, though, because he spoke again. "It's been a long time since Martha and I have heard from you," he said in that confident teacher voice of his.

"Please tell Dr. O'Connor hello," I managed.

"I will. Of course I will. But I wanted to see if you were all right."

"I'm fine." I let out a big breath. I kept forgetting I needed air.

"Are you?"

"Sure."

There was a pause on the other end and then, "I don't know if you've seen the news." He stopped. Waited for me to confirm or deny. When I didn't say anything, he continued on. "Don't get discouraged. The police are going to find out who did this."

"I know," I said. But I didn't.

"Maybe you and I could go down to the station and talk to them together," he suggested. "I'd be more than happy to do it. In fact, I'd like to be able to—"

"I'm actually headed there today," I said, not letting him finish, tears already pricking my eyes at his kindness. He was always so kind and this was of the fatherly variety, which made it even more potent. It's the kindness that kills you sometimes, I'd learned. "I'm okay to go alone."

"But you don't have to."

"Thank you for offering. I mean it."

"All right," he said, but he didn't sound confident that what I wanted was what was best. "Jane, Martha and I would love to see you. We want to have you to the house for dinner, though I know you haven't wanted to come here ever since . . ."

A single tear made its way out of my eye, despite my fighting against it. It slid down my cheek, a lonely raindrop. "I'd love to see you, too. But I haven't been able to get myself over there. I'm sorry." My last two words were all but lost, my throat too tight to allow them air. Professor O'Connor started to say something else, but I couldn't let him. I had a difficult day ahead, and I didn't want to break down completely. "I'm sorry," I said again. "But I have to go. Okay? Thank you. Thank you for calling. Really." The phone made a soft *click* when I pressed the hang-up button with my finger. I held it there a moment, in a daze of sorts, before I placed the receiver in its cradle.

To think that the very first moments of this morning held so much promise. Now the heaviness in the air only felt like it wanted to steal my breath. Suffocate everything. Take all the goodness this day might have had away.

I reached the police station quickly, more quickly than I'd wanted to.

Like everything else in our town, it was down by the wharf. It wasn't a pretty building, but it wasn't ugly, either. A nondescript concrete and glass structure that someone had painted dark blue a long time ago, whether to match the color of the ocean or the uniform was unclear. There were tall windows on the side that faced the water, to keep an eye on the happenings on the wharf, I supposed.

I was sweating underneath the long-sleeved shirt I'd put on, instinctively, before leaving the house. There was something about heading here that made me feel exposed and vulnerable. Like maybe jeans and a big shirt could hide me from view. I hadn't always felt this way, not when I'd come to visit my dad, but now everything was different, and the station had become a place not where I'd find family but where there were cops who needed something from me. Police with hopes that I could somehow give them a break in a case gone cold. Where now, when I walked through their door, what everyone would see was not simply Calvetti's daughter—they would see that, too—but Calvetti's grieving daughter who was also a witness.

A witness.

This was running through my head when I reached for the metal bar across the door to let myself in. I hesitated, holding it half-open or half-shut, depending on how you looked at it, waiting for someone to let me off the hook and tell me to go home. That I wasn't needed anymore because the police figured out who was responsible for the break-ins, or because some other witness had come forward. For a quick second I thought I saw Handel reflected in the tall panel of glass, far behind me on one of the street corners, but not far enough that he was too small to make out. When I turned to see if it was him, there was no one there at all. I stared at the corner awhile, willing him to reappear as if I might have that power, to no avail. Then I was left to heft open the door a second time, back at square one, trying to make myself go inside. I was saved the trouble by Michaela's father, who appeared before me as if he'd somehow known I was here. Maybe he had. Maybe he'd seen me through one of those big windows.

"Jane, let me get that for you," he said, opening the door the rest of the way easily. He filled the entryway. Wide and tall and strong. A man who ate a lot of pasta at home that his Italian wife cooked.

"Hi, Officer Connolly."

"Thanks for coming down," he said. "Michaela told me you would, and I'm grateful. Follow me." He started down the narrow hallway that would take us past the front desk and the big, open office where my father's former colleagues would be sitting, cups of coffee clutched in their hands, brown paper lunch bags decorating their in-boxes like cake toppers, sitting on top of tall stacks of files that will never get inputted into a computer because the police here worked the old-fashioned way. Michaela's dad was halfway to his office before I took my first step across the cheap tiled floor, grayed with age and years of scuff marks. He reached his door and realized I hadn't made it very far. "Come on, Jane," he called to me. "You don't have to stay very long. I'm gonna take care of you, okay?"

"Okay," I said when I'd caught up to him. "Okay," I said a second time, more to myself than to Officer Connolly.

My mind was on my dad.

I could see him so clearly, standing near the coffee machine, laughing with the other police. He was like a ghost within these walls, haunting me.

Once again, Officer Connolly held the door so I could pass through to his office, and I did.

He sat down in his big metal chair with the cracked red pleather upholstery, eyeing me, waiting for me to talk. He rolled it around his desk so we would be on the same side, the wheels squeaking and creaking in protest. His office was tiny and cluttered, too small for a man of his size and stature, his desk pushed against the left wall and littered with papers and pens and carbon copy forms that most places stopped using twenty years ago. The tall plastic shelves that went from floor to ceiling along the right wall were no different. Except for a few filing boxes, they were piled with paper that didn't seem organized in any particular way, giving me the urge to start fixing up the place.

Just like I used to for my father.

I pulled my eyes away from the mess.

His chair squeaked as he leaned forward. The freckles of youth had faded into tired lines on his face. "Can I get you anything? Water? A Coke?"

"No, I'm okay," I said, but I wasn't. Michaela got her mother's genes, except for her nose—she had her father's nose. I could see it on him now. I had my father's mouth. Could Officer Connolly see it on me, too?

He took a sip of his coffee. The big mug in his hand was white with black lettering that said SUPPORT YOUR LOCAL POLICE. He leaned backward, and the chair shrieked in protest from the shift in weight. "Jane," he began. "As I'm sure you know, we haven't had any more breaks in this case."

I nodded. My eyes darted to the wall above his desk, where he had a series of tiny, framed pictures of Michaela. Her formal school photos going back to what looked to be second grade. One of her in a swan ballerina outfit.

"Jane?"

I forced myself to look at him. "Sorry."

"We're sure the previous robberies are related to the one at the O'Connors', even though things happened differently there. The only difference was—"

"Me," I finished for him.

He let out a big breath, like he'd been holding it. "That's correct." His badge glinted in the harsh fluorescent light. "It's well known that when someone experiences a trauma, it can take a long time for memories to get straightened out. Details sometimes return months, even years later. I know this is hard on you, but I wanted to see if you'd remembered anything else. Any little detail, even one that doesn't seem relevant. You never know, it might be the thing that breaks open this whole investigation."

I closed my eyes. Told myself to breathe. In. Out.

Was I going to do it? Was I going to say something about Patrick? Or about his boots?

"Jane, you're like a daughter to me, you know that. I hate doing this to you. I hate that this happened to you. To your family. Your mom. Geez."

I opened my eyes again. Officer Connolly was shaking his head with sadness. His hand was red from gripping his mug so tightly. "I'm sorry I haven't been able to tell you much," I said. "I really am. I was in the dark, and a lot of the time I was blindfolded."

"I know, Jane, I know. But like I said, even the smallest detail could be important."

I stared into his round face, his kind eyes, all classic Irish features and classic red hair. My father and Officer Connolly had been friends. Ridden alongside each other one year in a squad car. "There is one thing," I said. The words tiptoed from my mouth. Tested the air. "It's probably nothing."

Everything about Officer Connolly lifted right then. Head,

eyebrows, chin, shoulders. He nodded. "Go on." Even his voice had more altitude.

"Before they"—I swallowed. My throat was sandy. The beach after the tide has pulled away—"before they tied the blindfold, there was this flash of metal near the floor. It was a boot. One of them had metal-toed boots."

Officer Connolly was nodding so hard he was bouncing. The chair squeaked with it. "Good, good." He grabbed a pen and wrote something on a yellow legal pad. The edges of the paper curled upward in the humidity. He smiled at me, all encouragement and approval. "You never know." He flicked the top of the pen once, then twice, the ballpoint disappearing, then reappearing. "That could be the missing piece that solves this."

"Okay."

Officer Connolly held the pen poised and ready for more. Black ink had stained his index finger. "Anything else, Jane?"

My lips parted. *Patrick McCallen.* Possible owner of the boots. His name was right there, heavy on my tongue. But he'd been so nice to me last night—or he'd tried to be. It didn't make sense. I needed to be sure before I gave him up. So I shook my head. "Nothing else," I told Officer Connolly.

"All righty, all righty," he said, still nodding, though less forcefully than before. "You done good today. You done real good, Janie." That name from his mouth, Janie, the nickname from my childhood, before I'd grown up to be just Jane. Officer Connolly stood, and the chair creaked with relief.

"Sorry I'm not more helpful."

"Nah, you've been helpful. Don't you worry. Thanks for coming down here today. I'll show you out now."

"That's okay. I know my way."

He sighed long and heavy, like the world was pressing him down. Looked at me with more sadness in his tired green eyes. "That you do now. That you do. If you're sure."

"I'm sure, but thanks."

Just before I left his office, he stopped me one last time. "Remember, if there's anything else that comes back to you, anything at all . . ." He trailed off.

"I know. Anything." My hand was already on the doorknob, turning it. "I wish I wasn't your only witness." I said this in a small voice, so small I don't even know if he heard me. "I wish with all my heart that the only other witness wasn't dead," I added in an even smaller one, before I was through the door and pushing my way outside into the gray of the cloudy day.

That night, I'd fallen asleep by accident. Head resting against the wall of the reading nook, face turned away from the lamplight. It was only a nap, but it was long enough that when my eyes blinked open, the short hand of the big antique clock on the wall was pushing ten p.m.

"Shit," I said to no one, my voice carrying through the grand, empty house, the shelves of books all around me eventually swallowing the sound.

The snow outside was coming down heavy now, thick and fast around the streetlights. There were two lonely cars parallel parked on the road out front, already buried in white. It was so quiet, as though the snow silenced the world, a mother's great long *shhhh* to her sleeping child as it fell toward the ground.

My phone blinked with a message. Was I so out of it that I hadn't heard it ring? I pushed the button for voice mail and listened.

"Hi, sweetheart, guess who?" said the voice of my mother. "I've tried your cell several times, but the ringer must be off. I don't know if you've noticed, but we are getting a surprise storm, and I'm worried about you being out so late. And before you hem and haw and even though I am still youthful enough for people to mistake me as your older sister, I *am* your mother and it's my duty to worry. Can you please call me and let me know you're all right? Love you!" There was a *click,* and the voice-mail system offered me a slew of options—save the message, erase the message, forward the message, followed by three more possibilities that I stopped listening to.

I called home. It barely rang once before my mother picked up.

"Sweetie! I'm so glad to hear your voice."

"I'm *fine,* Mom," I said in a tone that told her to stop being crazy. "Don't worry about me. I'm here late all the time, remember? I love this house."

"Yes, but not in a snowstorm."

"They didn't predict snow."

"But that doesn't mean it isn't piling up outside," my mother said. "And how do you plan on getting home in this? Hmmm?"

"I'll walk, like always."

"Oh, no, you won't." She was doing her best *I'm your mother* impersonation. "Not in this mess."

"Ma—"

"I'm calling your father. He will come pick you up."

"Don't bother Dad! He's working."

"Exactly. Which means he's already out and about and you'll get picked up in a big safe police car that can handle this blizzard. My little Jeep is a death trap in snow like this, and I don't want to risk it."

I stood by the window, taking in the scene outside again. It *was* piling up fast. If I tried to walk, I would be shin deep in snow the whole way, with all the watery slush freezing at the bottom. "Fine. Call Dad."

"Good. Though, let the record show that I was going to call your father either way, even if you did not acquiesce."

I laughed. "That sounded very TV-lawyer-ish."

"That's excellent since I've been practicing," she said, though the worry was still clear underneath the humor.

"Ma, I'm going to go now."

"All right," she sighed. "Just promise me you won't go out in this until your father shows up. I don't know how long it will take him to come get you, but you stay put until his car pulls up. *Inside* the house."

"Yesss," I agreed.

"I love you, Jane."

"I love you, too."

We both hung up.

The clock said it was five past ten. Everything was lit by a ghostly bright glow from the snow. As the minute hand made its way toward ten fifteen and onward to ten thirty and ten forty-five, I returned to my reading, occasionally glancing outside to see if my father had arrived. The hands of the clock passed eleven. A few more minutes went by, but not enough that the big hand reached a quarter after.

Then something strange happened.

The lights at the front of the house went out.

It must be the storm, I thought as I looked into the darkness of the snow and the night, trying to make out something, anything at all, now that the O'Connors' front lawn had disappeared into blackness. A power outage. A tree fallen across wires, the weight of the ice just too much. But then I remembered the glow of my desk lamp—no, I saw it—falling across the stack of books. My coffee mug. The skin of my own hands. Illuminating the reading nook where I sat. A new thought, a question really, came to me:

Why had the lights in the front yard gone out, but not the house ones?

Why the outside, but not the inside?

Could they be on different electric grids?

That must be it, was the next thought to cross my mind. I considered calling my mother, calling my dad, too, but then decided that would be overreacting. It was just a couple of lights. The clock on the wall said it was well after eleven. My father's police car would be pulling up any minute.

I decided to get back to my reading while I waited. I'd only turned a single page when something else happened to pull me away again, something that frightened me for real this time.

The light on the desk went out.

The darkness around me was complete.

I reached for my phone.

Quickly, I texted my father.

Daddy, are you close?

EIGHT

HANDEL DISAPPEARED FROM my life as suddenly as he'd appeared. Completely and totally. A week went by with no word from him and, in the summertime, that felt like a month. Signs for the upcoming Fourth of July festivities were being posted around town. Somehow I'd thought Handel and I would run into each other again, accidentally, which was when we would decide to go out a second time.

But this didn't happen.

It wasn't like we'd exchanged numbers, or that it even crossed our minds to do so. Handel was still on the list of people I needed to run into coincidentally, and without coincidence to bring us together, I was left to wonder if our date had been something imagined. Twice I'd gone down to the wharf hoping to catch a glimpse of him, and once to Levinson's to get another roast chicken, as if this was a magical combination that might produce Handel Davies walking through the door of the deli. In the end, all my efforts amounted to nothing.

My friends were split in their opinions about the situation.

"Stop thinking about him, Jane." Michaela stared at me hard before she turned over onto her stomach, flicking a few grains of sand from her beach towel. "It just means it wasn't meant to be."

"I wasn't thinking about him," I protested, far too forcefully to be believed by anyone. Not even Bridget. But then, Bridget wasn't having any of this *Handel and I aren't happening* business. She was too romantic to let it go.

"It's okay if you were, Jane," she said, all consolation and understanding. "In fact, if I were you, I'd go find him. He's probably down at the docks, working."

Tammy snorted. Looked at Bridget. "What are you, the lame-boy-excuse police?"

Bridget ignored her. "Or he's probably just busy."

This made Tammy snort a second time.

"Or he's probably just hanging around with a cross section of the town delinquents," Michaela offered, her voice muffled by the towel.

"Point taken, M." I hugged my knees. Rested my chin on them. Squinted my eyes against the sun. "The short reprieve you gave Handel is now over, and you're back to disliking him."

"You got it," Michaela said, lifting her chin just long enough to get these three words out.

Tammy's face got serious. "J, how do *you* feel? Are you disappointed?"

Bridget watched me. Michaela made a show of shifting onto her side so she faced away from us.

I turned to Tammy. "I am, kind of. No, not kind of, definitely. There was something special about that night we hung out."

"You were so excited about it," Bridget reminded me. "I hate to think that the bad boy isn't going to turn out to be a prince."

Tammy was about to snort again—I could see she wanted to—but she held off. Bridget was just being Bridget—sweet and romantic and meaning well. She always wanted a happy ending for everyone, and Tammy knew when to stop riding her.

"Well, just because he's of the boy species doesn't mean he doesn't get nervous like we do," Tammy said, surprising all of us, I think. Michaela shifted. This time she turned toward us and sat up on her towel. "Maybe you intimidated him, Jane," Tammy went on.

"What?" I shot her a look. "Me, intimidate *Handel Davies*? I don't think so."

"She might be right," Bridget said. "You are, like, perfect, and all that. Totally hot with good grades and going to college"—this comment made me roll my eyes, but Bridget went on, uninterrupted—"and here comes Handel Davies, townie, fisher-boy from a notorious family, who's going nowhere else."

"You mean, nowhere but jail," Michaela said in a huff.

Bridget and Tammy both shot her a look that said *shut up*.

I was about to respond when a tennis ball, ratty and torn, landed next to Tammy, just missing her leg, which made her shriek in disgust. It was followed by a big golden retriever running up, well, to retrieve it, its owner close behind, trailed by two friends. Two of the three were African American: the first one, the dog owner, light-skinned; the other darker; and the third one had the same coloring as Bridget. All of them were male, and all of them were obviously from out of town—far enough out that they were rich. You could see it written all over them. Plus, they carried lacrosse sticks. No one around here played lacrosse.

"Oh Lord," Tammy said as they headed our way. The dog panted next to her leg, and she patted its head absently.

The problem with out-of-town boys is that they always think they're better than us, better than everyone who's grown up around here. They go to their fancy schools and do their fancy activities and drive their fancy cars, and this makes them feel like it's okay to treat us like we're lesser somehow—less educated, less sophisticated, less valuable as people. More gullible about everything, especially when it comes to why they are paying us attention. It never seems to occur to them we might be as intelligent as they are. That we might be going places they'd never dreamed about, even with all their fancy money. And when they come to our beach, trying to mix with girls like us, it generally means trouble and broken hearts. We might be townies, but we still deserved respect.

Before they reached our beach setup, Michaela rolled her eyes. "Do boys actually think they're not being obvious when they use the *Whoops, can you give me back my tennis ball/Wiffle ball/ baseball?* approach at the beach? I mean, it's as bad as the *Do you have a light?/Do you know what time it is?* winter-season approach."

"Shhhh." Bridget's eyes locked on the boys. "They're cu-ute."

"Don't forget," I whispered to Michaela. I held the tennis ball to the dog's mouth, then dropped it to the sand, where it immediately picked it up. "There was a time, not long ago, when we would have cut off an arm for any attention whatsoever from even a single boy, regardless of the lameness of the approach."

"Yeah." Tammy adopted a bored look on her face, sunglasses on. "That was then, this is now, and this sort of attention is getting old," she finished under her breath.

"Not for me," Bridget sang softly. "Never for me."

"Sorry to bother you," said their leader, the light-skinned one and the tallest of the three, the one who looked like he must work out in one of those fancy gyms with machines designed to help sculpt muscles for athletes. Dark brows slashed over dark eyes and a bright broad smile. The lacrosse stick hung at his side. "Eric and I were playing fetch, and my last pitch went awry."

"Awry?" Tammy was all suspicion and distrust. I could practically hear her eyes rolling under those dark glasses.

"What? Lacrosse fetch?" Michaela asked.

"Your dog's name is Eric?" I asked next, surprising even myself with a question that might easily be mistaken as an invitation for further conversation.

"Jane, that's his friend's name, obviously." Bridget had strategically positioned herself on her towel, one gorgeous leg outstretched, the other bent at the knee. She alternated her attention between each of the three boys now that the other two had joined their leader.

The one with the dog grinned, his smile turned up to blinding. His father must be an orthodontist—he looked too rich for him to be a regular dentist. "Eric, come here. Stop flirting," he said, patting his thigh. The dog, obedient and wagging his tail enthusiastically, returned proudly to his owner. Bridget's eyebrows went up. "I'm Miles. This is Logan"—he nodded toward the boy on his left, the Irish-looking one who smiled on cue—"and this is Hugh," he finished, nodding toward the boy on the right, the one with the darkest skin, who also smiled.

Tammy laughed in disbelief. "Oh Jesus, you're serious, aren't you?"

"What?" Miles asked, like he really didn't know she was referring to their names, the kinds of names only the rich give their children.

"Just ignore her," Bridget said, trying to salvage the situation. "What brought you guys to this beach?"

The dog dropped the ball at Miles's feet. "Exploring the rest of the town. That sort of thing."

"We heard the girls were prettier over here." This from Logan, in a tone of voice that dripped *entitled asshole*.

Tammy got up from her towel, all confidence and sexiness and grace. "I don't have any patience for rich boys slumming it over here with us townie girls."

"Ouch," Miles said, but he never lost his smile.

Bridget opened her mouth in protest but stopped short of actually saying anything when she saw that both Michaela and I were starting to get up.

I brushed a few grains of sand from my legs. "I'm suddenly hungry."

"I've got frozen candy bars dancing in my little head," Michacla said, her left hip jutted to the side.

"Our treat," Miles offered, in a voice that said he was sure he wouldn't be refused. "It's the least we could do after disturbing your peace."

"No, thanks," Tammy said. "I've saved just enough pennies that I can afford some chocolate all on my lonesome. What about you girls?"

I smiled. Tammy's haughtiness could be annoying, but sometimes it was the best part about her. "I might need to borrow a penny or two, but I think I can manage."

Michaela shifted her sunglasses up so they pulled her hair

back from her face like a headband, showing off her brown eyes. "I'm good for an extra dime if you need it, hon."

"Thanks," I said.

Clearly outnumbered, Bridget finally joined us, though reluctantly. "Maybe another time," she said to the boys sweetly.

The four of us headed toward the snack bar, taking our time, knowing full well those boys would stand there and watch us walk away, taking in our bodies, mostly bare except for the bikinis each of us wore, long hair swinging across our backs, side to side with every step. We may not be rich like they were and we might just be townies like everyone else around here, but we knew where our power lay, and we were doing our best to learn how to use it.

It was in moments like these that I got a glimpse of the Jane I used to be before everything changed direction. The Jane who stuck with her friends no matter what, who would never let a bunch of boys come between us, who told and trusted her friends with everything. When you've done nothing wrong, it's easy to act that way. Carefree and confident. It was good to see that girl again, that version of myself. To remember that she was still there after all these months, that maybe I could call her up if I needed her and she would respond as though she'd never left. I just hadn't been looking in the right place.

Missy Taylor was coming out of my house just as I was returning from the beach. She was struggling with a garment bag that lay stretched across both arms. I sized it up quickly. Wedding dress. She was only four years older than me. Blond and perky. The cheerleader type in high school.

"I didn't know you were getting married," I said, helping her with the door. "Congratulations."

"Thanks," she said, whether for the help or the congratulations was unclear. The freckles on her face were dark from time spent in the sun. "The wedding is next week. Your mother didn't tell you?"

I shook my head. "No."

"Well, it's nice to know that someone in this town doesn't gossip."

I laughed. "My mother treats her client relationships like a lawyer or a doctor does. Total confidentiality. Whatever is discussed in the fitting room stays in the fitting room." I paused, thinking about whether this was completely true, of if there were any loopholes in the policy. "Well, unless she hears something about me. Then client confidentiality goes down the drain."

Missy smiled. "Good to know. I think her exception is forgivable."

"Don't know if I agree. Who's the groom?"

"Oh, he's from out of town." Her tone was almost apologetic. "He's really sweet. Different from the boys around here, you know?"

"I'm sure he's great. I like the boys around here, though," I added. Then I thought about Handel, how he hadn't been in touch. Maybe I should take a nod from Missy.

She cocked her head. Took me in with her big blue eyes. "There's a whole world out there beyond this town, Jane," she said, as if I might not have heard this before, as if four years and a proposal of marriage made her decades wiser. "You should go exploring. You especially."

"Hmmm. Well, good luck next week."

Missy stared at the thick garment bag in her arms like she'd just remembered it was there. "Right. I should go. So much to do in only a week. Tell your mom she's a genius. Bye!"

I gave her a wave. "Bye." Then I went inside. Kicked off my flip-flops. Felt the comforting grains of sand on the floor underneath my bare feet. It was still summer. There was still plenty of time for things to happen. Good things. "Hello?"

"I'm in my office," my mother called back. "Come visit your beloved parent."

My bag made a soft thump when I dropped it. I continued to shed things on my way to the sewing room. Hair band. Sunglasses. As usual, my mother sat amid a sea of fabric. This time it was violet chiffon. "Let me guess," I said. "You're doing alterations for Missy Taylor's bridal party."

She stuck a pin into the hem of one of the dresses. "You missed out. An hour ago I had eight girls in this house, all of them draped in violet chiffon. That's not counting Missy."

"You fit nine people in here?"

She laughed. "Not just in here. In the living room. On the porch. Sitting on my bed. There was a lot of giggling and a bit of complaining about being forced to wear violet or being forced to wear chiffon or, with one of the girls, complaints about both. All whispered, of course, while Missy was out of earshot."

"Out of earshot in this house?"

"She was in the yard investigating our flowers and thinking about whether to switch the ones in her bouquet."

"I'm kind of glad I missed all of it."

"You would've gotten annoyed." My mother looked at me, eyebrows raised. "There were comments made about the sandy condition of our living room floor. There was actually an offer to sweep it up while waiting."

I shoved a pile of fabric off a chair so I could sit, shin deep in a purple sea. "The nerve. What did you say?"

"I said—politely of course—no, thank you. That the sand on the floor was symbolic of summer in this house and was a welcome guest until after Labor Day."

"And they said?"

My mother shifted the hem so she could put in another pin. "Nothing really. Just an 'Oh' and a 'Hmmm.' Both of which were judge-y."

"Speaking of judge-y," I said. The chiffon was silky along the tops of my feet. "Missy is sweet and she means well, but she basically told me to get out of town because life would be better elsewhere. Or at least the boys would. Oh, and she said you are a genius. That part was okay."

"She's a nice girl. Awfully young to be getting married, though." My mother glanced at me warily. Accusingly even.

I gave her a wary look right back. "Who said I was getting married?"

"Actually," she said, shifting the dress from her lap to the worktable. "No one has. Not a single person has spoken to me about my daughter hanging out with Handel Davies over the last few days."

"So?"

My mother looked at me pointedly. "Jane."

I lowered my eyes. Purple fabric swam across my vision. "What?"

"The lack of gossip likely means you haven't seen him since the night you two went out."

"I thought you weren't interested," I said. "You never asked me about it."

"Of course I'm interested! I just didn't want to pry."

I crossed my legs, lifting them out of the chiffon. "Fine." Settled some more into the chair. "Handel and I had a nice time. Better than nice."

My mother was trying not to smile. "Nice? Nice and a Davies boy don't seem to go together."

"You sound like Michaela."

"Michaela doesn't like him?"

"She's just watching out for me. Like everyone else these days," I added, studying my hands and laying them in my lap. Trying not to fidget. "I liked hanging out with Handel. We clicked, or I thought we did. But I haven't heard from him since."

My mother swiveled her way toward me in the chair, moving fabric as she went. "Oh, sweetie, I'm sorry." She put a hand on my arm.

"I'm fine. We're probably not right for each other, anyway. And it's not like I need any complications this summer." I looked up, and my mother was right there, so close. Her eyes matching my own. My throat grew tight. "I need everything to be simple. You know?"

"Yes," she whispered. "I do." She leaned forward and brushed the hair away from my face. "There's something else I've wanted to talk to you about."

"What?"

"I think it's time," she began. Stopped. Took a breath and began again. "I think it would be good if we went to visit your father. You haven't been since the funeral."

Immediately, my head swung side to side, *no no no no*.

"It might be good for you. For both of us."

"I can't I can't I can't," I said on repeat. "I'm not ready," I tried, but what little voice I had left was gone.

"Okay. All right. But soon, Jane. I want us to go soon. You can't avoid it forever."

I nodded, though I wasn't agreeing. Deep breaths. I needed to get out into the air. Out of this room so full of fabric I might suffocate. But my mother wasn't done yet. Not done with me. She slid open the drawer of her desk. Removed a small white box.

Held it out to me. "I wanted you to have this," she said. "Take it." She placed it on my lap.

I lifted the lid.

Inside was a thin gold chain, at the end of which was a tiny mosaic heart. All shades of ocean and sky. Just like the one I'd lost—just like it, but different, too. This one had a pale sliver of green running through the center. Tears pressed into my eyes. "It's beautiful," I told her. "Thank you, Mom."

"Let me help you put it on," she whispered. Her voice was hoarse.

I got up, almost tripping over the fabric on the floor. Set the box aside. "Not now," I said. "Maybe another time."

My mother blinked. She was nodding. "Okay."

"I'm going to go out for a while," I said, glad I was still wearing my bathing suit underneath my clothes, thinking a swim might be in store for me tonight. Before my mother could say anything else, I grabbed my flip-flops and was gone from the house, staring up at the sky as it turned the red color of the evening.

I started to walk. Walk and walk and walk.

At first I had no direction, then I realized I'd walked so far I'd crossed into the next town. I doubled back, and soon found myself heading to the only place I wanted to be when I was hoping to forget. The beach. The smell of the ocean air, briny with salt and sea life, always calmed me. There was something about the sound the waves made, the constancy of them, their broken rhythm, that could knit me together again when I was afraid things were coming apart. Even the pungent smell on the wharf where the fishermen brought in their catch was soothing. My whole life had been spent coming down to this place with my mother and father when I was small, and on my own when I'd gotten old enough to do things by myself or with friends. It's where I always went when I wanted to think, even in the winter. The ocean provided the sound track to some of the most important moments I could remember. The best ones.

I passed the row of fancy bars and restaurants at the edge of town that catered to the city people that summered here, the ones who built big houses where they could have ocean views and catered parties on wide rolling lawns and park SUVs in long driveways. Where they didn't have to interact with the locals. These were people who typically never set foot on the town beach because they paid to go the private club far enough away from the wharf that the fishing boats going out for the day and coming back would never mar their view of the sea.

They had their own little world over here.

I passed the Ocean Club, with its big wooden deck looking out over the water and its glittering dining room, and the Pump House next door, all glass and minimalist white, its parking lot packed with BMWs. They looked like they belonged to another place, another town where bars like Charlie O's and O'Malley's Pub couldn't exist just down the road. The owners didn't even employ locals during the summer. They hired out-of-town kids looking for a quick buck or whose parents thought it would be "good for them" to find out what it was like to work for a change. No one would tell you that outright if you applied— that they didn't hire local kids to bus and wait tables—but everyone knew the deal and stopped applying for jobs on this strip of oceanfront long ago. There was almost an unspoken agreement between townies and the city people not to mingle, even though we all lived right next door to one another.

I stopped in front of Christie's, a martini bar that boasted drinks out over the ocean and quaint twinkle lights on the deck, watching as a tall, elegantly dressed woman emerged from a sleek Mercedes, handing her keys to a valet who would whisk it off to some unseen parking place. She had a white leather clutch under one arm and was dressed in a short, tight white dress and four-inch heels. Everything about her said rich and glamorous as she tottered toward the entrance.

"Hey, it's you."

The Mercedes pulled up in front of me with the valet I'd seen taking the woman's keys in the driver's seat. He was the same boy from the beach the other day, the one with the dog named Eric and the lacrosse stick. I was surprised to find out he had a job. He grinned at me with those perfect teeth, his crisp white short-sleeved shirt bright against his skin.

Okay, so he was good-looking.

I searched my brain for his name. "Miles, right?"

"So I *did* make an impression," he said over the soft purr of the car.

"Are you always this cheesy?" I tried to be annoyed, but I couldn't suppress a laugh. He was so different from the boys I was used to, so polite, all smooth lines and big winning smiles. His behavior was almost excusable. Almost.

"Nah, I'm just confident."

"Oh, oh-kay." I started on my way again.

He gunned the engine lightly. "Can I give you a ride somewhere?"

"In some other lady's car? No, thanks."

He looked at me strangely. "Don't worry. She won't care."

"Really, no," I said. "I like to walk."

"Too bad."

I didn't slow down. "Not for me."

He kept pace with me, the car nearly silent. "What if I came to pick you up one evening in a car of my very own?"

"Is it an SUV?"

"Why? Does that affect your answer?"

"Maybe."

The car rolled alongside me, the gravel in the road kicking and popping underneath the tires. "Maybe what? Maybe you'll hang out if it's an SUV? Or maybe you *won't* hang out if it's an SUV? Or is the maybe more about just the general question of whether you'll hang out with me?"

I laughed again, but didn't stop. Just shrugged.

"You could come to one of my lacrosse games. I'm really good," he added, with only a little irony.

"Seriously?"

"What? The girls where I'm from *love* lacrosse games."

I glanced his way. He looked so relaxed driving that fancy car. Like he belonged in a Mercedes. Like he'd never belong around here. "Yeah, well, you're obviously not at home anymore."

"Come on, girl! Give me something," he pleaded.

I looked at him one last time. He was almost charming in his exasperation. "I did give you something. I gave you a maybe," I said, then turned left, cutting across someone's lawn so he couldn't follow.

As my steps took me farther away, I could hear him idling there, waiting to see if I'd turn around, and my spirits lifted just a little bit. The rest of the way to the beach, I marveled at how the attention of a boy, even one that didn't interest me much, could be so wonderfully distracting, how it could cover over the cracks and dips of painful memories even if only for a little while. And I wondered, too, as I walked, how all those years before I'd managed to live without it.

NINE

THE TOWN BEACH WAS empty that evening, save a group of boys swimming way down at one end and a couple enjoying the view over the water, high up in a lifeguard chair. His arm around her shoulder. She leaning into him.

And me. There was me.

Alone on the sand.

I walked up and down the big curving C of beach. The breeze was slight, a soft whisper all around. I pulled off my T-shirt and considered going for a swim. I didn't have a towel, but I didn't much care, either. The air was hot and humid. The ocean ran across my toes again and again, bringing with it tiny shells and an occasional patch of stringy seaweed rolling by. It called to me. Finally, when I felt like I couldn't hold out any longer, I stepped out of my shorts, dropped my T-shirt on top of them, used my flip-flops to anchor everything so it wouldn't blow away, and headed straight into the water, confident and sure, not stopping for waves as they rushed toward me or when the cool temperature raised goose bumps all over my skin.

When I was waist-high, I dove in.

The beach, swimming, everything around me was magic. It could heal all things. Protect me from danger. I lay on my back, floating, eyes on the darkening blue above, the water lapping gently at my skin, soaking my hair. I gave in to the sea, letting it bob me around, buoy my body toward the shore with the tide. I don't know how long I stayed that way, but by the time I got out and headed up the stairs to the boardwalk, it was late. The rest of the light had disappeared from the sky. I slipped my shorts on and shoved the end of my T-shirt into the pocket of my shorts. I didn't want it to get wet. I knew what happened when a girl wearing a bikini went swimming and immediately threw on a shirt afterward, and how long those embarrassing spots took to dry. My legs were caked with sand all the way to my shins, but I didn't bother to wash my feet at the spout on the boardwalk. There was something satisfying about the way the sand would fall away, little by little, like shedding tiny, glittery scales as my skin dried and I got closer to home. My hair was heavy and wet, sending little rivers of water running down my arms and stomach and back. It felt good in the warm night air. I crossed the small parking lot, passing two old, battered station wagons, surfboards attached to racks on top, and started up the street toward the wharf, still barefoot. I could do that without catching stares—walk barefoot in summer, between the beach and my destination. Everyone could in our town.

Another perk of living in this place, I'd always thought.

With my flip-flops swinging in one hand, I combed my fingers through my hair with the other, trying to untangle it. The air was so thick with heat it was already starting to dry. I went around the bend, the wharf now in sight.

And with it, Handel Davies.

He stood on the corner in front of Levinson's, in the glow of the streetlamp, smoking a cigarette. Staring out to the water, his expression serious, like something was on his mind, and it wasn't something good. He wasn't alone. Another boy, big, stocky, whose name I thought was Mac, stood next to him, also taking drags of a cigarette. All muscle and brawn. Two more boys I knew by sight, but whose names I couldn't remember, were leaning against the wall nearby. One of them was tall and wiry, the look on his face unfriendly. Everything about his features twisted so as to seem angry, hair buzzed short on the bottom and longer on the top, all wrong, only highlighting his lack of bulk and his air of menace. The other was short, rectangular, and expressionless, like he was auditioning for the role of bodyguard. My mind searched for their names again but came up with nothing. I wondered if they'd been at the party that night in the dunes. It had been too dark for me to see their faces clearly.

Instinctively, my eyes went to their boots but came up with nothing.

I stopped walking. Unsure whether to go right on by or make a quick left. Duck behind Mr. Morgan's cobbler shop and cut through the alleyway behind it. Handel hadn't seen me yet. None of those boys had. They were all staring out at the water, saying nothing, some unspoken pact to avoid conversation.

But I couldn't put off meeting Handel forever.

I decided to go straight.

My feet took me forward, still barefoot, shins still caked with sand, though not as much as before. My hair was drier now, but still wet enough that the ends sent tiny streams down my skin, and my bathing suit top was too damp to put on my shirt just yet. When I got close, close enough that my footsteps slapping the sidewalk were audible, Handel turned his head, and with Handel, so did all the others. Michaela's warnings about him pounded my insides like waves crashing into the beach. It was one thing to gush and dream about a handsome bad boy paying me attention, and another to come face-to-face with one of the reasons he got that reputation in the first place.

Handel didn't smile when he saw me. All he said was, "Jane."

Before I could answer, I heard my name again, this time from across the street, and I turned.

It was Seamus. Seamus and Tammy. Together.

If I wasn't so unnerved by Handel, seeing those two hanging out would have made me happy. I would have better registered how great it was that Seamus was hanging out with one of my friends. But I couldn't. Not now. I was all about Handel.

"Hey," Tammy said once they reached me. She held a cup in her hand, and a spoon. Ice cream from Nana's down the block. Southern Apple Pie, her favorite. Tammy always ordered the same thing. She glanced at Handel, then at me. I could tell it was going to challenge her to be nice if I introduced them.

"I was just out for ice cream and I ran into Seamus," she said, which explained why she was with him.

Seamus seemed nervous, but the flustered kind. Like possibility was just around the corner, like this could very well be his chance with Tammy. "I was headed home from Slovenska's." He looked down at my feet. "Been down at the beach tonight?"

"Yeah. I went for a walk."

Tammy's ice cream was melting. "It's late, Jane. You didn't have to go alone." She didn't say *shouldn't,* but it was implied.

Handel stood there next to me. Waiting.

"It's fine," I said. "Everything's fine. Um, Tammy and Seamus, this is Handel. Handel, these are my friends Tammy and Seamus," I said, finally introducing everyone.

"Nice to meet you," Seamus said, putting out his hand, his face open and friendly, as always.

"You too," Handel said, and they shook.

I waited for Tammy to say something, anything, but she was studying her ice cream, pushing the pie dough bits around. I nudged her with my hip, and she gave me a begrudging look that said *fine*.

"Hi, Handel," she said, no offer of her hand.

Handel didn't seem offended. "Nice to meet you."

My eyes were pleading, first at Tammy, then at Seamus, who seemed to understand since he suddenly said to Tammy, "We should go."

"Should we?" she asked, eyebrows raised, watching me for confirmation. I nodded, ever so slightly. "Oh, all right. Bye, Jane. See you tomorrow at the beach. Bye . . . Handel."

Seamus hurried the two of them away, but Tammy lagged. It wasn't until they turned the corner and disappeared from view that Handel and I spoke again.

Well, I spoke.

"I had a nice time the other night after we left the party," I said. "I thought you did, too."

Handel's shoulders tensed, or maybe they already were. He didn't offer to introduce me to his friends. Instead, he gestured that I follow him. We walked a little ways down the block, just out of earshot if we kept our voices low. "I did," he said.

Boldness blossomed in me. It always seemed to when I was around Handel. "Then what's your problem?" I asked.

"I'm not sure I'm good for you."

"Why is that?"

Handel wouldn't look at me. Not at first. Then he did, but it was like he was trying to tell me something with his eyes instead of his words. "My life is complicated."

"This doesn't have to be complicated," I said, tossing my hair in that way I knew the boys found fascinating, the thick damp locks falling along my right shoulder.

I wanted Handel to find me fascinating—so much that he couldn't resist seeing me, even if he wasn't good for me. Especially because he wasn't. I was suddenly glad all I had on was my bathing suit top and shorts, that my T-shirt was still dangling from my pocket. I wanted Handel to forget I was a nice girl with a serious lack of experience with boys. I wanted to make him want me in all the ways I wasn't supposed to, to think about doing all those things that boys did to girls who weren't like me. I wanted to become that girl he did them to. I could feel her slipping into my body right now, taking me over.

"We don't have enough history for it to be complicated, so don't make it that way," I continued. "Right now, it's all very simple. Either you want to spend time with me, or you don't. If you do, great. If not, then the other night will become a nice memory of the time I had with Handel Davies, who took a sudden interest in me and then a sudden disinterest." I stopped there and wondered who this confident, sexy Jane was. I tossed my hair again—this time so it went over my other shoulder—because I'd noticed how intently Handel watched me do it the first time, pleased as his eyes traveled down my neck to my bare stomach to the place where my shorts hung low across my hips before flickering back to my face.

He smiled a little, so little it was almost imperceptible. Just a tiny curve in the left side of his mouth. "I don't know."

But I had him now. The way he stared told me everything.

I took the string of my bathing suit top between my fingers, twirling it, then letting it fall to my skin. "Yes," I said, so sure of myself. "You do know."

Then something—a shift in the air, a cough behind us—set me on edge. His friends' eyes were on us. I could feel them. When I turned, I saw that they had moved so they could see us. They were watching Handel. And me. The skinny one with the menacing stare most of all. The way he looked at me sent that other, bolder Jane running. "What's up with your friends?"

Handel glanced at them. Shoved his hands way down in his jeans pockets. He shrugged. Smile gone. "Ignore those guys."

"Really?"

"If you meant it when you said you want to hang out with me, you'll just have to endure them. They're . . ." Handel trailed off.

I finished for him. "A bit rough around the edges?"

Handel laughed a little, the first real attempt at levity since we'd started talking. "Yeah. You know. Townies. Born, live, and die here types. Like me."

"Like you, but not really," I said.

"You were born here, too," Handel said. "Grown up here, too."

"True. I'm not ready to think about where I'm going to die yet, though."

Handel was quiet. Pulled out a cigarette. Lit it. Took a drag. "Me neither," he said eventually.

The eyes of those friends, I could still feel them. Watchful. No: mistrustful. Suspicious. "Maybe we're not all the same, then."

"I don't know," he said after another long drag. "When you grow up around here and you come from a family like mine, there's something about this place that gets down deep into your bones and settles there. Makes you do things you never thought you would."

A chill ran across my skin and made me shudder. I grabbed the T-shirt from my pocket and pulled it over my head. "What's that supposed to mean? What things?"

The end of Handel's cigarette was a bright, burned orange, the ashes flaking away in the slight breeze. "That's a conversation for another day." He glanced at his friends, then at me one more time. Took a step closer, his face close, his breath close, everything about him suddenly so close. "I want to see you again. I do."

"So see me," I whispered.

His eyes were intense. Big and wide and all for me. "Tomorrow night?"

I nodded, ever so slightly. "Okay. Where?"

"How about down by the lighthouse?"

"The lighthouse?" I hadn't been out there since I was eight, maybe nine. When the girls and I used to ride our bikes all over town and didn't care so much about lying out in the sun and talking to boys.

"I go there sometimes," Handel went on. "When I want to get away." He stopped short of saying *what* he wanted to get away from. "How's eight?"

"All right," I said, and my heart raced at this, raced at the thought of seeing him in a place so remote. I imagined his lips on my neck, kissing bare skin. His eyes kept flickering there while we talked. "I'll see you then."

"See you, Jane," he whispered, then turned and walked toward his friends, who'd been watching him this whole time. Watching me. I doubled back the way I came, went down a different street. Took another route home so I didn't have to pass by all those staring eyes.

In my room, that night, the box with the heart was waiting for me.

It sat there, white and lonely, on my bedside table.

I didn't touch it. Wasn't ready to. Not just yet.

TEN

GOOD MORNING, SUNSHINE," my mother said, a tall glass of iced coffee in front of her on the kitchen counter. She was still weary-eyed from sleep, like me, neither one of us looking at all like sunshine.

"You look tired," I said, going into the fridge, retrieving the pitcher of coffee we brewed each day and left there to cool so when we added the ice it wouldn't get watered down. I poured myself a glass and dropped five big cubes into it from the freezer, along with some half-and-half that turned it the color of caramel.

"I was up most of the night finishing Missy's bridesmaid dresses." She swirled the glass in circles with her hand, the ice clinking against the sides. "Why didn't you come see me when you got home? My light was on."

"I was tired, I guess."

My mother gestured at the stool on the other side of the counter. "Sit."

So I did, and now we were face-to-face, elbows resting on the table, iced coffees in front of us. "What?"

"I want to discuss the fact that you ran out of here yesterday."

"I know. I'm sorry."

She blinked once. Twice. "We need to be able to talk about what happened. We need to talk about your father."

At this, I turned away. Stared at the hanging plant by the porch door, its leaves wilted from the heat, long green vines reaching toward the ground. Someone needed to water it. "It's too hard to," I said, my voice hoarse.

"Jane. Look at me."

But I didn't. Instead I turned my attention to the painting on the wall of an old fishing boat tied up on shore, stormy seas reaching up behind it, white caps dotting the tips of tiny waves farther out. My father had bought it at an art fair a long time ago, the kind that all beach towns seem to hold once a summer. I felt my mother's hands close around mine, her arms stretched across the table, trying to reach me.

"Look at me, Jane," she said again.

It took some effort, but I did. The subject—of that night, of my father—always snatched the breath right out of my lungs, threatening to choke me.

"What happened isn't your fault."

"But it is," I whispered. "It is."

"Jane, no—"

"If I hadn't stayed late, if I hadn't fallen asleep, if I hadn't called you back—"

"You might be dead," my mother finished before I could.

"But Dad," I croaked, unable to say anything else.

My father. My father, who taught me how to ride a bike. My father who took me swimming even when the water was freezing. My father who loved to order pizza after his shift was over and take it down to the beach with me, still in his uniform, socks and shoes off, dinner on the sand, extra pepperoni, just the two of us. My father who was big and strong and fearless and invincible—until one day he wasn't.

My father who was gone.

My mother squeezed my hands in hers. "Your father would be heartbroken to know that you're blaming yourself. You have to stop."

I blinked away tears. "I can't."

"It might help if you and I went to visit him."

A single tear escaped. It rolled down my cheek. "I'm not ready. Not yet."

"Just think about it. We don't have to go today or tomorrow, but soon."

I dabbed my face with a napkin. "Okay."

"I mean it."

"I know you do," I said.

My mother's hands slid away, returning to their place on the other side of the counter. Back around the cold glass of her iced coffee. "You have to face this. It's been long enough."

I didn't say anything. My throat was too tight.

"You're not alone, Jane," she said. "We will get through this together. We will. I am your mother and I love you and I'm not going anywhere."

Instead of running to my room, this time I slipped from my perch and softly padded my way to the other side of the counter. I leaned into my mother, and she took me in her arms and held me tight, as tight as that night after the police brought me home and everything was over. She didn't let go for a long, long while.

"I saw that guy again by the way," I said to the girls. It was midday, the sun straight above and glaring. Bridget had dragged an umbrella all the way down to the beach from her family's house and spent an hour anchoring it into the sand. We'd laughed at her, but now the four of us were huddled underneath it, desperate for shade.

Tammy peeked a foot into the sun, then quickly pulled it back. "If by *that guy* you mean Handel, *that* information has already been discussed."

"No," I said. "I mean *that rich guy* with the dog."

Bridget perked up. "The cute one with the friends? The lacrosse player?"

Michaela rolled her eyes. "How many other rich guys with dogs have shown up to talk to us recently?"

"I was just verifying," she said, offended. Her eyes flickered up to the green polka-dot umbrella above us. "Be nice or I'll kick you out from under my shade."

"I'm sorry, B," Michaela said quickly. "I don't mean to be impatient."

"It's fine. You can stay, then. For now."

I turned to Bridget. She always meant well. "Yes, it was the one with the friends, and I suppose he was cute. Though jocks aren't really my type."

Tammy nudged me. "Because your type is more"—she tapped her finger to her chin, made a mock-thinking stare—"young Irish mafia?"

My only response was to glare.

"Their names *were* pretty ridiculous," Bridget admitted, choosing to ignore Tammy's comment, or too distracted thinking about the boys to notice it. "What were they again?"

"I think one of them was actually Logan," Michaela said with a laugh. "Or was it Juniper? Or Jodper?"

"Miles was the name of their leader—you know, the dog one," Tammy said, finally dropping the Handel bit.

"He was their leader, wasn't he?" I agreed. "It's funny how that stuff is obvious. You see a group of guys and you automatically know which one is in charge."

"So, anyway, you saw him and . . . what?" Bridget wanted to know.

"I was walking along Ocean Ave," I said. "You know, over by the strip with the restaurants like the Ocean Club?"

"What were you doing there?" Michaela asked.

"Um." I hesitated. I thought about the conversation I'd had with my mother beforehand, the one that sent me running off, and the one from this morning about how I needed to deal with the stuff about my father. I decided I didn't need to start dealing yet. "You know, I just felt like being somewhere different. Other than the wharf."

"Well, that place is definitely different than the wharf," Bridget said with a laugh.

"I was walking by Christie's, and it turns out that this guy—the one named Miles—valets there, and he pulled up in one of the cars and said hello. He remembered me from the beach."

"I bet he did," Tammy said.

"I'm sure he remembers all of us, Tam," I said.

"Right."

Michaela looked at me. "Did he ask you out?"

"Yeah," I said with a smile, remembering. "First he offered to come pick me up in his car some night, and then he invited me to come watch him play lacrosse."

"You're not serious," Tammy said.

"Sadly, I am. I said no of course, and then didn't let him get much further than that."

Michaela looked at me. "You could give him a chance, Jane. See what he's like and all. He might not be that bad."

"Are you kidding?" Tammy and I both asked her at once.

"I'd go out with him," Bridget said.

"Well, we all know *that*," Tammy said.

"That's it. Out of my shade," Bridget protested, reaching around me to give Tammy a shove.

Tammy tipped a little into the sun and quickly scrambled to get her bearings again under the umbrella. "Sorry, sorry."

Bridget just sighed and let it go.

"Maybe it would be good for you to go out with someone else," Michaela suggested. "You know, someone other than Handel."

This time it was my turn to shove someone, and I gave Michaela a push. She didn't budge. Tammy might be bossy, but Michaela was tougher than all of us. "Can you, just this once, not judge Handel so negatively?"

"So we're pro-Handel again?" Tammy asked. "Just because you ran into him once down on the wharf?"

"I like him. I can't help it."

"It's okay, Jane," Bridget said. "You like who you like. And I don't blame you for liking Handel Davies. He is gor-or-geous."

"But of dubious character," Michaela said.

"So is the guy with the dog!" I shot back.

"He is *not*," she said. "He's a prep school athlete."

"Exactly. He's got 'entitled' written all over him."

Michaela pursed her lips and gave me a look that said *come on*. "And Handel Davies has 'bad idea' written all over him."

"I'm going out with him," I said. "Handel, I mean. Tonight."

Michaela took a deep breath. I could hear the disapproval in the way she inhaled. But she held her tongue.

Tammy sighed. "Oh, Jane." She sounded resigned.

"Exactly," Michaela said, finally letting out her breath. She sounded equally defeated.

Bridget looked at me, blinking those big eyes of hers. "If you see Miles *again,* and he asks you out *again,*" she said, the only one not to judge. "Tell him you have this friend."

I leaned into Bridget. Rested my head on her shoulder. "I will, B. Don't worry. I definitely will."

A spark of excitement flickered in me the rest of the afternoon, an urgent buzz underneath my skin as I lay in the sun, like something was about to happen. I had to keep reminding myself that this eager pulse was beating out its rhythm because I was going to see Handel, because we had another date. I wondered if this time we would kiss—I kept picturing it, what kissing Handel would be like, daydreaming about how it might happen. Then I moved on to fantasizing about where those kisses might go next, imagining his hands on my skin, sliding up underneath my shirt, and all kinds of other things I'd never allowed myself to do with a boy. I could feel the blood rising into my cheeks and coloring the surface of my skin. I used to be so in control, so focused, so disciplined, but there was something about Handel that undid me, or maybe it was just that lately I was easily undone. No—I was looking to be. I was still thinking about our imaginary kissing and the places it might lead when I heard my name being repeated.

"Jane? Hellooo," Bridget was saying.

I lifted my head from the towel and realized that she, Tammy, and Michaela were watching me. I hoped they didn't notice my blush. The umbrella was gone, and their blankets and towels were all packed up, bags slung across their shoulders and resting against their hips. "What's up?"

"We're taking off."

I sat up. "Oh?"

Bridget glanced over at Tammy. "Tammy has a date with Seamus."

This startled me. "Really?"

"It's not a date," Tammy said. "We're just going for a run."

I took off my sunglasses and rubbed my eyes. "How did I miss that part of the conversation?"

Michaela crossed her arms and looked at me. "You've been in your own world for, like, hours now."

Tammy smirked. "What were you thinking about?"

I shrugged. "I must have fallen asleep."

"Right," Tammy said. She cocked her head. "You might want to head, too. Don't you have somewhere to be this evening?"

I smiled. Started to get up from my towel. "Yes. But you ladies go. I'm going for a quick swim before I leave. It's hot."

Bridget was grinning. "I bet. Have fun tonight," she said. "And don't do anything I wouldn't do!"

Michaela rolled her eyes. "And by that, she means do *everything*."

"Exactly," Bridget said.

Tammy put her hand on my arm but spoke to the rest of the group. "Jane has always known her mind about this stuff, so I'm sure she knows her limits with someone like Handel." She looked at me. "Right, Jane?"

"Right," I said. "Tell Seamus hello."

Tammy nodded.

But as I watched my friends walk away up the beach, I realized how much I'd been keeping from them about what was really going on inside me, how different I'd become right before their eyes. The Jane to which Tammy referred was the girl who'd existed before February, the one who'd been living in a cocoon, tucked up and hidden and safe from the outside world. Now that this new Jane had emerged, it was as something unexpected. A butterfly, but one who awoke to find that her wings were black.

ELEVEN

HE WAY TO THE lighthouse was
rocky.

I was good at jumping from
one footing to the next, even if
the surface was jagged, avoiding the little tide pools that ebbed
and flowed with the surf. Years of doing this as a kid, scrambling
on my hands and knees, searching for green crabs and hermit
crabs and even lobsters farther out, made it almost instinctive,
my body and my legs knowing when to shift, to turn ever so
slightly, curving my foot to land just right on the slippery surface. The sound of the surf grew faint as I concentrated, all my
attention on getting to the next rock, measuring exactly how
much force to use, whether it required a step, a hop, a leap. The
sun was going down but there was still a lot of light in the sky,
the horizon big and colorful.

Then I misjudged the distance of my next jump and almost
slipped, barely landing, almost falling into a big tide pool full of
kelp. When I got my bearings again, I decided to rest. Catch my
breath. I was halfway down the narrow peninsula jutting out
from the very end of town, the remote one that was nearly un-
populated. It was illegal to build out here. The place was a nest-
ing ground for all sorts of birds, so the land and the dunes that
stretched up and out behind me were protected. The only visible
structure was the lighthouse, abandoned long ago.

I turned back to the shore, wondering if Handel would soon
appear, making his way out like I was, or if he was already waiting

for me, tucked up inside the lighthouse at the top, the round walls blocking out the wind. It was close to eight. Carefully, I stepped around that big tide pool, definitely not wanting to show up dripping wet and smelling like seaweed tonight.

Then I looked up and saw Handel.

Fair hair blowing and twisting in the wind. Hands in his jeans pockets like always. Watching me make my way, rock by rock. Suddenly everything felt different under his gaze. The stretch of my bare legs as I leaped, the way my tank top hugged my body in the breeze, my arms flying wide and open while I jumped. My pace quickened, even though at any moment I might fall, tumbling into the ocean out here where it was deep and angry and unforgiving. But I didn't care. I wanted to get there. To him. And soon enough the *there* became *here* and *now* and I was leaping onto one last rock, the one just before things flattened out and I could walk normally, one foot in front of the other, to where Handel stood waiting for me.

He smiled. Big and easy like he'd left all the weighty parts of life hidden among the dunes.

I smiled, too. Handel did that to me.

There we were, both of us barefoot and a little sandy. Hair knotted, faint lines of salt trailing along the bare parts of our skin from the spray and splash of the waves. The world was big out here, all ocean and sky. Remote and wild and beautiful. And the two of us, Handel and me, alone in the middle of it.

"Up here," he said to me, gesturing toward the top of the lighthouse.

I followed him inside.

This time with Handel there wasn't the surprise of talking

for hours under the stars or the drama of a thunderstorm and the pounding rain to go along with it, but the lighthouse had a romance all its own. It had been out of use so long that the white paint was chipped and peeling, and the long winters by the ocean and constant battering from salty waves had done their damage along the metal, inside and out. Rust had eaten through parts of the round wall, leaving a lacelike effect, tiny portholes that reminded you there was water just on the other side.

"Careful," Handel warned as we wound our way up to the top. There were jagged places in the handrail along the staircase, sharp enough to cut you if you weren't paying attention. His heavy work boots clanged against the old metal rungs, and I watched the way his body shifted beneath his clothes, the muscles of his arms tightening and loosening in the rhythm of his steps.

"Thanks," I said. The sound of the waves crashing into the rocks was distracting, loud enough at times to drown out our movements. I took the last few stairs and came to the landing. Looked around at the windows on every side, some of them permanently wedged open, two of them broken. A couple of wooden benches were lined up in the center like church pews. I supposed this was a church of sorts, for some people. "I haven't been here in years."

The sun was dropping over the land, and Handel watched it. "I love this place."

"Me too."

He turned. Looked at me a minute. "Yeah?"

I nodded. "I used to love all of it. The climb to get out here on the rocks, the tide pools along the way, the strength of the wind, the sound of the waves." I thought my list ended there, but then I realized I'd left something out. The most important part. "The way this room feels like a secret. You know, like for a princess in a castle."

Handel laughed, his calm audible in its sound. "You had me until 'secret,' then you lost me at 'princess.' But I like thinking about this room as a secret." Handel's eyes shifted, their color moving from blue to gray in the waning light. "It kind of is a secret, in a way."

I tried to read him, read into the last part of what he'd said. "I'm not sure what you're trying to say."

"What do you mean?"

My hand went to my hair, gathering it. I needed something to hang on to. Something to do with my fingers, since all they wanted was to reach out to Handel. "Are you talking about this place, or are you talking about me?"

He shook his head slightly. Took a deep breath. "I don't know. Maybe both."

"Do you want to keep me a secret?" I asked, a part of me loving the idea that I could be like this beautiful, haunting lighthouse, a mystery Handel kept from touching the other parts of his life. But part of me knew too well how secrets could be destructive.

"I told you," he said. "Things are complicated."

I took a step toward him. Then another. The thin strap of my tank top slid off my shoulder. "That's not a real answer."

Handel's eyes went to the place where the thread of silk came to rest on my arm, a loose bracelet. "You don't want the real answer, Jane."

"I do," I said.

"Are you sure?"

I nodded. I wasn't sure, though.

Handel walked over to the window farthest away, undoing all my work of getting closer. It was one of the broken ones, and his hair tangled and danced in the breeze. "I thought this could be simple at first. You know, hanging out with you."

I tugged the strap of my shirt back in place. "Your friends don't know where you are." I stated this because I sensed it, sensed that his friends were somehow part of his unease.

"No," he said. Just one word, like this was enough of an answer.

"Mine do."

"Your friends are different."

"They don't like you, either."

Handel seemed startled by this, though not for the reason I'd imagined. "How do you know *my* friends don't like *you*?" he asked, defensive.

"It wasn't difficult to figure out the other night."

"They didn't talk to you," he said, like that mattered.

"They didn't need to."

"Your friends really don't approve of me?" Handel asked, wanting confirmation.

I shook my head. Then remembered Bridget. "Well, all but one."

"Why not?" Handel asked.

It was my turn to be evasive. I wasn't ready to talk about the reasons my friends worried about me lately, reasons Handel probably already knew about from all the articles in the newspaper. I didn't want to ruin the evening. "My life is complicated, too."

"I'm sure," he said, but didn't press any further. Just turned to watch the water through the broken window. I joined him there, and the two of us stood staring out at the sea as it bobbed and churned, little whitecaps breaking through all that midnight-blue ocean. Handel and I were on the edge of something. I knew it deep down, instinctively. Now was the moment to turn back if we wanted to, if I wanted to, and step away unscathed. Seize this opportunity and go home, like none of this had ever happened, this thing between Handel and me, whatever it was. But it was Handel who spoke first, and I lost my chance.

"Do you want to keep seeing me?" he asked.

"Yes," I answered with a certainty I didn't realize I had in me.

He reached out and brushed a lock of hair from my eyes, the whisper of his finger along my skin nearly causing my legs to buckle. "Okay, then," he said.

Just like that, it was decided. Handel and I were headed over that edge, and I didn't care. I wanted it so badly, too, once the offer was officially there.

"I'm going to keep this from my friends," Handel said. "I think it's better that way."

This I hadn't expected. "Really?"

He nodded. "Maybe you should, too. It might be easier."

This raised a tiny red flag in me, but I ignored it. He could be right—it could be easier to just stop telling my girls about Handel, even though the idea of not talking to them about every little thing that happened was strange. Then again, I'd already been holding back so much, practicing that skill of not sharing details about something important, something that had woven itself into the core of who I am. Ever since that night in February, I'd been keeping so many things to myself. Sometimes it felt like poison coursing through my veins.

"Your friends don't like me much, anyway," Handel went on, making his case.

"No, I'm not like that," I said before I could change my mind, deciding I already had enough secrets. "They're not going to say anything to your friends about you and me. It's not like your friends and my friends hang out."

"Fair enough," Handel said.

And that was that—no more talk about the uneven pact we were making, the secret Handel was turning me into among the people in his life. We moved on to other topics of conversation on this beautiful evening, high up in the lighthouse, and the mood lightened as the sky darkened, my skin alive with Handel's nearness, my body as yearning as the moonlight. It was so easy, how this was all happening.

There was nowhere for me to go but forward, straight into Handel's arms.

There was something about him that drew me in and laid me bare, exposing my thoughts, my dreams, my vulnerabilities, my wishes. My desires, too, surfaced and sang out to Handel, calling him to me, making it clear I was already his. But it was more than this. It was like we had some invisible connection, one that I couldn't quite pinpoint, but I searched for it. It kept tugging at me, this tether between us, and I wondered what it would look like when it appeared. Even though Handel and I were different, maybe in ways that weren't easy to reconcile, we were also the same. I could feel it. He was better than he gave himself credit for and than everyone else did, too. There was a goodness in him, mixed in with all the bad. The bad was there, this I knew, but it was the good that I chose to trust more. I couldn't help it. It was written all over him, and I wouldn't turn away from it.

TWELVE

J ANE?" MY MOTHER CALLED to me. Her tone was urgent. Hopeful.

I could barely hear her on this bright summer morning. My eyes, all my attention, were caught by something else, one of the objects I feared most, something that simultaneously shattered my heart and reminded me of all the terrible things that had woven themselves into who I was and changed me.

A headstone.

It was small, rectangular, and a dark, dark gray.

It read: JOHN CALVETTI, DEVOTED FATHER, SON, AND POLICE with the dates of his birth and death. Those dates I couldn't bear to look at, especially the second one, from this past February. A little sapling grew next to the grave. I felt the urge to go to it, run my fingers over its soft green leaves, so full of life even in this heat, but I couldn't bring myself to move even an inch. I stood on a gentle incline a few yards away, close enough to see the words on the stone clearly, but far enough that I wasn't really there yet. Big, blooming white lilies were pressed against my chest, both arms gripping them, their scent strong and their stems long and thick and green. My mother had already laid hers on the sparse grass in front of the headstone, the lines from the newly dug grave still visible even as the earth tried to knit itself back together. She kneeled down a moment, her mouth moving in whispers, reaching out to run her hand over my father's name. Then she got up and turned to me.

"Jane," she called out again. "Come here."

But I shook my head. I couldn't even respond. There were no tears in my eyes or sobs in my throat. There was just a sense that everything in me was frozen, struck still with fear—of going any closer, of finding out that what I saw before me was indeed real. Here lay my father, gone forever from this life, from *my* life. Because of me.

He was gone because of *me*.

I suddenly wished for Handel, wished for his presence, the way he could distract me from the difficult things in life. Feel the deliciousness of having a secret.

"Jane," my mother called again. When I didn't reply and didn't move, she made her way to where I stood. "Oh, sweetheart," she said, and touched one of my hands, trying to unpeel it from my side. But I couldn't budge—nothing about me would. She slid the lilies out of my arms and pulled them close to take in their scent. "These are beautiful, aren't they?"

"Hmm," I managed, trying to remember to blink. My eyes had gone dry, unable to stop staring at the words on the stone, at my father's name. I breathed deep, in and out, then once more. "Okay."

"Okay?"

"Okay. I'm going to go put the flowers over there."

My mother held them out to me. "All right, honey. Do you want me to hold your hand?"

"No," I whispered, taking back the lilies.

"Are you sure?"

I nodded, the smell from the flowers so powerful it almost made me dizzy. I began to walk, tiny steps, all of them forward, first down the gentle slope of the hill and next along the side of the grave to the spot where my mother had been standing. I stopped there, staring at the ground, staring at the dirt in front of the carved stone, the way it was peppered with young blades of grass, all of them tender with the newness of life. The soil was that rich brown it always is when you are trying to grow something. It's strange to think how, right above the dead, we plant trees and flowers and grass. Or maybe it's not that strange at all. I couldn't decide. The one thing I knew for sure was that no amount of trees and flowers and new blades of grass was going to change the fact that my father was lying underneath this plot in a wood coffin that my mother picked out herself.

My father.

I didn't know what to do, what one was supposed to do when visiting a grave. I didn't want to talk, didn't feel like it, didn't know what to say and was afraid of what I might say. I didn't want to allow myself to cry, either, because if I started I might never stop, might never be able to leave this spot. I didn't touch the stone like my mother had. I didn't dare, because the cold rough slate under my hands was an unthinkable substitute for the real living body of my father, the arms that used to hug me and pick me up until I was too big and too old for him to carry me. I just stood there, still, unmoving, my eyes dry again from forgetting to blink, until finally, awkwardly, I bent just a little, enough to place the flowers alongside my mother's, careful not to touch anything. Not the grass or the sapling or the gravestone.

Especially not the gravestone.

Then quickly, very quickly, I turned around and began to walk away. I went up the gentle slope, past my mother, not looking at her, trusting that she would know to follow me, and she did. I could hear her footsteps. I may not have said anything out loud during those moments, but just before I left my father's grave, the words "Daddy" and "I'm so sorry" flashed through my mind.

I think it was okay that I didn't say them out loud.

I chose to believe it was, at least.

When we got home, my mind was a whirl. The name "Patrick McCallen" drifted in and out of it, stirring up guilt—guilt and a new sense of responsibility. I'd thought about him so much lately. Tried to decide what his involvement was that night, if any. Tried to decide if the boots I saw were his, or if they were common, if maybe they belonged to someone else who shopped at the same store he did.

I wasn't sure what I wanted the outcome of all this wondering to be. If I was hoping I'd find a reason to exonerate Patrick or if I was hoping to confirm he was involved.

But after this morning, I realized so clearly that his guilt wasn't up to me to decide. That *I* was the guilty one for not telling Officer Connolly all that I knew. For mentioning the detail about the boots but omitting the detail about Patrick McCallen. This wasn't a game. Not some cop show on television where they had to solve a random murder. This was about *my father,* who was lying dead at the bottom of a grave when he should be out and about in town, joking around with people on the wharf. Hounding me about going to mini-golf some night this summer.

I pulled open the top drawer of my bureau and started to dig around among the socks and underwear and bathing suits. At the bottom of it, underneath an old aqua-colored two-piece I wore the summer when I was twelve, I found the business card with Officer Connolly's direct number on it. Then I went to the living room and picked up the phone, the landline I'd come to associate with news about the break-in.

I started to dial.

I waited, nervous, listening to it ring.

Officer Connolly didn't pick up. I got his voice mail instead.

It was just as well, I decided. Easier to leave a message. I waited for the beep, the whole time tempted to hang up and try again later. I didn't, though—I knew I wouldn't try again later.

"Officer Connolly," I began. Then I stopped for a breath. "It's Jane Calvetti. I'm calling because I think I remembered something else important." Breathe, Jane. "The night of the break-in, those metal-toed boots I told you about?" Breathe. Come on, Jane. "I'm pretty sure I've seen Patrick McCallen wearing the same exact ones. That's all."

I put the phone down.

Listened to the soft *click* of the call cutting off.

I stared at the ancient thing. Those big fat numbers that I used to beg my mother to let me press with my little fingers so we could call Daddy. I was still staring at the phone, remembering dialing up my father, when it started to ring. The loud, piercing sound and the fact that I was hovering directly over it made me jump. I didn't answer. I waited until the call went through to the machine.

"Jane, it's Officer Connolly here, Michaela's dad," he said onto the recording, like I had more than one Officer Connolly in my life. His voice filled our house. "I just listened to your message, and I wanted to thank you for it. I'm gonna look into what you just told me right away, see where it leads. You just sit tight, and if you think of anything else, you call me, you hear? All right. Regards to your mother. Bye now."

There was a *click* as the call cut off.

I stared at the phone, like it might ring again. When it didn't, I started grabbing the stuff I needed for the day. To meet the girls in town and then head off to the beach. I moved around so easily, so quickly, at first I thought I must be numb from what I'd just done. But when I went out into the sunshine at nearly a run, I realized there was a lightness in me that hadn't been there before. I hadn't realized how heavy it was, carrying around my suspicions about Patrick all on my own. Now that I'd handed them off to someone else, to the people whose job it was to take on those suspicions and look into them, a great burden had been lifted.

Well—no. Not lifted altogether.

But I didn't have to carry it alone anymore. I'd take the relief, even if it was incomplete. A little bit was better than none.

THIRTEEN

THE GIRLS AND I were sitting in our booth at Slovenska's. Iced coffee and air-conditioning and, this time, a piece of lemon pie with four forks between us. I hadn't taken a single bite. I'd planned on telling them about my night with Handel, but the words that found their way out of my mouth were about my dad.

"I went to visit my father today," I said. My eyes flickered guiltily at Michaela across the table, knowing I should probably tell her I'd called her dad. But I wasn't ready to talk about that. Discussing my father felt like enough. "My mother brought me. You know. To the grave," I added, doing my best to be brave.

The girls were silent at first. Tammy, finishing her latest bite of pie. Bridget, already in the middle of scooping up another. Michaela let her fork clink onto the table. She put her arm around me in the booth. "Jane," she said softly. "How was it?"

"Weird," I said, thinking that was the only word I had in me for a response. But then came the others. "Horrible. Awful. Shocking. Sad. *Tragic*." This one nearly made me choke.

Bridget immediately shot up her hand and flagged down the waitress. "We'd like a piece of the chocolate cake." She smiled sweetly at her. "The biggest one you've got, if you wouldn't mind?"

"Sure, hon," said the waitress, the name GINA flashing on her badge. She headed off for the cake.

"My treat," Bridget said to me.

"Our treat," Tammy corrected.

"You don't have to do that," I said.

Bridget smiled, but her eyes were sad. "Of course we do. You've had a hard day, and it's not even two o'clock."

"Besides," Michaela said, "chocolate cake is your favorite, so maybe you'll eat some of it. You haven't taken a single bite of the lemon."

"Lemon just seems"—I searched for the right word—"kind of bitter."

Michaela laughed. "I think that's the point. Well, that it's bittersweet."

"So." Tammy looked at me expectantly. She wasn't going to let me get off that easily. "And?"

"And," I started, but I wasn't sure what to say next. I did my best to stay in control, monitor my breathing, my blinking. Describe this experience like I would any other. "I don't know. It was just . . . unthinkable, to realize that this grave was my father's. That he was gone. *Is* gone." The cake arrived. A giant piece. I couldn't bring myself to dig into it. "I guess I'm glad I went. Actually, maybe that's a lie. My mother thought it was a good idea, but I'm not sure."

"I think your mother is right." Bridget's fork hovered over the cake. Hesitant. Guilty. She wanted some, too, but wanted me to go first. "You need to start dealing with the stuff that's happened," she added, equally guiltily.

"Go ahead and have some," I told her, and when she didn't, I plunged my own fork into the part with the chocolate frosting and handed it to her. "Take it. Really." I knew I'd started this conversation by talking about my father, but now I didn't want to follow Bridget where she was going. "Um, B?" I asked, when she still hadn't eaten the bite I'd forced on her.

Bridget ignored me. "Are you ever going to talk to us about that night?"

"I already have," I said in a small voice.

"Not really," Tammy said, for once siding with Bridget. "It's good to talk about things, J. Especially the hard stuff. We're your friends."

"I tell you things," I protested, even though this was no longer true. I still hadn't told them about my night with Handel, but I would, of course. Soon. Just not now.

"Sometimes I worry . . ." Michaela started. She looked from Tammy to Bridget, then back to me, before continuing. "I worry that maybe you're still in danger," she finished in a rush.

"What? Why?" I stuttered. "How could I be?" I asked, like I didn't really know, when somewhere deep I did—of course I did. Whoever was responsible for what happened was still walking around somewhere, and they had an unfair advantage. They knew who I was. "It's all over now," I went on. "And here I am, safe with my girls."

The lids of Michaela's eyes lowered. "People are starting to talk."

"About?" I prompted.

Michaela opened her mouth. Closed it again.

"Tell me."

It was Tammy who finally spoke. "They're saying how, now that the break-ins have stopped, that the police might never find out who did it."

Bridget glanced at me. "Unless something else . . . *happens,* and they're caught."

I stared at the still-uneaten slice of chocolate cake. None of them mentioned how the "something else" that might happen, might happen to me. My friends kept on talking, debating the situation, and, slowly at first, I took one bite, then another, until all of the cake was gone. I'm not sure I even tasted it. Everything felt numb. Eventually they realized I'd stopped speaking and quieted down.

"I know you guys are worried because you care about me, but I'm fine," I told them. "I need you to believe me." I needed to believe myself, too. "I'm watching out for myself." They looked at me with skepticism written all over their faces. "I *am.*" I scraped the fork along the plate, digging for the last remaining sign of chocolate frosting, and the metal shrieked in protest against the glass.

"Maybe that's enough for today," Tammy said, being her bossy self and putting an end to this thread of conversation. "Let's change the subject." She eyed me, then the others. "We still haven't had the Handel report, but I think we should give Jane a break. For *now,*" she added.

I let out a long breath. "Thank you." I licked the dot of frosting I'd managed to salvage from the tine. "Why don't you update me on your lives? Please?"—then I stared hard at Tammy—"I know," I said all too loudly and eagerly. "Let's talk about Seamus and ice cream the other night and going running. I feel like I'm so out of the loop."

"I give you a pass and this is how you repay me?" Tammy

turned red. She was blushing—I hadn't thought it was possible, but she was. "It was just ice cream, and it was just a run."

"Oh, it's never just ice cream," Michaela said, and we all laughed as Tammy's blush deepened.

"It must be serious, Tam, if you're being evasive," Bridget said. "You love to tell us all the gory details about your boys."

"What are you talking about?" Tammy said.

The three of us took it as a challenge to see how far we could take Tammy's unusual shyness, and we played at this for a while, until a gust of hot air puffed our way from someone coming in the door of Slovenska's.

I was the one who turned first. Even someone showing up at Slovenska's for a strawberry shake was gossip enough to bother. You never knew what cute boy from town might walk in. I was surprised by who it was, though. "Look over there," I said, and everyone joined me in looking. The boy from the beach, the one I'd run into at Christie's—Miles—was standing at the register. He was alone. "I guess he's slumming it again."

"Jane," Bridget said with a giggle. "You promised to introduce me, remember?"

Miles looked over. He saw me and smiled.

I'm not sure what possessed me right then, maybe the reveal from my friends that they worried I was in danger, but I suddenly wanted to do something a little reckless, a little bit bad. So I let my laugh carry over the talk in Slovenska's, even though no one had said anything funny, sent it Miles's way like a hook to pull him in, and it worked. It was so easy sometimes, to play a boy. They always thought it was the other way around, that they had the upper hand. It didn't occur to them that girls could play games, too.

"Come on," I told Bridget, and we got up, ignoring the surprise on everyone else's faces.

"Right behind you," she said in a happy hush.

"Hi," I said to Miles when we reached him. It was all that needed saying.

He grinned like he'd won the lottery. "Hello, you." He glanced at Bridget next to me. "And you. If you told me your names, I could call you those instead."

She smiled back but didn't say a word. Bridget had coy down.

"I wouldn't guess you'd frequent Slovenska's," I said.

Miles shrugged. "The burgers are better here than over at the beach club, and I actually like coming down to the wharf, believe or not."

"I don't believe it," I said. "Actually."

The waitress handed Miles a big brown bag, filled to the brim. He took out his wallet, digging for bills. "So, is your answer still a maybe?" he asked me, glancing up. "About me taking you out, I mean."

I tilted my head. Bridget elbowed me and not at all subtly. "We might have changed our mind," I said, careful to include her in my answer.

"I knew you would eventually," he said after handing the waitress money for his food.

"I said 'might.' And I said 'we.'"

"I thought I heard a yes."

I looked at Miles, assessing. Then I looked at Bridget, trying to read her. He seemed like a nice enough guy, as arrogant as he could be. I turned to look at the rest of the girls. They were staring at us intently, like they were watching a movie, one that was about to get to the good part. Was I really going to make a date with this boy? What about Handel? "How about Friday at eight?" I asked, more to Bridget than Miles.

"I'm free then," she said.

Miles grinned. "The Ocean Club is good on Fridays."

I shrugged, like *of course* we knew all about the Ocean Club on a Friday. Like we'd been going to the Ocean Club on Fridays our entire lives. "Sure, we'll meet you there. And we'll bring the rest of our friends. So you should bring yours, too."

"I'll take it," Miles said.

I tapped the brown bag in front of Miles. "Better leave now before we change our minds, right, B?"

"Uh-huh," she said.

At this, we both turned around and walked away.

"See you Friday, then," he called after us, and Bridget and I smiled for Tammy and Michaela, who were watching our every move.

When I reached the booth, Michaela said to me, "So you and Bridget have a date?"

I slid in next to her again, and Bridget slid in across from me. "No." It was only after the looks of confusion crossed their faces that I explained. "*We* have a date. The four of us—with the other side of town," I added with a laugh.

Bridget broke into another fit of giggles. She reached across the table. "I love you sometimes, Jane."

"Well, I love you always, B," I returned.

Tammy was looking at me strangely. "I know I said I'd table

this topic, but, Jane, you don't think Handel will care if he learns you went out with another guy?"

I thought about Handel's desire to keep whatever was happening between us a secret from his friends. How if we happened to run into those same friends while hanging out with Miles and the others, that Handel might be relieved by this, rather than bothered.

"No, I know he won't," I said, and left it at that.

FOURTEEN

On the way home, I stopped at the wharf, straining my eyes to catch a glimpse of Handel pulling in his boat for the day. Plenty of fishermen were coming in, their clothes stained with guts and other remnants of life from the sea. Handel's friend Mac was standing at the bow of his father's boat, swinging his thick arms, like he wasn't sure what to do. Two of Handel's brothers, Colin and Finn, were nearby, caught up in conversation. But no Handel.

Not yet.

I had to wait awhile before I saw his long blond hair flying in the wind and that steely stare. He walked toward Colin and Finn. Ducked under a rope strung across the dock. Nodded at each one, then went to join Mac, both of them staring out over the water. My heart pumped with excitement and nervousness. I wanted him to see me, wanted to see his reaction, if he would smile a secret smile or pretend he didn't notice I was standing there, waiting for him, too concerned his friend and his brothers would notice. When he did see me, I didn't get a full secret smile, but I got half of one, the left side of Handel's mouth raised up in a way I'd seen before.

I wiped a hand across my face, pretending it was the heat, when really I wished that somehow with a swipe of my palm I could erase my own smile, the one that wanted so badly to appear on my lips in reply. Then I went to wait in the place Handel and I had decided the other night was far enough away from our neighbors' nosy glares and where his friends would never go—a coffee shop in the glitzy strip on the way out of town. Decided this when we were leaving the lighthouse in the protective cloak of the summer darkness. When I got to the café, I laughed a little to myself. I'd never once entered before, never even thought about it. It was so different from Slovenska's, with its tall glass windows shining in the sunlight and its carefully decorated interior, new couches and coffee tables made to look used and worn and scattered about in a way that was supposed to seem casual but whose places had obviously been choreographed to the last detail. It was almost empty. A pretty blond girl was working the counter.

"I'll have an iced coffee," I said.

She smiled. "Coming right up." The blond girl actually said this, like something out of a movie. At Slovenska's they barely acknowledged you were there and orders were shouted loudly in coarse voices with strong accents. I had a feeling this girl would pronounce all her syllables with precision.

"Thanks," I said when she handed me a tall frosty glass so unlike the plastic cups I was used to getting everywhere else.

"Are you visiting for the summer?" she asked.

The attempt at conversation was surprising. "Me?" I somehow needed confirmation from her, even though there was no one else nearby.

The girl laughed. Nodded.

"Um, no. I live here year-round." I almost wished for a mirror to see what I looked like, so I could figure out exactly what was in me today that allowed me to pass for someone other than a townie.

"Lucky," she said. "It's beautiful here."

"Yeah. It gets really cold during the winter, though."

"But you've got the beach. Even when it's cold, I bet it's beautiful."

"It is," I said, but ended our conversation by heading off to one of the couches. I shouldn't go making friends with the girl working if the point of coming here was to stay off people's radar. Though, it's not like I had a reason to think people would take special notice of me and Handel.

I sipped my coffee. Wishing he would hurry up.

Then the words "Hello, Jane" were spoken softly from behind me.

I turned to see Handel standing there, looking every inch the bad boy. I would have to take back what I'd thought before, about how Handel wouldn't get noticed in a place like this. Maybe I could get away with passing as the blond girl's friend, but how could people fail to notice someone like Handel?

"Hello, yourself," I said, even though it was a little cheesy to talk like that. "I have something to confess," I added, though I wasn't sure why this was what came out next.

A strange look passed over Handel's face. He didn't sit. Not yet. "Confess?"

Guilt simmered in my middle. "Another boy asked me out today, and I kind of said yes."

"Oh." Handel seemed relieved, even though I'd just told him he might have competition. He walked around to the front of the sofa and joined me there, sliding in close. Our legs touched. "You're going out with someone else?"

"Sort of," I said. "My friend Bridget likes him, or at least his friends, and then I made it a group date. You know, more like me and the girls are going out with someone else and that someone else's friends."

"Do I know him?"

"Definitely not. He's from out of town. He only summers around here."

Handel's eyebrows went up. "Interesting."

"I don't know. Maybe. I'm hoping he'll fall for Bridget. Or anyone else. He's nice, but not my type."

"What's your type?" Handel asked.

I walked right into that one. "I think you already know the answer."

"I'm not sure I do." He glanced around the coffee shop, taking in the two other people sitting across the room, a man wearing a business suit at one table and a woman at another, in a light dress that must have cost a fortune, high-heeled sandals on her delicate feet. Neither of them had any color from the sun. "You fit in easily in this place. I don't."

"Neither of us do and you know it."

"I'm not sure that's true." He covered his face with his hands. Slid them down to his chin. "Let's get out of here."

"But we just—" I started but didn't finish. Handel suddenly looked like he wanted to run away. "All right," I agreed. I would have followed him anywhere. Done anything he'd asked. I downed the last of my iced coffee, and we headed outside. Handel went around the building to the back of the coffee shop, where there was a little deck built on stilts that hung out over the water. He stood at the edge, watching me all the while until I joined him there. The water lapped against the shore. Everything about this part of the beach was soft and gentle, unlike the beach in our part of town.

Handel inched closer. "You're really going out with another guy?"

"I am. You never know." I leaned into him a little. I liked hearing the slight tone of jealousy in his voice. "It might be fun."

"I bet he's a good guy. Rich."

"Definitely rich," I said, thinking Handel was just kidding around. "But I don't care. I'd rather have a night for . . . for me and you." I couldn't quite bring myself to say "us" since we'd only gone out twice. But I wanted there to be an "us." I mean, I hoped there would be soon.

"Maybe you should care."

"Maybe, but I don't. No way." I stared at Handel, daring him to contradict me. I was sealing a pact between us by showing there wasn't room for any boy other than him.

He ran a hand through his hair, something he did when he was nervous, I was learning. Like when he reached for his ciga-rettes, his other nervous tell. "If the time comes when you realize this was all a mistake, just remember I warned you about me." He tried to laugh, like he was only joking, but there was some-thing else underneath the sound. Pain. Or maybe regret. "Jane Calvetti," he added.

"Handel Davies," was all I responded, because I was too caught up in the fact that our faces had gotten close. Really close.

I could say that this was the moment I'd been dreaming of

for so long, when Handel and I kissed for the first time, and how he looked into my eyes with his own, staring at me like I was the only girl in the world who could ever matter to him. I could describe in detail how his mouth felt on mine—soft but hungry, gentle but full of want—how his fingertips grazed the skin of my lower back, just underneath the hem of my shirt, giving me chills; how my knees turned to jelly as we stood there, kissing like we might never have another chance, and how Handel had to hold me up in his arms so I wouldn't melt away. I could explain all of these things, but then I would also have to talk about the part when Handel slid a finger across the tender skin of my neck, just under my chin, traced it right along the tiny red seam there, and whispered softly in my ear, "You have a scar."

If I talked about all of that, I would also have to explain how I'd nodded at Handel in response to those words, told him right then how I'd gotten it on that night in February. But I wasn't yet ready to discuss this with him, not just yet, nor the part about how after this exchange I decided it was probably time to go home, which also meant going our separate ways, all the romance of our kissing gone so suddenly, and all the life drained out of me, too.

February 19

"Be a good girl and don't scream," said the voice from behind me, male and cold and terrifying in the darkness. "Don't turn around."

I didn't do either thing. Didn't make a sound, not even a little one. Just stood there in the pitch black of the O'Connors' study, frozen, still halfway out of my seat in the reading nook, hair falling forward over my shoulders, hands pressed hard into the wood of the wall, knuckles turning white.

After the lights went out—first in the front yard and then inside—it wasn't long before I heard sounds, and not the kind that came from the heating system or an old empty house straining against the cold. These were the sort from people entering— people who didn't have keys, people who weren't supposed to be there—which would make it breaking and entering. It all happened so fast, and they were there before I even knew what was going on—the men, the boys, the robbers—whatever they were.

And I was alone.

"This place was supposed to be empty," hissed a second voice, also male, low and nervous. "She wasn't supposed to be here!"

"Don't you move," said the first voice again.

There came a crash. The overturning of a chair and something else. The smash of a vase, the shattering of glass, shoes, boots maybe, kicking the shards. The faint trickle of water as it dripped onto the floor between the sounds of other things breaking and crashing, and the crisp *snap* of stems underfoot. The *shhhhhh* of papers sliding to the ground. I couldn't see anything or anyone. There was the darkness, broken only by the occasional beam of a flashlight, and there was the fact that my captor had me facing away from everything and everyone. The only thing I could make out in all that black was the slight gleam of glass on the face of the clock, and the shine of metal on my captor's boot as it caught the glare of flashlights.

"Where does she keep the jewelry?" someone said, a third voice.

Doors opened and slammed shut. A table, or maybe it was a desk, overturned and a great resounding *boom* echoed outward.

"Hurry up!"—the second voice again.

Another pair of footsteps sounded along the floor, pounding out a run on the grand staircase that wound gently up from the entryway of the house, each step muffled by the rug until they hit the landing, where there was only wood. There was a sharp creak as the footsteps got closer.

I whimpered then. I couldn't help it, didn't even realize the sound was about to come out of me. With all the noise, all the banging and the searching, I thought it might be drowned out alongside everything else, but it wasn't. In a split second hands were on me, arms around me tight and unforgiving, and one of them, one of them went around my neck, put me in a headlock. I could feel the body, *his* body, the one of my captor, flat and tight against my back. More sounds escaped and kept on coming with a will of their own, that is, until I heard the man, the boy, whoever he was, whisper in my ear "Shut up or you're dead" so close and so frightening that my brain finally shut my voice down.

And then, then I felt the knife.

He held it to my throat. It was cold and it was sharp, so sharp it cut straight through the thin gold chain I was wearing like it was butter, the one with the tiny mosaic heart my mother had given me for Christmas. It fell to the floor with a soft *clink* amid the din. I was afraid to move, afraid to breathe, afraid that any little shift would push me toward that blade, so I stayed as still as I could.

It seemed like I might have to stand like that forever.

I stood, unmoving, for what felt like a hundred years.

Then, "What are you *doing* to her?" shouted a different voice, the newest one, the fourth, and it was shot in our direction like a bullet.

I flinched.

The man, the boy, the one who had me in his arms but not in a way that I'd ever wanted to be in a boy's arms, swiveled and shouted toward the fourth voice, "I'm taking care of loose ends." When he turned around, that knife sliced right across my neck, not a long cut or a deep cut but still a cut, and the pain was immediate—the pain and the blood. I felt it trickling, warm and wet along my skin.

Were they going to kill me?

The grip on my neck loosened, and I fought the urge to scream, but then I felt hands, more than two—I wasn't sure whose—at my head, my eyes—and my heart sped until I thought it would fly out of my chest. Two bodies at my back now, four hands fumbling around my face, and a bag being shoved over me—no, not a bag but a scarf, thick and suffocating across my eyes and falling down over my nose.

I was blindfolded.

The rush of blood to my head, the terror, all of it combined, made me dizzy. I thought I might faint.

There came the righting of a chair, Professor O'Connor's desk chair, I thought, and the scrape of it on the floor behind me, stopping at the back of my knees.

Hands again, two this time, different from the Headlock Man because these were gentler, on my shoulders and pushing me down. I was meant to sit, so I did. Then my arms were pulled behind me, behind the chair, then the feel of thick twine wrapped around them, tied together. I didn't struggle, tried not to. My breath came in great spaced-out gasps, my body forgetting to breathe after each gulp of air, head spinning, heart racing. I needed to get ahold of myself, so I began to pay attention to my lungs, pushing them open and closed in a rhythm. Tears burned in my eyes, but I refused their exit. I didn't want to die because I couldn't keep quiet and couldn't keep still. I had to give myself the chance of living through this.

"That's right, stay calm," went that fourth voice again. He'd whispered those words, his tone less violent than the others and more in control, a tone that said *trust me*. I wanted someone to trust right now, too, I really did. But then, how could I trust one of *them*? He was close, very close, I could feel his body, feel the heat pouring off him from the stress of the situation. From the stress of breaking into this supposedly vacant house and instead finding out it wasn't vacant at all. "No one's going to hurt you," he whispered, his voice low and husky and altered. "I'm not going to let anyone hurt you, all right?"

I wasn't sure if this was a question and it wasn't like anyone was giving me choices, so I said nothing. Stayed silent in the dark of the night with the blindfold over my eyes, the winds of the snowstorm outside howling.

But he'd wanted an answer. "All right?"

I nodded. I nodded, even though it wasn't all right. None of this was all right. I wasn't all right.

"Good girl," he said, those words spilling out at me for the second time, but this time with urgency, like my whole life depended on the ability to continue to be the good girl, the quiet girl, the girl who listened. "Just stay still," he whispered, closer now, next to my ear, like he really was trying to save me, as though it was in his power to do this very thing, his breath on my neck, fast and worried.

And I sat there—we sat there, me and him—I don't know how long, in the noise of the crashing and the destruction of the O'Connors' house, the shouting and the shattering, in this place that I loved and relaxed and relished the various books the professor left for me. My mind gone blank. My mind trying not to think anything at all. My mind wishing for this nightmare to end.

Then suddenly it seemed like it might.

There came a silence. A stopping. A gathering of footsteps nearby.

My body tensed with fear, and there came those words for the third time, rewarding the fact that I'd stayed still and quiet, that even in my terror I'd behaved.

"Good girl," my captor whispered, trying to soothe me I think, and for a moment he almost had me. I almost trusted him. I almost believed he meant well, wanted to save me after all.

But then came another set of footsteps, an unexpected set, loud and sure, the steady *thump, thump, thump* of heavy shoes pounding against the carpeted stairs and then the *thwack, thwack, thwack* across the wooden floor at the top, the sounds of a man approaching, a confident man. One with no idea what situation he was about to happen upon.

The footsteps came to a halt.

"Jane?" My name, called out in the darkness, cutting through the fear. Then again: "Jane?"

And next, "Daddy?" I called back.

FIFTEEN

WHEN I GOT HOME from seeing Handel, there was a surprise waiting for me in the living room—one I wasn't sure what to think about. When I reached the front steps of my house, I heard voices coming through the open windows. My mother's and someone else's.

I hesitated at first but eventually headed inside.

"Jane," Professor O'Connor said when he saw me. He got up from the couch in our living room, the springs groaning. It was strange to see him there, this big man dressed so formally, pressed into our little, sandy house. His hair had gotten grayer since the last time I'd seen him, and I was struck with the urge to weep.

"Hi, Professor O'Connor." I hovered by the door. Dropped my bag to the floor.

My mother was in the kitchen, fixing coffee. "It's nice of him to visit us, isn't it?"

I nodded. I wasn't sure what to do next, what to say, what to ask.

He stood there, waiting. Patient. Finally, he said, "I'm glad to see you, Jane. It's been too long."

I nodded again. Couldn't find my tongue.

"I was hoping we could talk."

My mother joined us while the coffee brewed, the machine stuttering to life in the kitchen. "Please sit," she said to him. "Sweetheart?" she said to me.

Normally I would go heap myself onto the sofa, but it was odd to think of sharing our old couch with Professor O'Connor. I pulled up one of the wooden chairs from against the wall, where I usually piled my things when I came home for the day, and positioned myself on the other side of the coffee table. Professor O'Connor sat down again.

"How are you?" I asked, finding my voice.

"I'm all right, considering."

"Considering?"

"That's what I'm here to discuss. Molly?" He turned to my mother, asking permission to say whatever it was he was here to say.

Her face was blank. "Go ahead."

"What's happened?" I cut in quickly, even as I wanted to cover my ears to shut out whatever came next.

Professor O'Connor leaned forward, elbows propped on his knees, hands clasped. The wrinkles lining his face left tiny shadows across his skin in the light of the table lamp. "It seems the police have a new lead."

"Really?" I asked, feigning surprise. I'd given it to them myself after all.

His eyebrows went up. "They haven't been in touch with you about it?"

"No," I said, which was only half a lie. I'd been in touch with them, and all Michaela's dad had done was leave a message confirming he'd gotten mine.

My mother chose this moment to get up and go to the kitchen to pour the coffee, even though we didn't need it. It was too hot for hot coffee. "Milk and sugar?" she called back to Professor O'Connor.

"Just black, thanks," he said.

She returned with three mugs, placing them on the table, mine so light with cream it was practically white. No one moved to touch them, the steam rising up through the air. A shiver ran through me despite the humidity, and I realized that my legs were shaking. I leaned over and grabbed one of the mugs, put both hands around it, the burn along my palms soothing me a little. "So what's the lead? Do they know who it is?" I asked.

Professor O'Connor glanced away a moment, his profile stark in the glare of the lamp. Then he let out a big breath. "They wouldn't tell me. I honestly don't know where it's taken them."

"Wait—what?" I was confused. "I don't understand."

"The police won't give out specific details, not even to me," he said. "I was hoping you might already know what was going on."

My back was straight against the wooden chair. I looked down at my hands, so tight around the mug I thought it might shatter from the force. I did know, of course. I'd given them a significant detail to look for and a name on top of it, one that must be panning out if Professor O'Connor was here talking about leads. But for some reason I couldn't manage to make myself confess all I knew—suspected—right now. I placed the mug on the coffee table, folded my hands in my lap, then unfolded them again. "But why wouldn't they tell you, of all people? You were the victim," I said, leaving myself out of the equation. "They should trust you," I added, even as I kept up my lie of omission.

"I don't think the police not telling me about the lead means they don't trust me," he said. "Or you, Jane. It's everyone else in this town that's the problem."

"What do you mean?" This question came from my mother. A worried look had settled over her during the conversation.

Professor O'Connor leaned forward. Rested his elbows on his knees and clasped his hands. "You know how everyone is around here. Everyone knows each other, everyone gossips. Word gets out fast, and the police seem to think whoever did this might live very close."

"How close?" my mother asked.

I took the coffee mug back into my hands, warming my palms. As close as the McCallen brothers, I thought right then. I couldn't stop shivering, even though it was anything but cold.

"It's very possible that Jane—that you and I"—he nodded at my mother—"might be acquaintances with the attackers."

At this, I stood, the coffee sliding right out of my hands onto the floor. The mug cracked in half. I bent down to pick up the pieces. Watched the milky liquid run in every direction. My mother got up and ran to the kitchen for something to help clean the mess.

"Jane," Professor O'Connor said, his face a mask of worry. "I'm not saying this is definite—the police still don't know who it is—but you need to be careful. I want you and your mother to be safe, and I'm concerned that you won't be until the police catch whoever did this," he added, in a way that said he wished this weren't true.

My mother returned with paper towels. She crouched down, glancing at me, in between sopping up the puddle of coffee.

I stood, the two halves of the cracked mug still in my hands. "But there's so much I don't remember. And I was blindfolded."

"You may have seen something and not realized it," Professor O'Connor said. "And you heard everything."

I didn't respond. This part was true.

"There's another reason I'm here," he said next.

My mother took the pieces of mug from me while I watched her, frozen. Waited for Professor O'Connor to go on.

"Martha and I have wanted to invite both of you over for a long time now," he began gently. When I inhaled deep and quick, about to protest, he stopped me with his hand. "I know you might not be ready yet, Jane, and I respect that. But I think it would be a good idea for you to stop by someday soon for a visit, the sooner the better. We could all have dinner."

My mother glanced up at him. "Is there any particular reason that's necessary?"

He hesitated. "It might help her remember."

"Mm-hmm," I said, but shaking my head no. "I've already remembered everything I can. I'm done remembering."

"I wouldn't push you, but—" Professor O'Connor stopped.

"But?" I asked. I couldn't help it. I wanted to know.

"The police think it would be a good idea as well."

Anger flashed through me, searing my insides. "The police made you come here?"

"No, no." He sighed long and big. "I wanted to come. I've wanted to see how you are for a long time. But it's my worry that finally brought me, and the fact that maybe the police are right and a visit might jog your memory a bit. It also might make you feel better. Going back to the place where you lived through a trauma can get you started on your way through all that dread you feel. It was a trauma, Jane, that night, a real trauma." His voice was pained. "You were there to take care of our house. All alone and we didn't think twice. Martha and I feel so terrible we put you in such a vulnerable position. We should've hired someone older. We weren't thinking."

My mother took her seat. "Everyone's blaming themselves," she said, frustration in every syllable of her words. "Jane blames herself, you're blaming yourself, I blame myself for not picking Jane up the second it started to snow. But the only people we should be blaming are the ones who did this."

Professor O'Connor stayed silent.

"You really think it would help Jane to go to your house?" she asked.

"I do," he said.

My mother looked at me, then at Professor O'Connor. "Can you give us a few days to think it over?"

"Of course," he said. "I should be going now, anyway."

Professor O'Connor's posture, usually so straight, was hunched. He seemed weary and sad. I felt the urge to weep again. He looked at me, his eyes pleading. "Jane, you must promise not to give away details about what happened that night to anyone other than your mother or the police. We don't want you or anyone else in danger."

"She understands," my mother said, answering for me, her tone tight with worry.

I nodded to show that I did, too. "Thank you for coming," I whispered to the professor, my voice nearly gone.

"I wish I'd done it sooner." He got up. "I think about you

all the time." He turned to my mother. "It was good to see you, Molly." Professor O'Connor turned to me now. "It was good to see you, too, Jane. I'm sorry for everything."

He was at the door in two long strides and was almost gone, but I stopped him just in time. I placed a hand on his arm, and as soon as I mustered the courage, I gave him a hug. He wasn't sure what to do, I think, not at first, but it only took a second before he pulled me in tight. For a moment, just a quick one, it could have been my father with his arms around me, and this feeling—I held on to it for as long as I could before it faded away.

"I'm going to bed," my mother said shortly after the professor had left, her voice heavy, her steps heavier. She wiped a hand across her eyes, then ran it through her hair.

"Okay," I said quietly. "Good night."

I stood there, in the middle of the living room, thinking awhile.

Trying to decide how I felt.

In some ways, certainly not in the ones that Professor O'Connor had intended, his mandate—*don't talk to anyone about that night other than the police or your mother*—had unwittingly offered me a way to assuage my guilt for not telling the people around me all I knew, all that I suspected. The notion that I should keep quiet for my own safety gave me permission to do what I'd wanted to all along, to let whatever was buried deep down in my memory about that night in February, hidden in the darkness, sink even further away from the present until it disappeared altogether.

When I finally went to bed, when I slipped my body between the sheets, they felt as cool and soothing as the mandate to keep silent about things. Everyone always spoke about how talking was supposed to make things better, but no one ever told you how silence could be healing, too.

The next morning, as I got ready for the beach, I put on my favorite string bikini, the same one I wore on the day when Handel first spoke to me. After I left the house and got closer to the ocean, I pulled my T-shirt over my head and stepped out of my shorts even as I continued to walk, the sand greeting my toes with soft sighs. I tossed my hair once, then again, its texture velvety against my shoulders and bare back. As I made my way toward my girls, there was a strut in my step, the ties of my bikini bouncing along the tops of my thighs. The stares from the boys were blatant as I passed, and I drank them in like lemonade.

"Hi, ladies," I said when I reached Michaela and Tammy and Bridget. I saw Seamus loping toward us from the water, and noticed his towel and flip-flops laid out next to Tammy's.

"Hey, Jane," Seamus said when he reached us.

I went to him and gave him a little hug. "I feel like it's been ages since you've shown up unannounced at the house."

Seamus blushed. "I've been . . . kind of busy."

I glanced over at Tammy, who was suddenly preoccupied with her magazine. "I bet."

Bridget smiled up at me from her towel. "You seem happy today."

"I am," I told her, removing my sunglasses from my eyes. "I really am," I said, and then lay on my back to soak up all the bright sun.

SIXTEEN

THE GIGGLING COMING FROM my mother's sewing room was becoming unbearable. An entire wedding party—four bridesmaids plus the bride—was getting their measurements done and talking to my mother about dress styles and possible designs. They spilled out into the living room, which was why I'd taken refuge on my bed, staring into my closet and wondering what a girl wears on a group date to a place like the Ocean Club. I thought of that woman heading into Christie's the night I'd seen Miles valeting, the way she'd walked along in her tight white dress and those heels, gripping a matching white clutch in her hand. I didn't have anything like that. It just wasn't my style. Well, it wasn't anyone's style around here.

"Oh, that's so beautiful," one of the girls in the wedding party cried out, followed by a lot of *ooh*ing and *aah*ing from the others.

Though I didn't really want to enter into the fray of Mom's current clients, whenever I was in doubt about attire, she was my consultant and savior, so I decided to brave the sewing room situation.

A pretty girl with long red hair, all spirally curls falling everywhere, was sitting on the couch in the living room. She looked up from a sketch in her lap as I passed through. Her face was freckled. "Hey there."

I searched the catalog of town families stored in my mind,

trying to locate her among them, but came up with nothing. "Hi. Are you the bride?"

She shook her head. "No, that's Jenny. She's in there with your mother and the rest of them. I'm just a bridesmaid."

"Can I see?" I asked, gesturing at the sketch.

"Sure." She handed it over.

My mother always outlined the designs for her clients as many times as necessary until they were satisfied. I could already tell this one was complicated, and what's more, three separate fabric swatches were stapled to the paper, all in different shades of green, and this was only for the bridesmaid dresses. That meant the bride had money. Lots of it. "Pretty," I said.

"Your mother's kind of a genius. She's determined to make everyone in the wedding party happy, and you know how difficult that can be."

I laughed. "She's good at what she does," I said as another shriek followed by more giggling spilled out of the sewing room. "All right, I'm headed in there."

"Good luck," the girl said, taking the sketch back.

"Mom?" I called, with a knock on the partially open door. The rest of the talk inside quieted.

"Yes, sweetie?"

"I need you a sec. Non-emergency, though. If you're too busy, no worries—"

The door swung open. A beautiful young woman stood there, long straight blond hair flowing down over her shoulders. Perfect pale skin. "You must be Jane," she said with a smile. "I'm Jenny Nolan."

Her recognition surprised me. My mother didn't usually talk about me to clients unless someone brought me up first. There was something familiar about this woman, too, but I couldn't tell what. And the name rang a bell. "Hi. You must be the bride. Congratulations."

"Thank you."

I glanced past her, seeing my mother in conversation with another of the bridesmaids. "Has my mother been talking about me?"

"No, don't worry. She hasn't been gossiping." Jenny cocked her head, her eyes assessing me. "It was my aunt who told me about you."

"Your aunt?" I racked my brain, trying to come up with a Nolan that I knew in this town. Then I remembered Billy Nolan, Handel's uncle who died. I wondered if Billy Nolan was her father or an uncle. That explained the familiarity in her features. "Your aunt is Handel's mother. Handel Davies?"

She laughed. "Yes. Is there any other Handel around here?"

I smiled, loving the idea that I was so important to Handel that his cousin I've never met had been discussing me with his mother. "I guess not."

She looked me up and down, unabashed. "Well, you're just adorable," she said. "Word gets around in our family about who the baby brother's been seen with around town, so of course you've come up in conversation. My aunt likes the idea of Handel going out with someone like you. Handel's a good guy, deep down. He just needs someone to redeem him from those brothers of his. Maybe you'll be the one to save him."

I opened my mouth. Closed it. I wasn't sure what to say in response to all this information, especially the part about my potential role in Handel's future. My mother's conversation with the bridesmaid halted during Jenny's speech. She was looking at me now, a curious expression on her face. I still hadn't responded when Jenny spoke again.

"You should give Handel another chance," she said.

I looked at her quizzically. "Another chance at what?"

"You know, go out with him. First dates don't always go that well, but sometimes second dates are the charm," she sang. Her bridesmaids responded to this with knowing laughter. "After all, that's how I ended up with Charlie," she went on, who I assumed was the groom. "If I'd given up on him after the first night we went out, there's no way we'd be walking down the aisle together this August."

"Right," I said, my face growing hot.

"I'm glad to finally meet you. You needed your mother, right? Let me get out of your way." Jenny Nolan stepped aside, and I saw that there were three other faces checking me out. The bridesmaids were apparently also interested in seeing the girl who was going out with Handel Davies. Or at least had gone out with him once as far as they knew.

It made me wonder how they'd look at me if they knew I'd seen Handel more than once—three times in fact. How when I went to bed at night all I could do was think about kissing him, dream about the press of his mouth on my neck, his fingers on my skin. That sometimes I thought maybe Handel would be the one to save me, and not the other way around.

"Jane," my mother said. "You had a question?"

I suddenly wanted out from under all this scrutiny. "Um, actually, I'm fine. You're busy. I can take care of it myself."

With that, I closed the door and hurried through the living room, the girl with the red curly hair watching me differently now. She must have heard Jenny Nolan's comments.

Suddenly, I felt special. In a way that I liked.

Sometimes, I can be a really good pretender.

Like when I arrived at the Ocean Club in a tight black tank minidress that shimmered with glitter, wearing black heels on my feet, as though this was how I usually dressed to go out, as though the clothes I had on were designer as opposed to discount, as though I was born to date rich boys like Miles and not townie boys like Handel Davies. The stones in the bracelet around my wrist were fake, of course, and I wondered how many people in this place looked at me and knew this instinctively, knew that, despite my attempts to fit in, I didn't really belong. That not one of us did. But my girls and I were all going to act like we did for the night. Act like we did for the boys.

Sometimes that's just what girls do.

"Don't you look hot," Bridget said when she saw me. She was waiting at the entrance, with all its stonework and glass.

I smiled, twirling the loop of the tiny black bag I had around my finger. "You too, B." Bridget was always gorgeous, but when she dressed up, she was stunning. There was something about all that fair skin that made her seem lit up from the inside. It gave her a vulnerability, too, that made the boys want to protect her.

Bridget's eyes went to my neck. "Pretty," she said. "It's good to see you wearing that."

I nodded. Fingered the tiny mosaic heart that lay against my skin, all shades of ocean and sky. Bridget knew what it meant—knew what it meant that I'd worn it, too. Tonight, when I was getting ready, I'd decided it was time to begin some things again, to try starting over bit by bit, remaking myself, now that so much in my life was just at the beginning. Now that Handel and I were at the beginning. The necklace my mother had given me to replace the one that I'd lost seemed a simple place to start. So I took it from the drawer where I'd hidden it and clasped it at the back of my neck.

I let the heart go. "Where are the others?" I asked.

"Michaela went to the ladies' . . . ," Bridget said.

"And Tammy just got here," said Tammy from behind us. She glanced around, staring at the large floral arrangement on a nearby table, brimming with white calla lilies. Tammy gave each of us a quick hug, and Michaela, too, when she returned from the bathroom.

"We're not at Slovenska's anymore," Michaela trilled.

"Yeah. Or Twin Willows," Tammy said.

We stood there awkwardly. "This is weird, isn't it?" I asked.

Bridget giggled. "This is fun. I like getting dressed up."

Michaela made it a point to look at each of us. "I think we dress up nice."

"Well, obviously," Tammy said. "And apparently, when we dress up, we all agree to wear black."

This got another nervous laugh from everyone.

I eyed Tammy. "Does Seamus know you're here tonight?"

"Why would Seamus care?" she shot back. "And, *yes,* he does happen to know. I saw him before coming here."

"Really!" Bridget was about to push Tammy for more information, but Tammy shot her down with a glare. "Fine," she harrumphed. "I'll ask later."

"So, what's next, J?" Michaela asked.

"I suppose we should see if they're outside on the deck," I said.

"Ooh, fancy," Bridget said, immediately turning to go. She headed through the restaurant with the kind of confidence I was lacking at the moment, so I felt grateful she'd taken the lead. The three of us followed after her.

The restaurant was filling up for the evening, alive with people chatting and eating, seeing and being seen. The Ocean Club was one of those places that wanted to seem no-frills and casual, a place where you could go following a long day in the sun at the beach, your bathing suit peeking out of your cover-up and your flip-flops still donning your sandy feet. In reality, it was anything but. Its patrons, especially the women, put on their evening best and were dressed to compete with one another for most glamorous, most elegant, most sexy, like they were there to steal each other's spouses and boyfriends and even one another's friends. Cutlery clinked daintily against china, and finely manicured nails flared out from hands holding crystal wine glasses. Hair was done up and perfect, everyone posturing for one another.

The four of us might not be regulars, but we filed through that room like we deserved the admiration of everyone in the place. More than one woman glared as we passed, and I'd like to think those stares were more about how we were stealing some of that coveted male attention and not related to the cheap fabric of our clothes. We went out onto the deck and made our way through the crowd. There were twinkle lights strung up in the trees and delicate lanterns hanging from their branches. The effect was beautiful. "Hey there!" someone called out.

We turned toward the voice, and Miles caught my eye. He was standing near the railing of the deck and waved us over, dressed in a button-down shirt and jeans, the typical prep school–boy uniform. He looked casual, but somehow he still had money written all over him. Maybe it was his good looks, maybe it was his confidence, or even his charm, but whatever it was, I almost wanted to turn back the way we came. Who were we kidding, imagining that the four of us could—or even would *want to*— hang out with guys like Miles? His friends were with him, the two we'd already seen at the beach and a new one, all of them wearing more or less the same outfit.

I took a deep breath and gave Miles a nod. Now it was my turn to be the leader. "This way, girls," I said with a reluctant shrug. We wove our way through the hands holding fine glasses, brimming with wine or cocktails. Miles and his friends were drinking beers so casually they didn't seem to realize they were underage. The four of us were unprepared in this regard. It wasn't like we needed fake IDs in the downtown bars, and mainly people hung out and drank on the beach or at people's houses.

"Hey," I said when we reached them, wondering what came next—a hug? A kiss on the cheek like we lived in Europe? A handshake? These options seemed awkward, so I stood far enough away from Miles that only words could comfortably be exchanged.

Miles grinned. "You made it."

"Obviously." I tried to return the smile. Tammy cleared her throat, and I remembered to introduce my friends. "This is Tammy, this is Michaela, and you remember Bridget," I said, gesturing at each of them. Only Bridget's little smile and wave was genuine, and Miles's friends' eyes were glued to her now. I was sure they thought she was adorable because, well, she really was.

"And you are?" he asked me.

I laughed as I realized I still hadn't told him my name. "Jane. Now it's your turn," I said to Miles, nodding in the direction of his friends.

"It's nice to meet you, Jane," he said wryly. "You remember Logan and Hugh," he said, pointing to the two boys who'd been with him during that first conversation on the beach. The friends each had that jock look and the bodies to match, muscled arms peeking out of their finely made, finely cut shirts.

"Not really," Tammy said. Then I elbowed her and Bridget elbowed her at the same time, and she flinched. "Oh yes. Of course I remember. Now it's all coming back to me."

Sometimes Tammy's dry attitude rolled up into all that natural suspicion was hilarious. It was all I could do not to burst out laughing.

Miles obviously wasn't taking Tammy's sarcasm personally. He just kept on grinning, his dark eyes dancing as he finished the introductions. "And this is James," he said about the fourth boy, with reddish-blond hair and the faintest of freckles dotting his skin. If he wasn't dressed in such expensive clothing and hanging out with the other three, he could pass for an Irish townie. "What would you girls like to drink?" Miles asked.

I bit my lip, then just said it. "None of us have fake IDs."

All four boys' eyebrows went up in surprise, like they might have practiced the reaction. "How is that possible?" asked the one named Logan.

Michaela rolled her eyes. "We don't usually hang out at bars like this." Her tone implied that this should already be evident and that, in fact, we were above such places.

This wasn't going well.

"What *do* you do, then?" asked Hugh, shifting so he could rest a hand on the railing behind him, his muscles rippling under all that dark skin as he leaned.

Bridget chimed in, trying to save the night from getting off to a bad start. "We hang out at people's houses and go down to the beach a lot. It's hard to pass up the allure, you know? Even for a place as nice as this one."

"Don't worry." Miles held up his hand to flag down a waitress. "We all have connections."

"Connections?" went Tammy, the eye roll implied but not acted on this time, thankfully.

"I'll just have a Coke," I said quickly, before Tammy could snort or say anything else sarcastic. I didn't want a beer or one of those fancy drinks that made you sloppy by the time you reached the bottom of the glass. I would start slow and decide from there.

"Tammy and I will have Cokes, too," Michaela said, after it was clear Tammy wasn't going to speak up for herself.

Bridget batted her eyelashes. "If one of you boys can get me one of those pretty drinks, I would certainly be grateful."

All four boys looked at one another, engaged in unspoken competition for helping fulfill this one willing damsel's request.

Bridget was going to be a hit this evening. This made me smile. Bridget reveled in boy attention no matter who they were, and she was too sweet to begrudge her the vice.

Cokes were gotten for Tammy, Michaela, and me, and Bridget was handed a tall martini glass filled with a faintly pink liquid and very little ice. She exclaimed, "Ooh!" in surprise after taking the first sip. I was relieved it didn't take long for all of us to fall into something like normal conversation, Tammy talking to James, Michaela and Bridget with Logan and Hugh, and me with Miles. Somehow, he seemed to have laid claim to me. His friends had barely even looked my way.

"Is this where you guys usually hang out?" I asked him.

"You mean when I'm not slumming it at the town beach or Slovenska's?"

"Tammy can be tough sometimes," I said.

"So can you," Miles said.

I swirled the ice around my glass with the dainty straw. "Not really."

"Just because I don't live in town year-round doesn't make me a bad guy."

"Maybe not." I looked around the deck, taking in the people laughing and drinking and flirting, the sheer gorgeousness of a bar when it's built on money and elegant patrons. I saw the delight in Bridget's eyes, how she was so excited to be here, and how even Tammy and Michaela seemed to be enjoying themselves now, despite all attempts to resist the possibility. "I used to dream of hanging out somewhere like the Ocean Club," I admitted, surprised by my own honesty.

"Dream?" Miles said with a laugh. "Wow. The Ocean Club is open to the public, you know."

"Maybe for someone like you. But people like us"—I nodded at the girls—"we don't think to come here on a Friday."

"But here you are," Miles said, a bit triumphantly, like he was glad to have given us the opportunity.

I turned toward the water. Rested my glass on the rail of the deck. There were sailboats out on the ocean, floating leisurely in the harbor, and a couple of yachts. "Part of the dream involved being here with a bunch of boys like you and your friends."

Miles shifted to let two girls in stilettos pass. They were draped in jewelry, the real kind, and were giggling nonstop. "Is that a joke?" he asked. "I never know whether you're being sarcastic or serious."

I shook my head. Took a sip of my Coke, the bubbles in my throat fizzy like the atmosphere around us. Maybe I should've asked for a beer. "No, that part is true."

"Now I'm feeling really good," Miles said with a smile, but from his eyes I could tell he was taking this seriously, that he was glad to hear this confession of mine. "I hope we can live up to the dream."

"I don't know . . . ," I began slowly.

"Ouch," Miles interrupted.

"Calm down. I wasn't finished."

He leaned against the rail, eyeing me. It was the first time I'd seen his confidence falter. "Sorry," he said. "Finish away."

"Now that I'm here," I went on. "I'm not sure this place is really me. Or any of us. Well, maybe except for Bridget."

Miles turned and watched her laugh at something his friend said. "She seems to be having a good time."

I took another sip of my Coke, watching Miles from above the rim of the glass. "Bridget can have a good time anywhere."

Miles seemed to relax again. As people drained their drinks, the crowd around us was getting louder. Miles bent toward me so I could hear him. "So what else can you tell me about yourself, other than that your name is Jane?"

"Well . . ." I bit my lip, trying to decide what to say. It was such a date-like question, but then, I'd agreed to go out in a date-like situation. "You might think this whole town is all Irish, but there are a lot of Russians around here, and Italians, too. I'm of the Italian variety."

Miles grinned. "I love Italian."

I smiled a little, and tried to hide it behind my glass. "Are you always this cheesy?"

"Only when I'm with a girl who I like."

I rolled my eyes. "Oh my God." But I laughed, too, for the first time tonight. Underneath all that confidence, there was an earnestness to Miles. He might come from a different back-ground, but he was turning out not to be so bad after all. And cute. Definitely cute. And yes, winning. His charm was starting to work on me.

Miles flagged down the waitress and ordered another beer. Then, "I want to know more," he said.

So I told him. Soon, conversation was flowing easily between us. We moved to a couch set beneath one of the tree branches, the hanging lanterns floating and glowing above us, getting brighter as the sun dipped below the horizon and the evening grew dark.

I was starting to enjoy myself.

Miles picked up his beer from the coffee table. "So let's see if I can recap what I know so far." He took a long gulp and swallowed. "You've lived in this town your entire life and attend the local high school, where you're going to be a senior this fall. Your mother is a seamstress. You hang out with those three"— he gestured at the girls, who were still over by the rail of the deck—"down at the wharf and the beach during the summer. Nearly constantly."

"Yes," I said, laughing. Then I did my best to effect a haughty tone. "And you want to go to an Ivy League school, ideally, to play lacrosse. Because the girls go crazy over lacrosse where you're from."

He smiled. "They really do. I wasn't lying about that!"

"And this is your first summer here," I finished.

"Right again," Miles said. "So what else do I need to know about the mysterious and Italian Jane . . . ?" His eyebrows were a question. He wanted me to finish the sentence.

"Calvetti," I said. "Jane Calvetti."

"Wow, that *is* Italian."

I laughed. "I know."

"Wait a minute—I know that name. Calvetti, Calvetti. Jane Calvetti." Then Miles stopped, his lips parting with surprise. His eyes clouded over. Suddenly he was looking at me differently, his expression serious, all that playfulness gone. "You're not *that* Jane Calvetti, are you? The one from the—"

"From the break-in. Yeah." I said the words before he could get to them. The glass in my hand was frosty from all the ice. A shiver went through me, and I set it down on the table.

"I'm sorry," he said.

I clasped my hands in my lap, staring at them.

"I mean it, Jane. I had no idea that was you." Miles sounded shocked. Then he shifted, leaned toward me across the couch. "If you ever need to talk, I'm happy to," he said, just like everyone else always did.

I looked away. It was all I could do not to shrink from him, even though he was just trying to be nice. "Um, thanks, but no, thanks."

"Do the police—?"

My head went left, right, left and right, saying *no, no, no, let's not do this*—not now, not here. No more. "Let's change the subject."

"Okay. But I mean it, Jane, if you ever want—"

"To talk, you'll talk," I finished for him. "Got it. And just so you're not offended when I don't, you should know that the police don't want me talking to anyone but them," I said, this mandate lifting me up from such weighty requests, lightening the burden. "New topic," I pressed, when Miles hadn't yet responded. I waited for him to go where I wanted. Willed him to.

Miles looked at me then, trying to force the sadness from his eyes. I wanted to see that confident grin on his face, feel the relief of having this moment pass. I wanted to move on, to get to a place where we could relax, but I could already tell from the way Miles was looking at me that this wasn't going to happen.

Suddenly, I wished for Handel, wished for the boy who made me feel like I could be whole again, who knew my world inside and out because he'd lived in it his entire life, who didn't push me into places I didn't want to go and who looked in my eyes in a way that made me feel I was the only girl who'd ever existed. I realized right then how much I hated the thought of being a secret in his life. How I wanted Handel to keep up that conversation he'd started with his mother that spilled over into a conversation with his cousin that had somehow reached all the way to my mother's sewing room.

"You okay?" Tammy whispered softly from nearby. She was standing next to the couch. Maybe she'd overheard what Miles said. She sat down on the armrest next to me. Her fingers reached for mine and squeezed.

I nodded, squeezing back.

Miles looked at me guiltily. "I shouldn't have been so cavalier, bringing that whole thing up."

"It's okay," I said. "It is."

"I'm not so bad, really," Miles said, a bit pleadingly, and waited for me to respond. The hope in his voice was almost painful.

"No," I said after a while, looking up at him, trying to focus on Miles instead of Handel. "You're really not." Then I did my best to dial up pretend Jane, the girl who could have fun at the Ocean Club for a night, the one who belonged with a cute, nice guy like Miles, and who could exile painful memories far, far away, even if only for a short while.

SEVENTEEN

YOU LOOK . . ." HANDEL stopped before he finished the sentence.

It was late, almost midnight.

Handel and I decided to meet up on the docks by the wharf after I left the Ocean Club, way out over the water where the fishermen kept their boats. There was no one around on a Friday night at this hour.

I could barely wait to get there. Here. To see him.

He was all I wanted.

"I look *what*?" I asked him. "Like someone I'm not?"

I followed Handel to the place where his father's boat was tied up. My high heels dangled in my right hand. It felt good to be on solid ground again, heading along the boardwalk, that familiar rough wood underfoot, the type you had to know how to walk on so you didn't get splinters. It was a relief to be with this boy who made me swoon just by standing there and looking at me. Handel got under my skin without having to try, and I think I got under his, too. I could tell, the way the electricity was flowing off him and reaching out to me, wanting me with such intensity, that this was true.

"No," Handel said, glancing at me. "You look beautiful, and you're always beautiful, which means that you're being exactly who you've always been."

My face flushed. I loved what Handel just told me. "You think I'm beautiful?"

"Yes." His reply was so blatant. So unabashed.

"That's new for me."

"What is?"

"Someone saying I'm beautiful like it's a given. A boy, I mean. Like you."

Handel held out his hand to help me step onto the boat. "How could that be new?"

I climbed over the bow and hopped to the floor. His fingers were gentle but firm. "I haven't dated too many people before." I hesitated, then decided to keep going. "I've always flown under the radar, I guess."

"That's hard to believe."

I gave Handel a skeptical look. "You can honestly say you knew of my existence before this year?"

Handel busied himself arranging a place for us to sit on one of the benches that lined the side of the boat, piling lobster crates off to the side so there was more space, pulling out a couple of cushions from a storage cubby. "I might not have known," he admitted.

"See. I told you."

When the seat was ready, Handel settled himself onto it, and I settled myself next to him. "But once I did notice you, I couldn't stop seeing you. Or thinking about you. You have that effect." He took my hand into his, inspected it, drew his fingers across the lines on my palm.

"I do?"

He raised my hand to his lips and kissed the back of it. "Yes. It's like you're . . . fragile and unbreakable at once."

"I don't feel unbreakable. But it's a nice thought." Handel's mouth brushed my skin again. The feel of it stole my breath.

Then he looked up at me with a grin. "So how was your *date*?"

I laughed. "It wasn't a date. Not really."

"How was your *group* date, then?"

"Fine. If you insist. It was fun actually. Not as bad as I'd feared."

Handel's eyes were amused. "You actually felt fear? Now you've got to tell me more."

I elbowed him. "You would, too, if you were expected to show up at the Ocean Club."

He whistled. The sound cut low over the water and the dinging of the boats against the docks. "Fancy."

"Very."

"Did they pay for your beer at least?"

"Yes. Though it was just a Coke. An *expensive* Coke," I added.

Handel nodded over at my heels, now piled one on top of the other next to an orange life jacket and a lobster crate. "So the shoes and the dress tonight were for them and not me?"

"Afraid so."

"Did they behave themselves?"

This question got a look of disbelief from me. "Of course. What, were you worried?" I asked with a laugh.

"I am human," he said, laughing along with me. "Most of the time."

"And don't forget, I'm part unbreakable, so you don't have to worry so much."

Handel looked down at his hands. "It's the fragile part I worry about."

"I want my friends to like you," I said suddenly.

"Oh yeah?"

"If they got to know you better, they would."

Handel pushed aside a lock of hair that had fallen across his eyes. "You seem confident about that."

"I am," I said, reaching up to shift it aside after it had fallen right back. Handel's eyes were so steady, so full of feeling. He made me never want to look away. "How could they not, when I like you so much?"

"I like you, too," he said, so sincere.

Those words washed over me like the tide, leaving me with chills.

Handel reached over, his fingers grazing the tender skin just above the dip in my dress. He took the blue mosaic heart into his palm. Inspected it. "This is new."

I swallowed. Nodded. He placed it gently back against my chest. His hand lingered there a moment, eyes flickering up to mine again. I leaned in for a kiss, just a quick one, but just as quickly, the kiss turned into something else, something much more intense. Handel's mouth parted, and his hands went to my face, gently pulling me closer. The light touch of his fingers along the curve of my jaw, then sliding down across my neck and over my shoulders, stole the air from my lungs. I don't know that it was a conscious decision—I don't remember there being a decision at all, honestly—but I found myself shifting positions, moving in such a way that I had one knee pressed into the seat next to Handel's left thigh and the other pressed near his right, sitting across him. We never stopped kissing, not even for a moment, and now I was looking down at him from above, the blue heart of my necklace swinging and swaying between us, my long hair flowing around us like a curtain. The low back of my dress was gripped tight in Handel's fists, as though he were afraid of where his hands would travel if he let go. His lips tasted of salt and the sea air and I couldn't get enough of him; I could *never* get enough of him, so I pressed myself closer until there was no room left between us. I didn't even care that the hem of my dress was riding up my legs, or that I could feel the fabric of Handel's jeans rough along the inside of my thighs. It's what I desired. It's *all* I desired. Wherever this led was where I wanted to go.

When we finally pulled apart, we were both gasping for breath.

My heart pounded and pounded in my chest.

Handel's eyes were wild. Then he said, "You make me want things, Jane."

I felt a sudden burn in my cheeks, laughed nervously, a little shocked at myself, at whatever possessed me to act the way I just had, so uninhibited, as though I was a girl with far more experience. As gracefully as I could manage, I extracted myself from Handel's lap and returned to the seat next to him, adjusting my dress, tugging it lower.

"I didn't mean it that way," he backtracked. "Though you make me want those things, too."

I combed my fingers through my knotted hair and tried to steady my breathing. "What did you mean, then?"

Handel was silent awhile, and I let him think. It was so quiet out here. Just the sound of the waves against the dock, the activity along the beach by all the bars too distant to interrupt all this peace. The moon shone bright over the water, shimmering and sparkling with the gentle movement of the boat as it rocked.

Handel took my hand again. Ran his finger in circles across

my palm, and I felt the electricity of it in my core. "When I'm with you, I think I could have a different life."

This answer surprised me. "Do you want one?"

"Sometimes."

"Why?"

"I wonder what it would be like to have been born into a different family."

"Speaking of, I met your cousin today," I said, his comment reminding me. "Jenny."

Handel seemed startled. "What?"

"Jenny Nolan. She was at my house for a fitting with my mother. I guess she's getting married?"

"Jenny Nolan," he repeated. "I guess she is. Yeah, she's my cousin."

"She's pretty."

Handel just nodded.

"Was it her father who died? Your uncle?"

"No. Her father's brother," Handel said. "How'd you know she was related to me?"

I smiled a little, feeling a tad smug about the fact that members of Handel's family would find me important enough to gossip about. "She told me straight out." I leaned into him. "Apparently, your mother liked the idea of us going on a date. She told Jenny about it, and how she was disappointed we didn't work out."

Handel shook his head. "God, my ma is always talking."

"Everyone's ma is always talking," I corrected.

"True enough."

I watched Handel. There was a look on his face that made me sad. He was like a lost boy in that moment, the bad-boy mask

fallen away to reveal the lonely boy who'd seen enough tragedy in his life to have it change him forever. "Sometimes I think
you're more vulnerable than you give off," I said. "That you're
completely different from what people think you are."

"Nah. I'm probably just the way they say."

But I shook my head. "I don't buy that. And if you don't want
to be, you don't have to."

"If only it were that easy."

"It is, though," I said. Closed my eyes. The circles Handel
was still making on my palm lulled me into a swoon. I wondered
if that's what he'd intended.

"I wish that were true," Handel said.

Then I felt his mouth on mine again, and that was the end of
our conversation.

EIGHTEEN

MY MOTHER LOOKED UP from her sewing machine. It was early in the morning, and her eyes were still weary. This time, pale yellow chiffon covered every available surface and the floor like a layer of butter. Despite the air conditioner humming in the window, she was sweating. It was the only room in the house that had one. "Do you want to talk about it?" she asked.

I placed her iced coffee in the only available space, right against the wall behind the giant red pincushion. "Talk about what?"

She pushed aside the chiffon. "Jane, don't play dumb."

I sighed. "I'm not."

"I'm worried about you, and we haven't had a real talk in a while. Then Professor O'Connor comes over and says the police have a lead. You didn't know anything about it? Nothing at—"

"It's not like I remember anything else," I cut in. Walked away from her. Stopped only when I stood in the doorway, ready to disappear down the hall.

My mother took a sip of the coffee. "All right. I'm not going to push you."

The dark cloud lifted. "Thank you." I wanted to change the subject. I took a step forward, now that the conversation could go somewhere safer. Glanced at all the fabric everywhere. "Who's forcing bridesmaids into yellow chiffon?"

My mother closed her eyes a moment. Like she was trying to

forget her worry. Then she took a deep breath and opened them again. "Lizzie McCreary."

"The oldest McCreary sister?"

My mother nodded.

"All that fair freckled skin and she couldn't have chosen another color?"

My mother made an ick face. "I know. It's awful, isn't it?"

I grabbed a yard off the floor, held it up to my body. Even my olive skin looked washed out. "It really is."

My mother took some of it into her hands. "The fabric is lovely, but that color is death to anyone who wears it, regardless of how pretty they are. I tried to convince Lizzie to choose blue or green to go with her sisters' pretty strawberry-blond hair, but she wouldn't hear of it. Something about her bridesmaids matching the center of the daisies in their bouquets."

"Wow. How horrible."

"Truly."

"Promise me something," I said.

"And what's that?"

"When I get married, you will not allow me to inflict such trauma onto Tammy, Michaela, and Bridget. You'll remind me what good friends they've been to me all these years and how a bride should always be kind to her bridesmaids."

My mother laughed. "I'll do that." Her face grew serious. "You're not about to tell me you're engaged, are you?" Her tone was half kidding, but only half.

I put a hand to my chest. "Me? Getting married? Any time this century?" I shook my head like she was crazy. "Have you been drinking?"

The look on her face lightened up. "Well, that's a relief," she said. "Though, the way Jenny Nolan was talking about you and Handel Davies, it sounded like she hoped you two would be married off already."

"Jenny Nolan has no idea about anything."

"You do, though. Care to share?"

"Don't you have work to do?" I dodged.

"I'm here when you want to talk about it."

"I'm aware," I said, halfway out the door again.

The pedal of my mother's Singer began its slow rhythm, then stopped. "Jane, one last thing."

I'd already turned around, but I stopped. "What's that?"

"It's not your job to save anyone," she said. "Not even if you fall in love with them." Then the pedal started up, the sewing needle pricking the delicate chiffon mercilessly and leaving a trail of stitches behind.

"Bridget's got a boyfriend," Tammy was singing when I arrived at the beach.

Bridget leaned over and whacked Tammy with her magazine. The "Us" in Us Weekly just barely readable on the curve. "What are you, twelve?"

"Sometimes," she said, rubbing her arm.

"Yeah, well, Tammy's got a boyfriend," Bridget sang back to her.

"That's not fair," Tammy said. "I don't have a magazine to hit you with."

"I take it last night at the Ocean Club ended well," I said, laying out my towel, watching as it floated down onto the sand. I threw my flip-flops onto the far corners.

Bridget was busy guarding her magazines so Tammy couldn't get ahold of one. "Tammy's luck had nothing to do with the Ocean Club, though she's not quite ready to admit it," she whispered to me. Then she mouthed *Seamus* and put a finger to her lips.

I nodded. I couldn't help but smile, too. I loved the idea of Tammy and Seamus together. "What's this about you having a boyfriend, B?"

Michaela huffed. "If you'd stayed with us until we left, you'd already know the answer."

I let my hair fall from its knot on my head so I wouldn't feel the bump when I lay down. "I was tired."

"Tired of us?" Michaela asked.

I shook my head forcefully. "No way."

"The lady doth protest too much," Tammy said.

"Someone's been doing their summer reading assignment," Michaela said wryly.

Tammy shrugged. "We can't all be as smart as *Jane,*" she said, her voice singsongy.

"You really are twelve," I told her.

"She totally is," Bridget said with a sigh.

I took refuge on the other side of Bridget. Slathered on sunscreen. Waited for the conversation to continue without me, but when it didn't, I turned to the girls, wondering what was causing the silence. The sun burned on my bare skin. "Did I miss something?"

Michaela seemed exasperated. "Jane!"

"Fine." I knew what they were waiting for, and it was about

time to give in. "I have another story to tell. A longer one this time. About Handel," I added.

"I knew it," Bridget chirped.

"So did I." Michaela sighed. She shifted on her towel, turning onto her side so she could face me. "I just hoped I was wrong."

I put my sunglasses on to cut the glare. "I'm not telling my story if you're going to prejudge."

"Tell it, tell it," Tammy said. "No prejudging on this part of the beach."

"I will, as long as you guys spill after I do."

"Of course," Bridget said, her eyes sliding to the lifeguard who had just loped past on his break. "I'm dying to tell you my updates, anyway."

Michaela's exasperation turned on Bridget now. "You're too easy, you know."

This time, Michaela got whacked by Bridget's magazine. A different one. *People*. "Well, you're too bitchy. How 'bout that?"

"Ladies, please," I said, laughing. "We're all friends here."

Bridget harrumphed. "I always *thought* so, but maybe I was wrong."

"Sorry, B," Michaela droned. "You've got quite an arm."

Bridget smiled sweetly now. "I might be easy, but I'm definitely not weak."

"That you are not," Tammy said. "You were saying, Jane?"

My sunglasses provided adequate cover from their stares—I was glad I had them. I took a deep breath, then launched into the details. "I went down to the docks to meet Handel last night. And, um, we've seen each other more than I may have told you,"

I admitted, then shrank back a little, waiting for possible contact with one of Bridget's magazines.

Bridget's mouth opened in surprise. "You've been keeping things from us!"

"I told you it was a longer story this time."

"Uh-oh," Michaela said. "You really like him, don't you?"

A smile wanted onto my face, but I tried to hold it off. Handel didn't even have to be nearby to make me swoon. "I do." Michaela was about to say something else, but I didn't let her. "He's different from how you guys think. He's different from how everyone else says for that matter. I know he's got that bad boy thing, but after spending all this time with him, I really don't understand what's so bad."

Tammy's laugh was full of sarcasm. "Um, he's a Davies."

"Which means he's also connected to every single hoodlum in our town," Michaela went on, but she wasn't laughing. "Your father would have—" she started, but then was halted from finishing by another hard whack of a magazine, this time from Tammy, who'd grabbed one off Bridget's towel to do it.

The smile fell from my face. "I swear, Handel's not like that. My dad would have liked him. Because of how Handel likes me," I added.

Bridget placed a hand on my arm. "I believe you, Jane." Then she turned her glare on Michaela. "And I think if you want to tell us more about how you feel, there will not be any more judgment or negativity. Will there? Hmm?"

"Sorry, J," Michaela said. "Really."

Tammy just nodded. "Promise."

I reached for the remains of Bridget's iced coffee, the cup anchored in the sand.

"Go ahead," she said, nodding.

I picked it up, avoiding the wet chunks falling off the bottom. The sun was so hot, and I was suddenly so parched. I sucked down all that was left, my eyes widening at the shock of how sweet it was. Bridget always put in way too much sugar, but I wasn't about to complain. "Thanks," was all I said. Then, "I want you guys to like Handel. Actually, I *need* you guys to like him."

Bridget's face lit up. "Oh my God. Do you, like, *love* him?"

"No," I said too quickly.

Michaela, who'd been holding her breath, let it out.

Tammy stared blankly.

The burn in my cheeks had nothing to do with the sun overhead. I was thinking about last night and all that had happened between us. Things were starting to get . . . intense. "But there was quite a lot of, well, kissing, et cetera."

Michaela's eyebrows went up. "Define *et cetera*."

Tammy glanced at Michaela. "Jane doesn't *need* to give us details. It's not like *you* ever give us details."

Michaela huffed but didn't push any further.

Bridget cocked her head, looking at me. "I don't think you're being honest with yourself, Jane. Maybe you do love him. And I say that because of the, well, *et cetera* you just mentioned. It's not like you to, you know, go anywhere with a boy besides kissing—not that I'm disapproving because I'm absolutely not," she added quickly. "I approve wholeheartedly if it's what you really want."

I waited for the blush on my face to subside. "Maybe Handel and I are heading in that direction. You know, toward *love*." It was strange to say that word out loud in reference to a boy and me. It tasted like a foreign substance. "But I'm not quite ready to decide that love is what's happening. It feels serious, though, which is why it's so important to me that you guys like him."

Tammy shifted positions on her towel. She was nodding. "Okay. Maybe all we need to do is spend some time with him. Maybe he's suspicious simply because he's an unknown."

"And because," Michaela began, but Bridget shot her a glare, to which she replied, "I'm not gonna say anything bad," with gritted teeth, before continuing her response. "Because we *love* you, Jane, and want you to be okay. We want you to be with someone who's going to make you happy."

"I am happy," I admitted. "He makes me happy."

"It's settled, then," Michaela said.

"What is?" I asked.

Michaela picked up her suntan lotion and began applying some to her arms. "You're going to arrange for all of us to get together so we can start feeling about Handel the way you do."

This got Michaela a confused look from Tammy. "I don't know about you, but I am not planning on liking Handel Davies the way Jane does."

Michaela switched to her legs. "You know what I mean."

I waved a hand in front of their faces, trying to get their attention back. "Um, I can try to make that happen, but Handel is a pretty private guy."

Bridget sighed dreamily. "Mystery is half of what makes the bad boy seem so bad."

"If he cares about you, then he'll do it," Tammy said simply. "We're your girls."

"Right," I said.

But I wasn't sure it was that simple.

"Great," Michaela said.

"Oooh," Bridget nearly squealed. "I've always wanted to get up close and personal with someone like Handel."

I laughed. "I think it's about time you told me how *your* night ended, now that I've told you about mine."

Michaela rolled onto her stomach, like she couldn't bear to go through the details, but on her way there, she said, "Bridget had three guys fighting over her."

"It was *wonderful*," Bridget sighed.

I smiled. "And what were you two doing while this was going on?"

Tammy snorted. "Making bets."

Michaela lifted her head an inch. "I thought Hugh might win."

"But it seems Logan has the edge," Tammy said. "Then again, James was in the lead at one point. Bridget, would you care to share?"

"You girls make it sound so pedestrian," she said.

"Pedestrian? Apparently it's not just me who's been studying," Tammy said.

Bridget took off her sunglasses. Batted her eyelashes at us, then put them back on. "I've got plenty of SAT words up my sleeve."

"You're really good at that, B." Tammy was sincere. "The batting-your-eyelashes thing, I mean."

"You should try it," she said with a slight pout. "Boys love it. All it takes is a little practice."

"We're getting off-topic," I said. "Which boy has the edge, B?"

There was that dreamy smile of hers. "They're *all* really sweet. Ask Michaela what she thinks of Hugh, for example."

Michaela shook her head. Then shrugged. "Fine. Hugh is kind of hot. I've never dated a black guy. Maybe I should."

"Maybe you should," I echoed, giving her a smirk.

"Perhaps," she said noncommittally.

A woman lugging two beach chairs and an umbrella nearly knocked into me as she walked by our setup. I ducked away just in time. "And Miles?" I asked, righting myself again. "What about him in all of this jockeying?"

Tammy tsked. "He was rather shattered when you took off."

I dug for an elastic in my beach bag, but it was stuffed with so many things I couldn't seem to find one. I needed to get my hair off my neck. It was too hot to have it down. "Nah."

"*Yeah,*" Tammy said, tossing me one of her elastics. "Don't deny it. He has a thing for you."

Bridget got serious. "Jane, you shouldn't let him hang on to hope if he hasn't got any. He's a nice guy."

Guilt sprung up like a weed. I tried to distract myself from it by focusing on putting up my hair. "I know he is."

Michaela rolled over. Looked at me. "Unless Miles has a real chance?"

I finished fixing the knot, then shrugged. "I'm with Handel. We just went over that."

"We've yet to see this for real, however," Michaela said. "If you're with Handel, then where is he now?"

"Working," I said. "Why would you even ask that?"

"Do you know this for sure?"

"Yes," I answered, even though I didn't really know the answer. She was right. I just assumed that's where Handel was. That this was where he was all day every day. "I thought you guys were going to try to be nice about him now that—" But I didn't get to finish.

"Incoming," Tammy interrupted, looking off into the distance, toward the lifeguard chairs at the far end of the beach. Miles and company were headed toward us. "From the left."

"Ooh," Bridget cried. "Make yourselves pretty for the boys!"

"Jane, since you're not all the way toward love with Handel yet, why don't you make yourself available to Miles," Michaela suggested. "Maybe a little? That's all I'm asking. A teensy bit."

"I'm not justifying that with a response," I said as the four of us watched the band of boys approaching, moving across the beach like the tide, picking up shells and sand and more than a few glances from the other girls lying out in the sun.

"Hello, hello," Miles said cheerily when they reached us. Then he gave me one of those blinding, golden-boy smiles, the kind they must have you practice at prep school. "Can I sit here?" he asked, gesturing at the space in the sand next to my towel.

"Sure," I said, smiling back, but immediately felt a little bit guilty about it. Bridget was right: Miles was a really nice guy, and he had no idea that right after seeing him last night, I'd gone out to meet Handel at his boat. I really shouldn't lead Miles on. It wasn't right. It wasn't the kind of thing I did.

Miles and his friends set their towels in a circle around us, doubling our little beach setup. Miles sat down next to me, that easy smile never leaving his face. He didn't seem to have a care in the world, and I realized right then that I liked this about him. It was infectious. Even a relief. Miles wasn't even the smallest bit bad or dangerous, or from a notorious family like Handel. He was good all the way through like I used to be, a nice boy who thought of me that way, too.

So instead of telling Miles immediately and honestly that I had a boyfriend—well, more or less—I let myself soak up all the ease that was rolling off him in waves.

I have to admit, as I looked around at my friends who, despite their protests, were obviously enjoying this literal circle of male attention, I saw how simple it would be for my friends to approve of someone like Miles. How, if I chose him, I could have one of those fun summer romances I used to dream about when the boys didn't know we were alive, the kind that aren't weighty or dark or serious, but as light as the cotton candy they sold by the baseball field near the wharf. A tiny part of me wondered, too, if Michaela wasn't a teensy bit right and I should leave myself open to the possibility of Miles, even if, in the end, it was really only a little part of me that thought this was a good idea.

NINETEEN

STOP FIDGETING," MY MOTHER said. "Do you want me to stick you?"

I looked down at her warily. "It's hot." She was holding pins dangerously close to my chest as she worked on the bodice of the wedding dress I was modeling. "If you stop threatening me with a sticking, maybe that will help with the fidgeting. You're making me nervous."

She took a step back and put her free hand on her hip. "How many years have you been doing this for me? And how many times has there been a pin-related injury?"

I rolled my eyes, the only part of my body I could easily move. "Once."

"And that happened because?"

"Because I slipped off this pedestal thing you make me stand on."

My mother went around to the back of the dress, stepping carefully around the train. She bent down to fix the snap on the bustle. "And you slipped off because?"

Thank God she was too invested in her work to see the expression on my face. "I slipped off because I was trying to get to the phone."

"Exactly," my mother said, her words slightly muffled. I didn't need to look at her to know she had pins in her mouth. "It wasn't me that was the problem."

"Bridget had important news!"

"Not so important that it was worth a serious stabbing."

I put my hand over my mouth, trying to hold back the laughter. Laughter would be bad right now. "Definitely not," I admitted, the laughter spilling out of me, anyway.

My mother came around to the front of the dress again. "No giggling," she protested, trying not to laugh herself. She stopped working for a moment. Looked up at me with a smile. "My silly daughter."

"I'm not silly."

"It's not a bad thing," she said. "Giggling and silliness are nice to see. It's been a while since I've heard you so relaxed."

I stiffened a little at this. "I guess so." I didn't want to think about the reasons why I hadn't been silly lately. That same morning, I glimpsed a headline about the break-ins on the front page of the newspaper. I'd gone to retrieve it from the front steps, the clear bag it came in covered with dew.

SUSPECT IN RASH OF BREAK-INS TAKEN IN FOR QUESTIONING; POLICE WON'T REVEAL IDENTITY

My mother was still in bed, so she hadn't yet seen it. I grabbed the paper and took it inside, shoved it far underneath my bed so she wouldn't. Just like I'd erased the messages Officer Connolly had left on the machine about needing to talk to me before my mother knew they were there. If I avoided these things, I could almost pretend that life was normal, protecting myself and my mother from further worry.

"So, my darling daughter," she was saying as she bent low to the ground to touch up the hem of the gown, "what are you doing for the Fourth of July? Going to the beach with the girls? Or anyone else?"

She didn't mention Handel directly, but I could tell that she was fishing for information. Her tone said it all.

I felt my cheeks reddening. Even the thought of spending an evening with Handel was enough to make me flush with want, with all the desire I felt for him—an embarrassing reaction to have in front of my mother. "I'm going to watch the fireworks like always. Probably up in a lifeguard chair if I can get ahold of one." If I just referred to myself, then I didn't have to do the work of figuring out who else to mention in the equation—the girls, Miles, his friends, Handel. Handel and I still hadn't made plans for that night, and Miles had already said he wanted to hang out with me if I was around.

"Hmmm," my mother said, gently tugging along the edge of the fabric. She obviously didn't believe I'd be spending the Fourth alone. She stood up and stepped back to admire her work. "Now, *this* is a beautiful wedding dress."

The fabric was ivory, a thick rough silk, so thick that when my mother worked her magic she could mold it almost like a sculpture. It was strapless, simple on the top, and fitted all the way down my body to below my hips, where it belled out. No beads were sewn onto this one, no pearls or buttons or lace. The simple beauty of the fabric and the style are what made this dress stunning.

I looked at myself in the mirror on the far wall. "It really is."

"Mary is going to love this design when she sees it. I'm feeling proud of myself, I have to admit."

"You should feel that way."

The doorbell sounded.

My mother put down her pincushion on the sewing table. "I'll get it. Don't move."

"Yup, I'll just wait here," I said sarcastically as she left me trapped in all these heavy yards of silk, flowing down off the pedestal into a train that trailed off a good few yards behind me. I was so pinned that if I tried to remove the dress, I risked serious injury. "Don't worry about me. I'm fine!" I yelled after her, a bit grateful for the interruption, honestly, so I had time to banish my sexy Handel thoughts before I had to look her in the eyes again.

Then I heard voices.

One of them was male.

Maybe it was a fabric delivery.

But when my mother returned to the sewing room, singing, "Jane, you have a visitor," along the way, I knew it wasn't the deliveryman approaching or the mailman. Oh God, I thought. It's Miles. He's found my home address and surprised me with a visit.

But it wasn't him, either.

"Hi, Jane," Handel said, hovering in the doorway of my mother's office, smiling. "I got the day off."

I covered my mouth with my hand, unsure what to do. Unable to move.

"Jane," my mother said from behind him. He stepped aside so she could come in the room. "You didn't tell me you were expecting company."

I removed my hand. "That's because I wasn't."

"Right," she said.

Handel's eyes traveled up and down my body, then stopped when they met my eyes. "That's a beautiful dress, Ms. Calvetti," he added quickly.

My cheeks burned.

"And an even more beautiful model, don't you agree?" she asked, glancing at Handel, who was still not quite inside the sewing room.

I wanted to die. "Mom!"

Handel laughed. "I thought that was already understood."

My cheeks were on fire, even though I was secretly pleased by Handel's appraisal. I gave my mother a look that said *we are going to have a serious chat about your behavior later.* "Um, can I get out of this dress now?" I asked her.

"I'll go wait in the living room," Handel offered. "Then maybe we can head to the beach?" he asked me.

I nodded.

"It'll take a few minutes, just so you know," my mother warned him. "These gowns are complicated."

"I've got time," he called out, already gone from the doorway.

My mother hadn't moved. She studied me. One hand on her hip. "He's nice, Jane."

The blood that started to drain from my cheeks with Handel's departure immediately returned. "I know."

My mother began undoing the row of tiny pearl buttons all down the back of the gown. "And he's *very* good-looking."

"Mom," I protested. This was going to take forever. There must be a hundred buttons for her to undo, and she'd only gotten to about five. I was trapped in this conversation.

"It was just an observation," she said, the smile on her face audible in her tone.

"I could probably do without that particular observation about my boyfriend," I said, finally able to breathe now that my mother was more than halfway down the bodice. "And please lower your voice."

"So he *is* your boyfriend," she said in a whisper. "Interesting. How come you didn't tell me?"

"It feels kind of private."

"Not private enough that he couldn't stop by."

She finished with the last buttons, and I let out a long breath. "I'm as surprised as you are."

Now she got to work on the bustle, trying to let it down without losing any pins in the process. "Interesting."

"You keep saying that," I said.

"Because it's true," she sang.

My mother finished with the bustle and came around to the front of the dress again. Escape was in my near future. I could practically taste freedom. "Well, I'm glad I could add some excitement to your day."

She stood there, looking at me. "Jane, you know you can talk to me about anything."

"Yes, I know."

"Including about the . . . *famous Handel Davies*," she added, in an exaggerated whisper.

"Mom!" Maybe she was going to make me suffer in this gown all day. "Can you please help me here?"

She laughed gleefully.

"You know," I said, about ready to step out of the dress on my own, yet finding I was still surrounded by so much fabric that this wasn't about to happen easily and I didn't want to ruin any of my mother's work. "I always assumed that since you're such a *young* mother that you would be much *cooler* than the other ones I know."

My mother got a look of concentration on her face and started fiddling with the hem of the dress, studying it. "Really."

"But suddenly I find that I am wrong."

She took out a pin and wove it through the bottom of the fabric. "Don't hurt your mother's feelings," she said.

"Right. Like you sound so hurt."

"No. You're right. I'm not. I'm enjoying this."

"Mother!" She finally stood and gave me her hand so I could step out of the dress. When it was safely away from harm, I hopped down from the pedestal, threw on my shirt and shorts, and sprinted by Handel, who was standing near the screen door. I ran into my room and got dressed, gave myself a quick look in the mirror, and, satisfied, sprinted back to see my mother in the sewing room. "I'm leaving now," I informed her.

"Jane," my mother said, stopping me with her hand.

"What now?"

"You *are* being safe, aren't you?" she asked.

"Oh my God. I'm not even close to needing to be. Can we please drop this?"

"Well, when you do get close, we should go to a doctor and make sure you have everything you need."

"I am not doing this right now. I love you, bye," I added, my cheeks as red as the bolt of taffeta leaning against the wall. I shut the door behind me, took a deep breath, and walked the very short four steps into the living room, where Handel was still waiting. "Please tell me you didn't hear every word of that," I said to him.

"I didn't," he said. But he was grinning.

"You're lying."

"It was a white lie," he said. "I was trying to make you feel better."

I covered my face with my hands. "I'm mortified," I said, my words muffled.

"Don't be. Besides, I told you the mortifying story about my name. Now we're even. Your mother loves you. She just wants to know things about your life."

I still didn't remove my hands. I couldn't look at Handel. My cheeks burned like I'd stayed an entire day in the summer sun without any shade or sunscreen. The only thing that was even the least bit consoling was the familiar grains of sand on the floor of the living room under my bare feet. Slowly, I uncovered my eyes. "You sound like you speak from experience."

His grin slipped but only a little. "My ma wants to be a part of my life, too."

"And is she? Does she know about . . . me and you?" I still couldn't quite bring myself to say "us."

Handel didn't answer. Instead, he said, "Maybe we should head to a place where, you know, your mother can't overhear our entire conversation."

"I can't hear anything!" my mother called from the sewing room.

"Yes," I said immediately. "That's a fantastic idea."

"Have fun! Don't be home too late!" my mother yelled out.

I slipped my feet into my flip-flops. "Come on," I said to Handel, already opening the screen door. "Bye, Mom," I called back to her.

Once Handel and I were outside, even in the heat, I could breathe easier—at least at first. Then I noticed how patches of the grass in our yard were growing out of control and others were burned from the sun. My dad had always been the one to come over and maintain it. I pushed this out of my mind, deciding I'd deal with it later. "Where do you want to go?" I asked Handel.

"I was thinking," he began, then stopped.

"You were thinking . . . what?"

"That we should go public. Again."

"Public," I said. "About me. And you. Like before."

Handel's hand kept going to his back pocket. "Yeah. That we should stop hiding this. Us," he added. "We started out that way, and I don't think it makes sense to pretend we aren't together."

I looked at him. "You want a cigarette," I said.

"How'd you know?"

"You're nervous," I said. "You always want one when you get nervous. Well, that and the fact that you keep the pack in your jeans pocket and your hand reaching for it gives you away."

He hooked his thumb into his belt loop. "I'm not nervous."

"But you want a cigarette."

"Yes." He glanced at the house. "But I'm not going to light one up in your front yard."

"All right. Let's walk somewhere, then. In public. Together."

"Let's," he said.

"Here we go," I said, then stopped at the edge of the grass, like it was a line of demarcation I wasn't sure we should cross. "You're really not worried about your friends anymore?"

Handel already had the cigarette out. The lighter poised. "I guess not."

I took a step forward. Crossed that line. "What changed?"

"I don't know. Things. Today life feels different for some reason." Handel put the cigarette in his mouth. The flick of his lighter sounded. Then after one long drag, he crossed that line, too, joining me on the other side. "And it's not right to hide. I want to do this right with you." Handel's eyes were serious. He took the cigarette from his mouth. "Jane, from the very first time I noticed you, *really* noticed you, I was sure you could only be good all the way through. I want that good to rub off on me, too."

I reached out to him. "I'm not *that* good."

"You are, though," he said, and his hand closed around mine. "And I love it."

Handel and I began our walk through town toward the beach. Once again, we braved the stares of the neighbors, the way they stopped sweeping their front porches and put down glasses of lemonade, pausing conversations to take us in as we passed. The daughter of a fallen cop, hand in hand with the youngest son of one of the town's most notorious families. I was sure my mother would get more gossip in her sewing room, but then, she could say she already knew about it, how her daughter's boyfriend was none other than Handel Davies, who'd stopped by the house to say hello and meet her.

Despite the attention, the nosy busybody-ness of everyone

around us, my mind was elsewhere. It was stuck on the last three words Handel said before we started on our way. He'd used "love" among them, used it to refer to how much he *loved* how I am. He hadn't said he loved *me,* not directly, but what he did say came awfully close. The very proximity of the two made me feel a little light-headed, like I was glowing brighter than the sun, everything about me lit up from the inside, or about to float away like a balloon. I could see it happening within Handel, too, from the way he couldn't stop smiling as we walked along, even though he kept trying to. From the way he kept looking over at me, with eyes that reached right inside to my heart, and how he didn't simply hold my hand—he couldn't stop playing with my fingers, tracing circles at the center of my palm. Each time we turned down a new street, he'd lift my hand to his lips and kiss the tender skin just above my wrist.

By the time we reached the path in the dunes that led to the beach, by the time we'd gone past all those staring eyes on the wharf, Handel had his arm around my shoulders. Then it went to my back, then my shoulders again, as though he couldn't get enough of touching me. I leaned into him, my hair cascading down his side. Occasionally I looked up into his eyes only to see that he was looking down into mine. We held each other close, held on to each other like a real couple, one without a care in the world, enjoying the summer and romance and falling in love because that was all that mattered.

TWENTY

MILES'S FACE FELL the second he saw Handel and me approach. He'd set his stuff up next to the girls and was chatting away enthusiastically with Bridget.

Suddenly I felt terrible.

I loosened my grip on Handel's waist. Pulled apart from him, a slight westward tug. I hadn't been thinking about Miles when Handel and I were on our way here, that we might run into Miles and his friends at the beach. But that was the thing about Handel: I could hardly think when I was around him. I hoped Michaela and Tammy and Bridget wouldn't mind that I'd shown up with Handel, unannounced. They wanted to get to know him. Now was their chance.

By the time Handel and I reached everyone's setup, Miles had plastered a grin on his face. It didn't reach his eyes, and that nagged a little at my heart. I had no interest in hurting Miles, yet obviously I already had. I should have mentioned something about Handel to him on Friday night, that there was another boy in my life, but I didn't, so now I was a jerk.

"Heya, Jane," Miles said enthusiastically, getting up from his towel to greet us. He must have picked up the local "heya" from spending time around here.

"Heya, Miles," I returned with a nervous smile, my public display with Handel suddenly awkward instead of thrilling. Everyone else was staring at us from behind Miles. The girls had their sunglasses on, so it was difficult to gauge their reactions, all except for Bridget, whose mouth was open wide in an excited sort of shock. No one else got up from their blankets. "Where are the rest of your friends?" I asked.

"They'll be here eventually," he said to me, then looked at Handel. "I don't believe we've met."

I cringed. Miles was extra polite. Formal. Which made him seem like a rich out-of-town guy. Which, of course, he was, technically, but a nice one all the same. "Um, Miles, this is Handel."

Handel's left arm never left its place along my back, not even when he reached out his right to shake Miles's hand. In fact I felt his fingers curl along the curve of my side. "Nice to meet you, Miles."

I swallowed. Looked from one boy to the other.

Right there, with the two of them standing so close, it was clear Miles was no match for Handel, not as far as I was concerned. Miles with his nicely built body, his prep school–boy charm, his perfect tan and easy smile, easy because he'd grown up with money in a good home with a good family. Miles was attractive and could be smooth when he wanted, which was almost always. But Handel was something else. There was beauty in Handel, a rough, unpolished kind. I could see it all over him now, in the way his long blond hair was whipping around his face in the wind, the way his skin glowed in the sun, his dark eyes suspicious and vulnerable and deep and wanting. The strong bone structure, his jawline, the way he carried himself, cigarette half dangling from his lips, the muscles in his arms and back and legs that came not from working out in a gym but from working out on the docks, which led to the kind of strength that has nothing to do with a person's ability to lift weights and every-thing to do with his ability to weather the toughness of life. It was true that Handel's last name gave him his reputation as a bad boy, but it was the rest of him that made a girl like me want to do anything she could to win him over from that dark side or, if this wasn't possible, to join him there.

I think Miles knew all this right then. We both did. How could I fall in love with Miles when there was someone like Handel to fall for instead? Despite this, Miles would be a sport, be-cause that's the kind of guy he was.

"Why don't we set up our stuff?" I said stiffly, half to Handel, half to Miles, not quite sure how to deal with both of them at once. My feet were burning in the hot sand.

"I'll make room," Miles said, shifting his towel, tugging it with his foot, so that Handel and I could sit next to each other. So that he was just a little farther out from the rest of us, a lonely island in a great sea of sand.

Bridget hopped up and bounced our way. "I'm Bridget," she announced to Handel, putting out her hand.

Finally, Handel's smile was genuine. He extended his own. "Handel."

"Well, I already knew *that,*" she said, flirty and adorable, not in a way intended to make me jealous but instead to make me feel included, to make Handel feel included, for which I was grateful.

"Hey, B. You're the best."

She grinned at me. "Well, I already knew *that,* too."

Handel matched her grin. "Jane talks about me?"

Bridget twisted and turned, coy, her blond hair swishing and swaying. "Only when we make her. Don't worry. She's very discreet." When we didn't move, she added, "Come on, join us," and plopped back down on her towel.

Handel raised his eyebrows. "You know, I'm not really prepared for the beach. I don't have a towel."

"They'll have extras," I said. "We'll just stay for a little while."

Michaela and Tammy were smiling at us now, but I couldn't tell what sort of smiles they were: forced, genuine, halfhearted?

"Hi, Handel," Tammy said. "Nice to see you again."

"I remember you," he said. "The ice cream."

"Tammy," she reminded him. Her tone was . . . confusing. Neither friendly like Bridget nor unfriendly. Neutral, maybe.

Michaela didn't get up. Didn't say anything. I nudged her foot with my own.

"I'm Michaela," she said, unmoving, her body propped by extended arms, her knees bent and pointed toward the sun. Our casual *look at me* pose, the four of us had decided two summers ago, back when we were all trying to crack the code of whatever unlocked the boy mind and his accompanying boy attention.

"Nice to meet you," Handel said.

"Hmm," was Michaela's response.

I glared. Made a show of moving the towels that Bridget had set out for us away from Michaela so we didn't have to be near her. Sometimes she made me so angry with her judging and her patronizing attitude. Like I couldn't fend for myself and needed her to do it for me.

Handel shrugged. Smiled sheepishly at me. "I don't have a bathing suit on. I was just imagining a walk."

Bridget laughed. "What, you don't live in one like Jane?"

"You're the same way," I shot back playfully. Then I began removing my T-shirt and jean shorts a little self-consciously.

Even though I had my bathing suit on underneath my clothes and even though I'd done this a million times in front of a million people, including Miles and his friends in this same spot on the beach, undressing in front of Handel made me nervous. It felt intimate and public in a way that was both thrilling and strange. I wanted to know what he was thinking as he watched me raise my arms to pull my shirt over my head, then undo the buttons on my shorts one by one, slipping them from my hips and letting them slide along my legs to my feet, if Handel was thinking about the other night on his boat when we'd kissed or if he was imagining doing this very thing himself sometime later on when we were in private. That's certainly what I was imagining him doing as I performed this beach striptease, and why my cheeks were burning by the time I kicked my shorts to the side and sat down, nearly naked, next to him. It wasn't embarrassment that was turning my skin a deep red, though. It was desire. Intense and hot as the sun above us. It made my heart flutter like the wings of a hummingbird. I wanted Handel to see it on me, the way his gaze made me flush with it. I wanted to make him as hungry for me as I was for him. I liked feeling this way.

"Are you okay?" Bridget asked, bringing me back to reality. Reminding me that I was in the middle of a summer crowd. "I think you might be getting some color in the sun. Take some of my lotion." She handed it over.

"Thanks." I opened the tube and began rubbing some into my cheeks and over my nose, unable to look at Handel as he made himself comfortable on the towel next to me, yet aware that his eyes were on me the entire time. When I finally turned to him, the way he stared was exactly the way I'd hoped he would. The smile he gave me so small it was almost imperceptible, except that I could see it and he knew that I could. A secret passed between us. Or more like it was exposed. I suddenly felt free of something, though I'm not sure what it was, exactly, that had been tossed aside like all of my clothing. Maybe it was some of the good I carried on my body like a heavy backpack. Maybe it was some of that.

"So, Handel," Tammy said, surprising me by starting up a conversation. Shaking me out of my daydream. "You've got the day off?"

Handel turned to her. Squinted in the sun. "I do. It's rare, but occasionally it happens."

"Summer job?" Miles inquired.

My heart sank once again. Miles was so obviously an outsider sometimes.

Handel just shrugged. "More like a job for life. I come from a family of fishermen. Generations of fishermen, really."

"Oh," was all Miles said. He probably had no idea how else to respond, since he was more accustomed to someone discussing their Ivy League future after a question like that, or at least some kind of university future.

"I'm putting off college for a year," Handel added.

"You are?" I asked, surprised. "I mean, you're planning to go?"

"I'm thinking about it. Lately, a lot."

I smiled. "That's great."

"You're a good influence," he said, smiling back.

Out of the corner of my eye, I saw Michaela take a deep breath to make some snide remark, I was sure, but Bridget got there first with an elbow and Tammy, too, squeezing her other arm tight. Michaela closed her mouth.

"What about you . . . Miles?" Handel asked, pronouncing the name carefully, giving it two distinct syllables. "What's your future plan?"

"Relax this summer. Finish high school next year and then college directly after." He eyed me. "I'm hoping for Harvard, but it's tough to get in, of course. If not Harvard, then maybe Dartmouth."

"Of course," Handel said with a laugh.

My heart was perpetually sinking for Miles. I wanted to help him sound more down-to-earth. More like us, I guess. "But you've got a summer job, too."

He gave me a confused look. "No, I don't."

"Yes, you do! I saw you, remember? You're a parking valet over at Christie's."

Miles laughed. "That night you saw me, I was driving my mother's car."

The pretty, ritzy woman all in white with the clutch. "That was your mother?"

"The one and only."

"So you don't have a job," I confirmed.

He shook his head. "Is that a problem? I mean, it's not like you do, either."

Bridget bit her lip but didn't say anything. Tammy and Michaela glanced at each other.

"I used to," I said, determined to reply. "But I'm taking some time off."

"Michaela," Handel said suddenly, cutting through the awkwardness that had settled over everyone. "Your last name is Connolly, right?"

She looked startled. "It is."

"I knew it," he said. "Your older brother is Jason Connolly. You guys have the same eyes."

She smiled at this, a genuine one. Michaela loves her older brother, and without realizing it, Handel said about the only thing that might cool off some of Michaela's attitude. "You know Jason?"

Handel nodded. "From hockey. He, uh, took me under his wing, I guess you could say, back when I was a freshman."

Michaela's smile grew. "Jason's like that, isn't he? I didn't realize you would have played together, but I guess that makes sense," she added offhandedly.

Much to my surprise, Handel and Michaela fell into a conversation, bonded by their mutual admiration for her brother.

Bridget leaned close. "This is good."

I nodded. "I know. Though unexpected."

We switched places on our towels, so Handel and Michaela could better talk and Tammy was closer.

"He's not so bad," Tammy whispered to me.

I rolled my eyes. "Gee, thanks."

Now Tammy rolled hers. "No, I mean, I might even like him."

"Good. Because I like him a lot."

"I know, J," Tammy said, growing serious. "I can tell. That much I can definitely tell."

"Well, I think it's great," Bridget pronounced.

"We already knew that," Tammy said with a laugh.

An hour passed, then another, and as the time ticked by, I began to realize that, without planning to and nearly without any effort, Handel had not only met my friends but was getting to know them, too, and best of all, they were taking him in as though he might even be one of us. Between their acceptance and the looks Handel kept giving me, looks that were full of laughter and ease but also longing, I felt as though I was soaring. Like I was both in my body and out of it at the same time, watching this scene from above, a scene I had dreamed about before, the one that involved a boy who'd taken an interest in me, who'd decided he'd wanted me and only me, a boy who made my head swim and my mind full of daydreams. We'd be at the beach together, hanging out in the summer with my friends, as though this was somehow normal, as though it was meant to be, just as it had seemed with the older girls we used to watch enjoy the very same thing, who owned such attention, basking in the adoration of boys even as they basked in the sun and the sand.

The only person who didn't seem to be enjoying himself was Miles. The only person who left early that afternoon was him.

And I admit, it made me a little sad to see Miles go. But only a little.

TWENTY-ONE

I WAS THINKING WE could go to this place near the docks to eat," Handel said after we left the beach. It was evening. We headed toward the wharf. "It's kind of hidden—I bet you don't know it. You hungry?"

"I could eat," I said, reveling in the wonder of spending an entire day with Handel, a day that had been wonderful from the start. He had his arm around me again, and our pace was slow, leisurely, like we had all the time in the world. My flip-flops slid across the concrete of the sidewalk. "Though it's tough to imagine there's a place in this town I don't know about."

Handel grinned at the ground. "You wait. I've got secrets for you."

My heart was pounding. "Yeah?"

"This way," he said, and led me toward an area near the docks that I'd always thought was deserted. "Under here," Handel directed when we reached a part of the beach where the dock rose up over it on thick wooden pilings.

"There's nothing—" I started, about to protest there wasn't anything but beach on the other side followed by a long jetty of rocks that stuck out into the ocean, dividing one town from the next.

But Handel had disappeared. After I passed the last piling, I looked right toward the water and left toward the seawall towering above. Then I noticed the buoys stacked like a welcome sign in front of a wooden shack almost hidden from view. I saw

Handel pass by the doorway, stop, backtrack, and beckon, so I went to join him. I ducked inside after him, and the remaining sunlight of the day was cut away by the thick boards that made up the roof of the little house.

A pile of sand on the floor marked the entrance. Whoever maintained this place didn't care if it got everywhere, just like at home. Two lightbulbs hung naked from the ceiling, and a make-shift bar divided the room in half, with a few stools in front of it. Behind the bar was the bare bones of a kitchen—a silver sink and counter where some dishes had been piled to dry and a short fridge at the back, a wide chopping block for cutting with a set of knives standing at its corner to the left, and what looked to be a small oven and gas stove to the right. A round outdoor grill was shoved into a corner, the kind you had to light the old-fashioned way and took forever to catch but was always worth the work because it made the food taste so good.

I slid onto one of the stools in front of the bar. "What is this place?"

Handel was opening a cooler packed to the brim with ice. He dug into the middle and pulled out a giant codfish and laid it on the chopping block. "It's a place for us."

"Us?"

He glanced at me before pulling out the biggest knife I'd ever seen, like a cleaver, but with a fat, curved blade. He put on a pair of thick gloves and began to expertly gut and clean the fish, removing its head and tail, which he dropped into a bag and shoved in the fridge. "The guys who work on the boats. We can come here whenever we want to cook up the day's catch. Make some dinner. Drink some beers. Hang out. You know."

I watched as Handel carefully pulled out the skeleton of the fish, then went to work on the smaller spines. "Am I allowed to be here?"

Handel turned for a sec, grabbed a pan blackened with use, and threw it on the stove, turning the flame to high. "You are if you're with me. There's some beer in the fridge. Help yourself, and if you wouldn't mind, I'd love one, too."

"Sure," I said, coming around the bar, still watching Handel deal with the fish, picking out the tiniest of the bones. I was used to watching this—we lived in a fishing town. But there was something fascinating about seeing Handel Davies doing it, and for the purpose of what appeared to be our dinner. A dinner he was going to cook for me. A dinner cooked by a boy who'd never spoken to me before only a few weeks ago—no, that hadn't even known I was alive before then. The fridge was packed with beer, the bag with the fish head and tail shoved into the only remaining space. I grabbed two and opened them, leaving one at the edge of the chopping block for Handel. Then I returned to my perch at the bar. "Are you bringing the leftovers to your mother for later?" I asked, referring to the head and tail, which people around here used to make stock.

He grinned. "Yeah. I keep her in good supply." He slipped the glove from his left hand and took a swig of beer. "She's a fine cook."

"From the looks of it, so are you."

"Nah," he said, his eyes on me now. "It's just knowing how to clean the fish right, then some high heat and salt. There's no skill in that."

I took a sip of my beer, breaking our stare. "Maybe. We'll see, I guess."

"We will." Handel threw two long, thin pieces of fish into the pan, where they made a satisfying sizzle. He began opening and shutting cabinets, pulling out plastic spice bottles and a couple of plates. While Handel cooked, I got up and stood in the doorway, staring out at the ocean, watching as the last of the day's light seeped away. I couldn't stop smiling; I couldn't stop glowing, really; and I couldn't stop loving the fact that Handel felt like he was wholly mine. Unlike before, when I was unsure what to call us, I suddenly knew that I *had* him—had him like I'd never had a boy. And he had me, too. There was no doubt about this, either. All my worries, the despair of that night in February, the danger everyone feared would rear up in front of me like a killer wave, it all seemed so distant now, like I might have imagined it, and I loved that Handel did this to me, too, that he *gave* me this.

Eventually, the delicious smell of fish pulled me from these thoughts, from the sounds of the ocean and the breeze rolling across the evening. I was just in time for Handel to place a perfectly charred fish in front of me at the bar, a couple of lemon wedges on the side. A big bowl of potato chips followed.

Handel pulled up a chair next to mine and began squeezing some lemon over his own dish. "I hope you like it," he said.

I detected a trace of nervousness in Handel's tone. That I made Handel nervous meant that he really liked me, that he really cared about what I thought. "I'm sure it will be great," I told him, but that was before the first bite of dinner melted in my mouth. "I meant *amazing*," I corrected. Suddenly I was ravenous.

The two of us ate in silence, the only sound the *clink* and clatter of cutlery. After a while I spoke again. "I really like this place." My fish was nearly gone.

So was Handel's. He speared the last of it with his fork. "Good. Me too."

I set my empty plate to the side. "Thank you for bringing me here."

Handel took a sip of his beer. "I thought about bringing you the first night we went out, but I decided maybe it was too soon."

"Really?"

He nodded.

I grabbed the two dirty plates from the bar and brought them to the sink. I was about to turn on the water when Handel stopped me.

"I'll do that later," he said. He placed a hand on my back. "Let's you and I go sit on the beach. It's a nice night."

I could barely breathe with him touching me.

I followed Handel out of the shack. He'd grabbed a blanket from a small wooden chest against the wall and carried it between his left arm and body. When we reached a spot that was tucked away from the prying eyes of our town, we set it out on the sand. Then we sat down and started to talk, watching as the moon showed its crescent self. It wasn't long before Handel leaned forward, kissing me softly at first, then less so, his fingers brushing the tender indent at the base of my neck, hovering over the top button of my shirt, hesitant.

All day, ever since our time at the beach, I'd been replaying in my mind the thought of Handel's hands doing this very same thing, this act of undressing, even a little bit, that before now only I was permitted to do. So I gave this power over to him with only the slightest of nods, and the softest of yeses, and that was all he needed to take the next step, to twist his fingers so that the first button slid from its loop and my shirt fell open just a little at the neck. I might have stopped breathing then. With his eyes on mine, full of just the sort of desire I felt, one by one he opened the rest until there weren't any more left to undo.

My heart pounded. I was lit up like a star.

Handel smiled that nearly imperceptible smile again.

And then I dared to do the same to him, to start at the button at his neck and work my way down until I could slide his shirt open and run my finger from his chest to his navel, something I had never done before to a boy, had never dreamed of doing before this boy. We stayed like this for a long while, hands exploring, softly, slowly along tanned skin, like we had all the time in the world, lids lowered, smiling with pleasure, a smile I'd read about in novels but never understood until now, the most wonderful ache building all through my body. Eventually, finally, Handel's fingers danced along the ends of my bathing suit ties, tugging, teasing, loosening. By the time the strings fell away down my back, I was the one reaching behind my neck and lifting it the rest of the way over my head, setting it aside.

"Jane," Handel said after leaving a trail of kisses along my neck up to my ear.

"Yes," I said, more of a statement than a question.

"I'm crazy about you."

He said this so simply, so intensely, and I opened my eyes to look into his, feeling half like an animal and only half like the girl who I am. Chest heaving. Hair knotted and falling everywhere. Shirt hanging wide open and nearly slipping off my shoulders. Handel leaned down and kissed the skin around the mosaic heart. His fingers traced the curve of my breasts.

I closed my eyes. "I'm crazy about you, too." My voice was hoarse.

"Would you believe me if I said that I'm falling in love with you? Or maybe . . . maybe I already am."

I nodded, half dazed. Everything was full of feeling. The ocean. The breeze. The air. We lay against the blanket. Pressed our bodies together. I opened my eyes again. "Why wouldn't I believe you?" I whispered in his ear.

Handel watched me. "I want you to feel special, Jane. I want you to feel perfect."

"No one is perfect. I don't want to be perfect." I reached out, took his hand, and placed it on my stomach, just above the top button of my jeans. When at first he didn't move, I pushed it lower, until his fingers were touching the round piece of metal. I wanted Handel's hands everywhere. I'd allowed myself to imagine what this might be like, to have Handel wanting to do this to me, this thing that I knew about and talked about with the girls but had never done with anyone.

Then Handel said something I wasn't expecting. "I think we should wait."

"For what?"

He was silent a moment. "For the right moment. The right time."

I pressed at his hand. Patience had long ago fled. "That time isn't now?"

He took his hand back. Sat up. "Not yet."

My breathing slowed. My heart didn't. "Why not?"

"I want to know everything about you. And I want you to know everything about me."

"Everything?" I said, half laughing at the impossible thought, half serious about what that would mean.

He nodded. Answered simply, "Yes."

"What else is there to know?"

"Plenty."

He trained his gaze on the water. The rhythm of the waves became audible again. I'd almost forgotten where we were, the sound of their crashing so far off in the distance, so far away that I'd stopped hearing it. But now it came back loud and clear.

"Okay." I sat up now, gathered my shirt together, closing it over bare skin. "But I want this. I want you," I added with confidence because I was sure it was true.

"I hope you still do once you get to know me better."

I looked at Handel. Reached my hand to his face and turned his cheek so I could give him a soft kiss. "I will."

His smile was almost sad. "Sometimes I wish we'd met under other circumstances."

"What do you mean?"

"You know, like if I was from a different town, a different life even. A different family for sure. And I came here for the summers and saw you for the first time, talked to you on the beach. Made you fall in love with me."

My smile wasn't sad at all, hearing this. "Half your wish has already come true."

"I'll never be like your friend Miles."

I laughed. "I don't want you to be Miles."

"You say that now."

"And I'll say it again come the end of summer. And winter and spring, too."

Handel leaned forward for a slow, heart-melting kiss. Then he pulled back. "I should take you home."

My heart sank. How could I go home after all this? "Really?"

Handel did the buttons on his shirt while I watched. "I want your mother to like me," he said.

"She already does."

"I don't want that to change."

I grabbed my bathing suit top and shoved it in my bag. Closed the snap. Buttoned myself up. "All right. I'll go."

"I'm going to take your reluctance as a compliment."

I smiled, the glow of the evening's events returning and with it a kind of confidence that I liked. I turned to Handel. "You should."

The way Handel looked at me then, I thought we might start up again, unable to leave each other. There was so much want between us, and it was exhilarating. It made my heart pound and my skin tingle and my body ache. It made me feel like a girl, too, a feminine thing, who suddenly knew just what the boys wanted. And more important, what she wanted from the boys. The great mystery finally revealed.

But just when I thought Handel was going to reach out to me, the want disappeared, replaced by a darkness, one I'd seen before in his eyes and one I was trying so hard not to see because I wasn't sure what it meant, or if I wanted to know what was behind it, either. Instead of running his fingers along the side of my face or over my shoulder, Handel got up and walked me home.

That night in bed, half covered only by a thin sheet because of the heat, I lay wide-awake. The crickets were loud outside my window, singing their midnight serenade. My fingers went to the heart at my chest. Over and over my mind replayed the various moments of my evening with Handel, his lips on my skin, his fingers, and the mere memory made my body light up all over again.

I smiled to myself.

I couldn't help it. I felt utterly and completely taken by Handel Davies, and it was what I wanted. I couldn't imagine wanting anything less. Or more for that matter. It was the first time in months that my nighttime thoughts were wholly occupied by something so delicious and exciting and wonderful, never slipping into that haunting, darker place I always tried so hard to avoid but where my mind inevitably went. The allure of such escape was impossible to resist. It was a relief I thought I'd never feel again. But only something as violent as the desire and the want I had for Handel was powerful enough to pull me away from my past. Only something as violent as the love I was beginning to feel for him could do it, and it was strange to notice how this sort of aggression could be welcome, and it was strange to think of what this meant for my understanding of love, how it changed my understanding, really.

Falling in love was not gentle, I was learning. Not at all. Back when I didn't know anything about love, at least not the romantic kind, I used to imagine that the falling part was like a leaf plucked from a tree branch in the breeze, floating and swirling lightly to the ground, the slow trip of dandelion fluff as it makes its way toward a soft landing in the grass during the spring. I never dreamed it could be violent, like someone reaching into your body and closing their hand around your heart. Reckless and dangerous and maybe even wrong. If someone had told me before I met Handel that love could sometimes be wrong, I wouldn't have believed them. I was too romantic.

Today I know different.

It was Handel who was reaching straight into my chest to grip my heart, Handel who was showing me how desire could come upon you like a thunderstorm, with flashes that would light up your insides, maybe even leave you burned. It felt so reckless that I was letting him do it, too, so dangerous in so many ways.

But sometimes it's dangerous and you know it and you just don't care.

Sometimes it's the part that's dangerous that makes it exciting.

As I tossed and turned and twisted in my sheets in the early hours of the morning, my thoughts took a different turn, a turn toward that darkness I kept seeing in Handel. Despite all the wonder, all the good, there was something off about him, too, something I couldn't quite put my finger on. It would appear in his eyes or be tucked just beneath a word. Hide in that moment when he pulled away from a kiss—like he'd wanted more but something inside had told him to stop. Just like tonight.

I could sense all of this.

But the thing about falling in love, the thing that makes it truly dangerous, is how you refuse to see those moments, those warning signs, with any clarity, and it doesn't take long to find out that you've nothing left to hang on to on your way down.

TWENTY-TWO

"OH MY GOD," Tammy said the moment I arrived at Slovenska's and slid into our usual booth the next day. "Someone is changed."

My cheeks were on fire. "What are you talking about?"

"What *are* you talking about?" Bridget seconded.

"The look on Jane's face. Can't you tell?"

Michaela sat down next to Tammy. "Tell what? What did I miss?"

"Sex, apparently." Tammy lowered her voice. "Jane's having sex. With *Handel*."

Michaela's eyes widened. "Tell me that's not true."

I closed my mouth, which had been hanging open. "It's not. It's absolutely not."

Michaela let out a sigh of relief. "Well, that's excellent news."

Bridget leaned into me. Whispered, "Are you sure? I'd totally approve of having sex with that boy. He's obviously in love with you. Not to mention hot and sexy."

Tammy rolled her eyes. "I think 'hot' and 'sexy' are synonymous."

Now Bridget rolled hers. "No, they're not."

Tammy flagged down the waitress. Her iced coffee was down to just ice. "Then what's the difference?"

Michaela cut in. "Can we not go off on a tangent?"

"Sorry," Tammy said. When the waitress arrived, she tapped the top of her glass, and the waitress nodded.

Bridget looked at Tammy. "Are you apologizing to me or Michaela?"

She shrugged. Smiled. "Both, I guess. But back to our current subject."

"Oooh, yes," Bridget agreed. "We were talking about sex with Handel Davies."

"Which I did *not* have," I confirmed.

Tammy studied me. "But you're thinking about it. No wait"—she cocked her head—"you *almost* had it."

"Did you?" Michaela asked, her voice shrill.

This time I didn't respond.

Bridget's face lit up, and she had to cover her mouth not to shriek. She'd taken my non-answer as a yes.

Michaela glared at Tammy. "I thought you said Jane knew her limits."

Tammy made a face. "I didn't say what those limits were. And I've come over to the pro-Handel camp. I thought you had, too, given that he knows your brother and all that."

"I was trying to be nice," Michaela said. "But just because Handel played hockey with my brother doesn't mean he gets to have sex with Jane!"

People in the diner were starting to turn and look at us. The waitress arrived and placed Tammy's iced coffee in front of her, then stopped to linger. She obviously wanted to hear whatever came next.

"Michaela," I hissed. "Why don't you just make a formal town announcement?"

Tammy gave the waitress her death stare. "We're fine, thank you."

Bridget uncovered her mouth. When the waitress was finally out of earshot, she whispered, "So how was it? Almost having it, I mean." She sounded envious.

I bit my lip.

Tammy's expression softened. "J, you have to tell us. We're your girls."

"But Michaela hates him," I said.

Guilt flitted in Michaela's eyes. "I don't hate him. I just worry about you getting involved with someone who might hurt you."

"Handel doesn't want to hurt me, so you can rest easy about that," I said. "He's the one who stopped things from going, you know, as far as they could have."

"And how far was that, exactly?" Bridget asked. "Wait a minute, I totally need to be eating something for this." She flagged down the waitress we'd just sent away. "I'll have a piece of the key lime pie. And the rest of them will have the apple crumble." The waitress nodded as she wrote down the order, then took off, this time quickly. Bridget stared guiltily at Michaela. "I know you don't think you like apple crumble, but if you'd just try it, I think you'll change your mind."

Tammy was staring at Bridget like she was crazy. "B, shut up. Let Jane talk. Talk, Jane."

Bridget huffed. "What are you, Tarzan?"

It was Michaela's turn to glare. "You're doing it again. The tangent thing. Apple crumble? Really?"

Bridget shut her mouth.

I had the floor once more. I took a deep breath. "It wasn't even that far. I mean, it was far for me but not in general. Do you really want the details?" I asked, glancing toward the back of the diner where the waitress was serving up our desserts onto plates. I didn't exactly want to be getting specific about what I'd done with Handel when she was delivering them to our table.

Tammy laughed. "Are you asking that as a joke?"

"We always give full details when it comes to sex with the boy species," Michaela reminded me. "That's what we promised each other."

I hesitated. Then I peeked over the divider between booths to see if I knew anyone nearby, to make sure there wasn't anyone from school the next row over or some of my mother's more popular clients. But aside from a few tables of older people sitting by the windows, the other diners had mostly left. "I don't know," I said, lowering myself into my seat. "It feels . . . kind of private."

Bridget seemed taken aback. "Private even from us?"

I was about to answer when the waitress arrived with our desserts. She left the key lime pie in front of Bridget and the big bowl with the apple crumble in the center of our table with four spoons. I immediately grabbed one of them, for something to do, and dug into the ice cream on top of the crumble. "Why don't you ask me questions and I'll answer. That's somehow more . . . okay." I shoved the dessert in my mouth, the cold of the ice cream mingling with the warmth of the apple but still making me shiver. Or maybe I was just nervous to talk about this stuff.

"I'll go first," Bridget said immediately.

Tammy grabbed a spoon and scooped up only apple and the crumbly part, avoiding the ice cream. "Of course you will."

Bridget was undeterred. "Where were you when it happened?"

"*It* did not happen," I reconfirmed. "And keep your voice down."

Bridget glanced around. "Nobody's listening." She cut the corner of her pie and stuck her spoon into it. "Then where were you when whatever happened *happened*?"

"On this private spot on the beach," I said, my eyes on the dessert and my spoon excavating more apple, grateful for the distraction. "Way away from the wharf."

"Oooh, romantic," Bridget responded. "Were you on a blanket? Could you see the stars?"

Michaela laughed. "What are you, writing a novel?" She was the only one of us who wasn't eating.

"Yes and yes," I replied to Bridget. "Next?"

"Let's get to the important things," Tammy said. She set her spoon down on the table and looked me straight in the eyes. "Were your clothes on or off?"

"Tammy," Bridget protested.

"She said we could ask questions, so I asked a question!"

"We kept our clothes on," I said, not wanting Bridget and Tammy to continue bickering. "Mostly."

Bridget squealed, but quietly this time. "So they were *half* off."

I smiled sheepishly. "More or less."

"Shirt or jeans or both?" This from Michaela.

"You girls seriously lack the romantic gene," Bridget complained.

"Jeans on, shirt half off," I answered. "But I wanted it to be *everything*," I added, noticing that everyone else had set their utensils on the table and I was the only one left eating.

Bridget's mouth was hanging open. "That's so exciting! Was it? Exciting, I mean?"

I didn't respond to this. Just smiled.

"So why didn't you do *everything*, then?" Tammy asked.

I scooped up the last bite of dessert, since no one else seemed to want it. "I told you, I would have. Handel is the one who stopped. If it had been up to me, we would have had sex. I mean, I wanted to," I confessed, finally warming up to giving out the details of my night to the girls, suddenly realizing that I wanted to talk about it with them and that I was glad to have the chance. "I really wanted to. I've never felt like that before. Sometimes it seems like I know everything there is to know about sex, you know, from school and from books, how to have it, what you're supposed to do and not do, how you're supposed to protect yourself from all the bad things that could happen and everything in between. But there's a huge difference between knowing everything there is to know, and then being in the moment and *wanting* it to happen with this boy who's sitting right there, wanting you back just as much. It changes *everything*."

"Wow," was all Bridget said, finally remembering her half-eaten pie and taking another bite.

"I'll second that—*wow*," Tammy added.

Michaela's expression was indecipherable. "Handel is moving up in my estimation for halting things before they went too far."

Bridget rolled her eyes. "Jane, I think you should go out with him again tonight and finish what you started."

"Believe me, I want to," I admitted.

"So it was *that* good?" Tammy asked.

I nodded. "Better."

Bridget sighed. "I want to get to feel that way."

"You have your pick of boys, B," I reminded her. "You'll get to feel that way as soon as you decide among them."

Bridget looked thoughtful. "But deciding to date someone doesn't guarantee they're going to make you feel like Handel makes *you* feel," she said. "I can hear it in your voice, how much you *like* him. Or maybe *love* him?"

The blush returned to my cheeks. "Maybe."

Michaela seemed alarmed. "You don't have to go so fast."

I looked at her. "Things haven't gone fast, though. Well, until last night. And then I wanted them to go faster."

"You should wait," she said.

"Are you the virtue police now?" Tammy asked.

"And wait for what exactly?" Bridget asked.

Michaela pursed her lips. She reached for Bridget's pie plate and slid it toward her. Then cut a huge hunk out of the back of it, crust, whipped cream, and all. Surprisingly, Bridget didn't protest. "There's nothing wrong with getting to know someone before you have sex with them."

"I *do* know Handel," I said.

Michaela gave me a skeptical look. "But you don't *really* know him, do you? I mean, have you met his family?"

This question was like a punch in my stomach. "No."

"Seriously, M?" Tammy asked. "This isn't the Victorian era. Next thing we know you'll be advocating marriage."

"I told you," she said as she polished off the rest of the key lime pie. "I'm feeling protective of Jane." Michaela set her spoon down on the plate. She looked hard at Tammy, then at Bridget. "It seems we've all agreed not to mention the latest headlines about the break-in." Michaela looked hard at me. "You have so much going on. This isn't a good time for you to be acting reckless with Handel."

I wanted this conflict to end, and I didn't want to talk about all those things Handel helped me to forget. To Michaela I said, "I know you don't want me to get hurt, and I appreciate that, but it's not your decision what I do or don't do with Handel." To Tammy and Bridget I said, "And I appreciate your enthusiasm, I really do." I closed my eyes a moment before continuing. "But I can decide for myself what's best and how fast and if Handel's feelings for me are real."

"Of course you can," Bridget said, quick and generous with her confidence.

"New subject," I said. "Benign subject, please," I added.

But as the conversation moved forward onto other topics, Handel's hesitations hovered somewhere in the back of my mind, and I wondered if Michaela's caution was somehow warranted or if Bridget was justified in thinking that I was the one who knew best. I just didn't know which one was closer to the truth.

On my way home, the gaze of the McCallen brothers was heavy from their corner—they were all there, save Patrick. I'd managed to avoid them for days now, but my luck had run out. I picked up my pace on the other side of the street. Maybe Patrick was locked up. Maybe that was why Officer Connolly kept leaving me urgent messages. Regardless, I was sure the McCallens knew I was the one who told the police about their brother. Their conversation came to a halt as I passed, and Joey McCallen took in an audible breath, made like he was about to speak, but, in the end, didn't say a word.

Then I saw why. Three policemen, all of whom knew my father about as well as anyone in this town, appeared from around the corner. I waited for one of them to call out my name, stopping me, forcing me to face the uniform my dad used to hang up so carefully on the outside of the door of his closet each night. The beloved attire of a man so devoted to his job he was willing to sacrifice his life for it.

The three policemen watched as I went along. So did the McCallens.

Too many gazes on my back.

It sent chills up my spine even in all this summer heat.

When I thought I was safely away, when I thought somehow I'd escaped more than one of these uncomfortable encounters, I breathed a sigh of relief.

But then I heard: "Jane Calvetti, come over here."

I swallowed. Joey McCallen had followed me. I turned and saw that he was across the street. "Hi, Joey," I said, but my feet stayed planted where they were, a couple of old Buicks parallel parked between us.

Joey waited there, arms crossed. When I didn't move, he came to me.

"You told the police to look into my baby brother," he said. "How could you do that? You're killin' me, Jane. I told you I was looking out for you."

I shrugged, like this was no big deal, but my heart was in my throat. "Maybe you're only looking out for me because you've got something to hide and you're worried I'll figure it out," I said, surprised at my own boldness. I looked around. There was no one else in sight. No one to help if Joey got angry. "Besides, I was just telling the truth. The police asked if there was anything else I remembered, and a couple of weeks ago when I saw Patrick, he was wearing those black boots of his. I saw a pair just like it the night of the break-in. I had to tell someone." I wasn't sure why I felt the need to defend myself, but I did. Maybe because I was afraid of Joey, or maybe because there was something about the look on his face that made me doubt myself.

Joey's eyes narrowed. "Yeah, well, lots of people wear them boots."

I looked at Joey straight on. Did my best not to let him intimidate me. "But his are different. They've got a metal band across the toe."

He was shaking his head. "There's something else you didn't realize, Jane."

"Oh?"

"Patrick found 'em next to the garbage bin down on the wharf. Perfectly good boots and someone tossed 'em. Makes you wonder why they'd get rid of 'em, eh?"

"Patrick found them," I whispered.

"That he did." Joey sounded pleased. "There were about ten witnesses, too, and the police have already ruled my brother out as a suspect."

My lips parted. "Maybe Patrick just pretended to find them. Maybe they were his all along."

"Well, *I'm* gonna pretend you didn't just say that. I don't know what the police got in terms of evidence, but I know for sure that Patrick is no longer on their radar. They're looking elsewhere."

Joey was staring at me hard. I stared hard back, even as my

heart lurched. If it wasn't Patrick, then who? "The police haven't told me they're looking elsewhere," I said. I left out the part about how maybe the police had tried to tell me, but I hadn't let them.

Joey cocked his head. "You're at square one again, I guess."

My eyes dropped to the ground. "Yeah, I guess," I said, my voice hoarse. "I've got to go," I added quickly, already turning to leave, disappointment roaring through me. I had to get out of there. I'd thought what I wanted most was to forget, but I'd been lying to myself. What I wanted far more was for this whole nightmare to be over. I'd wanted that memory to be a real lead, one that would put an end to this terrible chapter of my life. Maybe that was why I couldn't seem to make myself call Officer Connolly back. I couldn't bear the possibility that he would tell me how the little detail I'd finally confessed led them nowhere.

"Despite what you did," Joey called out as I walked away, "I'm still gonna be looking out for you, Calvetti."

I didn't turn around. Didn't say thank you or tell him not to bother.

It was all I could do to keep moving.

TWENTY-THREE

I WORRIED THAT JOEY was following me. Levinson's was ahead, and I decided to stop in to get myself off the street. Make sure I wasn't alone for long. I could walk the aisles until my heart stopped racing. My hand was already reaching for the bar across the door to the deli, but I retracted it. Tried to turn back quickly enough to escape a whole other kind of attention I didn't need right now, but I was too late.

Miles was coming out of Levinson's, a paper bag gripped under one of his arms. He smiled when he saw me. The fact that he could still be so nice after I'd led him on made me feel guilty. The bell over the door jangled as it shut, and the two of us stood there looking at each other, neither of us uttering a word at first.

I took off my sunglasses. "Hi, Miles," I said softly.

"Hi, Jane." He looked like he wanted to say something else, but he was hesitating. "You and I can still be friends. Right?" he asked finally.

"What do you mean?" I really didn't want to do this now. Then again, if I was talking to Miles, Joey McCallen wasn't about to come up to me. "Of course we're friends."

Miles shifted the bag to his other arm. "I mean I can handle you being with that guy," he clarified.

"Handel," I said, glancing behind me.

No Joey in sight.

Relieved, I turned back and saw Miles nod in answer.

I used my hand to block the glare in my eyes. Squinted at

Miles in the bright sun. Our neighbor, Mrs. O'Malley, was trying to get to the door, so I stepped aside. She looked tired, forehead shiny with sweat, breaths audible, but she perked up once she took in the scene of Miles and me.

"Hello, Jane," she said politely. Gave Miles a once-over.

This sighting was sure to make its way to my mother's sewing room within the next few days. "Hi, Mrs. O'Malley," I said awkwardly. "Nice to see you."

She nodded. Headed into the deli, a whoosh of cold air spilling out.

"Do you know absolutely everyone?" Miles asked.

I thought about the McCallens right then, how sometimes living in a town like ours could be oppressive. But I wasn't about to explain this to Miles. "Most people, by sight if not by name." I made an effort to sound casual. "The women especially, because of my mother's work."

Miles half smiled. "You don't sound happy about that."

"No, it's fine. I just end up being the subject of gossip a lot, though my mother does her best to fend it off. Sometimes people around here can't resist telling her things."

"And what will Mrs. O'Malley tell your mother about you now?" Miles asked in a way that was definitely flirty, his confidence returning.

I felt my cheeks redden. Miles was fishing for compliments, and for hope, I realized. He might be able to handle me being with "that guy," but if he could wedge his way between us, he would do that, too. Between the police, the McCallens, and now Miles, I was feeling overwhelmed. "She'll say she saw me with a boy who's obviously not from around here," I said. I knew this was what Miles wanted to hear, and somehow I thought that if I satisfied this need of his, we could say our good-byes and part ways.

"And what else?" he asked.

"Miles, quit while you're ahead." Frustration broke through into my words.

Miles grinned, ignoring my signal. "Ahead of who?"

I put my sunglasses back on. "There isn't a competition. I have to go." In a huff, I pulled open the door, welcoming the cool air that ran over me head to toe. As it swung shut, I could hear Miles's protest of "Jane, wait, I was just kidding around," but I pretended not to. Instead of letting him finish what he had to say, I plunged forward into the icy deli, unsure of what I was doing there, or what it was that I wanted, which left me to wander the aisles aimlessly until I was sure that Miles had gotten tired of waiting for me to come back out.

"I'm on my way to the door," Seamus called as he crossed my front yard later that afternoon, making my head turn toward the open window. "I didn't want to startle you this time."

"Come on in," I yelled back, setting my novel aside on the couch. "Stranger," I added softly when Seamus's freckled face peeked inside. Seamus was one of the few people I could handle being around at the moment.

He picked up the mail scattered on the floor. I'd ignored it when I arrived earlier. Picked up my book instead, in an attempt to distract myself from the encounters of the day so far. Seamus parked himself next to me. The couch spring creaked loudly. "I've had stuff going on."

"Too busy even for me?" I asked gently.

He handed me the mail. "Nah. Never."

"Does this have to do with Tammy? You've been hanging out with her a lot."

Seamus's face colored. The luck of the Irish always ran out on the embarrassment front. His freckles were darker from spending time in the sun. "Yeah, but just to go running and stuff."

"You should ask her out for real," I said, relieved to have someone else's life to think about, to advise about. "She's going to say yes. I mean, aside from going running, you guys had ice cream together."

"But that was just an accident."

I shifted positions to face Seamus. Crossed my legs underneath me. "It doesn't matter. You hung out. It's almost like a . . . practice date."

"A practice date?" Seamus's blush deepened. "You really know how to make a guy feel manly."

"I was just trying to help." I regretted kidding Seamus in a place that made him feel vulnerable. I hated when people did that to me. "I'm sorry."

"It's okay. I know you're looking out for me."

I nodded. "Forgive me, then?"

"Yes." He drew the word into two syllables. "So, are you going to tell me what's going on with you and Handel Davies, or are you going to make me wait even longer?"

Seamus's question made me take a sudden interest in the mail. I had to hide my own blush now. I flipped through the letters that had arrived, one by one. Electric bill. Credit card bill. Postcard for a pizza special at Tony's down on the wharf. I opened a catalog to the middle and stared at the pictures of couches we could never afford and wouldn't want to, anyway. "I think there's still plenty more to discuss about Tammy."

Seamus leaned closer, looking at the catalog with me. "Oh? What else?"

"I think she likes you. *Likes* you, likes you," I clarified.

Seamus turned red and pointed at the white china teapot in the middle of the page. "I should buy that for my mother's birthday," he said.

"With what? Your charm?"

He laughed. "My charm is useful sometimes."

I got serious again—I didn't want to embarrass him anymore. "You should turn it on Tammy, then. For her. And for you," I added.

Seamus didn't respond. Just pretended to read the teapot description for a moment, before shifting the subject back to Handel. "Do you like him or what?"

"I do," I admitted, setting the catalog aside. Seamus was nice enough to distract me from the earlier events of the day, even if he didn't know it, so I owed him some honesty.

He smiled shyly. "That's great, J."

"Really? You mean you're not going to scold me like Michaela?"

He looked at me strangely. "Why would I do that?"

"Who knows? Why would she?"

"That's a good question," he said, picking up the catalog and starting to flip through it but not really looking at anything on the pages. "What does Michaela have against Handel Davies?"

My eyes dropped to the mail again as I thought about how to answer. There was a thank-you note from one of my mother's brides. The phone bill. Then an official-looking envelope. Suddenly I couldn't breathe. My lungs stopped and wouldn't start, a car that wouldn't turn over. Someone was sitting on my chest. I tore my eyes from the letter.

Seamus was watching me. "Jane, you're scaring me. What's wrong?"

In one big gulp I finally got some air into my body, my lungs expanding greedily. I got up. "I need you to go. I need to be alone."

"Did I say something—"

"It's not you." Tears pushed into my eyes. "Please don't be mad."

"I'm not. I'm here if you need me."

I nodded. I almost couldn't talk. I watched Seamus walk out of my house, glancing back twice. It was only after he'd disappeared down the street that I looked down at the letter in my hands for the second time.

My father's life insurance check had arrived.

"Were you even going to tell me?" I asked angrily when my mother got home from the beach. I was sitting at the kitchen counter, on the side facing the door, waiting for her. "Did you think I wouldn't find out?"

Her face went white underneath all that color from the sun. "Jane," was all my mother said.

I held up the letter in my hand. "You know exactly what I'm talking about. I don't even need to say it."

The screen door banged shut behind her. She walked across the living room and slid onto the stool facing me at the counter.

"Your father wanted you to have that money. That's why he had the policy."

"Well, I don't want it," I said. "Ever. It's money for his *death*."

"Honey, I know how upsetting it is to think about it that way, believe me I do. But you can go to any college you want with it. You need to be practical about this and think about your future."

I looked at her in horror. "You want me to build a future on . . . on Dad's *murder*?"

"Jane—"

"You signed for me, didn't you? As my guardian? That's the only way this check would be cut. The insurance company said so when I called them."

She tried to take my hand from across the counter, but I snatched mine away. "I'm sorry, sweetheart," she said.

Her apology did little to ease the guilt raging inside me and pumping my heart like I was on a run. "There's a reason I refused to sign those papers. How can I go to college on money I got because someone killed my father?"

For the first time since my mother arrived home, her face flushed. "There's a reason why your father took out a policy in your name only! Have you thought about the part where you're not honoring his wishes? Do you really think he'd like that, Jane? Do you think that would solve everything? Do you think it would make him happy that you refused this money he left you?"

Tears burned my eyes. I blinked them back. "I don't know," I said, my throat choked with a sob. "It's my fault he died. He was there because of me, and now he's dead."

My mother gasped. "It's not your fault, Jane. It never was. You have to let that go."

I could barely hear her words. "Dad's not here anymore to ask, and I feel so lost without him," I choked out, finally giving myself over to the sobs that came, one after the other. "I don't want any money, Mom, I want Daddy back. I want Dad."

"Oh, honey," my mother said, coming around the counter and putting her arms around me. This time I didn't push her away. Her mouth pressed into my hair. "I know you do. I know you do. I feel the same way."

"Daddy?" I shouted a second time with all the breath in my lungs.

"Oh my God, Jane," said my father when he reached the top of the stairs. Everything seemed to stop in that moment, to freeze like the world outside in its icy blanket. The noise ended, all movement ended, and everything grew quiet. Silent. The breathing of the boy who had me stilled. To my captors, my father said: "And I thought better of you, especially you."

Who? went my brain.

Chaos erupted all around me. I was blind at its center, the eye in a storm out of which I could not see, and in the chaos I was pulled and I was shoved and I was screaming and then I was going down, down, down, crashing to the hard wooden floor until my head knocked into it.

There was a gunshot.

One.

And then a second.

245

I don't know how long I lay there in a daze, noise all around me, noise and shouts that I could hear but as though far away, my head under a heavy dark cloud. But when I finally came to, reality rushing to me like a parent to a lost child, everything was suddenly so clear again, as clear as the icicles dripping from the trees outside.

I sat up. Pulled the blindfold off. Put a hand to the back of my head where it pounded.

Saw the destruction around me.

My captors were gone.

My father, though, my father was still there, lying half-in, half-out of the doorway to the library.

I tried to get up, stumbled and fell, then dragged myself across the floor. My father hadn't moved. "Daddy?" I called to him, voice full of fear.

But he didn't say anything. Not *I'm all right,* not *Jane,* not even *Help me.*

I bent down over his chest, saw that it was still.

Took in the blood next.

A great pool of it spilling from his body.

Staining his uniform.

His eyes, his big brown eyes, gone vacant.

Then the tears came in one great wave. They swept through me like a hurricane, rising and drowning and pouring out over everything, sobs so big and powerful I thought I was suffocating.

My father, my beloved father, was already dead.

TWENTY-FOUR

BEFORE I WENT TO SLEEP, I got down on the floor of my room, flipped up the bed skirt, and searched around in all that darkness, reached beyond the newspapers I'd hidden there for a large, shallow cardboard box. When the tips of my fingers brushed the edge, I flattened myself even further to reach it, carefully sliding it out from its resting place. Box retrieved, I shifted positions, legs out, back against the bed. The lamp on the table just above me provided a soft glow. After one deep breath, and another, I removed the top and set it aside.

There he was. My dad.

In his uniform down by the wharf next to the station, stormy clouds hanging over everything, implying rain that hadn't yet fallen.

I moved on to the next keepsake, and there he was again, this time in the form of his handwriting. LOVE, DADDY written on a birthday card for when I'd turned seven. Then his script on another card, from when I turned ten, this time with a whole line of *X*s and *O*s across the bottom of it, something I'd started to do that year on the cards I'd given him for his birthday and Christmas and Father's Day. He'd been returning the favor. I had cards for eleven and fourteen and sixteen, too, but that was all. I don't know why these were the cards I'd saved as opposed to birthdays eight and nine, or even fifteen. It seemed so random to have these and not the others.

Now, in retrospect, I wished I'd saved them all. The fact that I wouldn't get another card from my father ever again, that when I turned eighteen there would be cards from my mother and my friends, cards sent in the mail by my grandparents who lived in Massachusetts, but not one from my dad, made the ones I'd kept seem precious. The ones I'd so carelessly tossed away or lost seemed like the most foolish, ungrateful thing I could ever have done.

I set the cards aside and peered back in the box.

There, sitting on top of everything else, was the most important thing of all I'd salvaged.

My father's policeman's badge. Number 2877. Gold against a black background with black lettering.

Michaela's dad had given it to me. Handed it to me at the wake, pressed it into my hand without a word as he passed by my mother and me in the long line of mourners come to give their condolences. I didn't know where he'd gotten it, if my dad had a spare or several, or if Officer Connolly had reached right into my father's coffin and plucked it off his uniform before it could be lost forever to burial.

All I knew was that I was grateful he'd given it to me.

I'd held on to it so hard that night I thought my palm might never lose the impression of it on my skin. When I'd gone to bed, it was still tight in my grip, and it was only in sleep that I'd finally released it. I woke to find it on my bedside table, shadowed and lifeless in the dim morning light. My mother must have come in to see me and placed it there. After the funeral, I put it in this box with everything else that reminded me of my father and hid it in the safe darkness underneath my bed. I couldn't bear to see so much evidence of my father's life.

But just looking at it now, holding the badge in my hands, running my fingers along the rough, scalloped edges, made it seem like he might be here with me. And when I held it up to the light, held it away from my body high in the air, I could fill in the rest of my father around it, remember the way he used to wear it on his uniform, picture things as though he was standing there in the room with me, dressed up and about to go to work, come to visit me to give me a hug and a kiss on the cheek before he left, even though I might be too old for that now.

I kept that badge as high as I could hold it, until my arm began to ache and until the moment that image of my father had faded and all that was left was the air around it. Then carefully, gently, I placed it on my bedside table.

I owed it to my father—and to myself—to do whatever it took to find out what really happened the night he was killed. To remember any and every detail, however small—like Officer Connolly had said—because who knew what answers that tiny detail might reveal? And now that the lead I'd given the police about Patrick McCallen didn't pan out, I had to try for another one.

So I got up from the floor. Tiptoed across the sandy house.

"Mom?" I called softly from the doorway of her room.

She shifted in bed. Then roused a little, sitting up. "Jane?"

"I want to call the O'Connors tomorrow," I said into the darkness, my mother's outline just visible in the moonlight. "I think I should accept their invitation to dinner. And . . . you know. The other thing."

"I think that's a good idea," she said, her voice thick with sleep.

"Will you go with me?"

"Of course."

"Good night, Mom," I said.

There was more rustling. "I love you, sweetheart," she whispered. "So much. And so did your dad. More than anything else in this world." Then she laid her head on the pillow and went back to sleep.

TWENTY-FIVE

MY MOTHER AND I were having breakfast. Coffee and a jelly doughnut for her, and coffee with so much milk that it was almost white for me, with my favorite morning sandwich on the side: toasted peanut butter and jelly. Mom was silent, the paper open to the movie reviews. The letter from the life insurance company wasn't anywhere in sight.

"Why did you name me Jane?" I asked, unaware this was about to come out of my mouth. But then, I'd been thinking about family all night.

She looked up, mid-chew of her latest bite of doughnut. She swallowed. "Where did that question come from?"

In my mind I answered *Handel,* but out loud I said, "I don't know. I was just wondering. Jane is such an . . . ordinary name."

"It absolutely is not!" Her protest was passionate, her eyes fiery as she said the words, a nerve touched.

"I'm sorry," I said quickly. "That's not what I meant. I like my name. I didn't mean to hurt your feelings."

She let out a big breath and closed her eyes. "No, it's all right. It's fine. It's just been an intense couple of days."

I waited for her to continue.

When she opened her eyes again, they were glassy. Tears brimmed. "It was your father's idea."

"Dad?" I said, surprised, my voice hoarse, both from the mention of him—so many mentions in the last twenty-four hours—and from seeing my mother so emotional.

My mother picked up her empty coffee mug. Studied the stray grinds clinging to the bottom. "He was such a romantic. And we were in love. He would do just about anything I asked, and to prove how much he loved me"—she smiled through the tears streaking her cheeks like rain against glass—"he read every one of Jane Austen's books."

I laughed, but it came out more of a sob. "Dad read *Jane Austen*? You have to be kidding me. He was so . . . not . . . feminine at all. Or literary."

It was my mother's turn to laugh. She wiped her face with her napkin and left a trail of sugar from the doughnut across her cheek. "No, that he wasn't. Not either one. But that first summer we met, he'd seen me reading *Pride and Prejudice* on the beach and wanted to impress me, so he got a copy out of the library and threw himself into it."

"That *is* romantic." I smiled despite the tight feeling in my throat.

"Well, your father, much to his grave dismay and stubborn complex about his masculinity, got addicted to Miss Austen and confessed one day that if we ever had a girl we would name her Jane, because little girls should start out life with auspicious names so they could one day grow up to be young women who would make their own marks on the world."

I put my hand over my mouth.

My mother cocked her head. "What?"

I took my hand away. Swirled my milky coffee around in its mug, staring at it like it might tell my future. "It reminds me of a story someone else told me once. About his name."

"Handel," she said simply.

"Yes."

"You really like him."

"I do."

She nodded. Took this in. Then switched the topic suddenly. "I called the O'Connors," she said. "They're expecting us at six this evening. We'll go together. Okay?"

"Okay." I swallowed. "I'm going to take a walk."

My mother looked away. "Be careful. It's been a hard year."

I looked away, too. "I know."

"If I wanted you to read a novel by Jane Austen, would you do it?" I asked Handel.

I'd gone down to the wharf to see if Handel's boat was docked or out on the water. I'd found him alone, smoking a cigarette, staring out at the ocean, no boat in sight.

He laughed. Brushed a lock of hair from his face. It kept blowing into his eyes. "How do you know I haven't already?"

"Because unless boys have to read Austen in school, they just don't."

His eyes narrowed as he took another drag of his cigarette. "Maybe that's true."

I wanted to reach out and grab his hand, but I didn't. Standing here on the docks, we were so out in the open. Exposed. Anyone could see us, and after our last meeting I was feeling private about sharing intimacy. To be honest, I couldn't wait to be in private again. "So you haven't, then."

"No," Handel admitted.

I could feel his eyes on me. It made my skin burn hot. "But would you? If I asked you to?"

"Tell me why you're smiling first."

I didn't look at him, but my smile grew. "I was thinking . . ."

"About what?"

"The other night. And . . . what happened."

"You have regrets," Handel stated, like this must be obvious. His voice was pained.

Now I did turn to him. Looked him in the eyes as seriously as I could. "Not at all. I was thinking about . . . when we'd get to do it again."

"Oh." He sounded surprised. Relieved. Then that lustiness I was learning to love seeing in Handel's eyes appeared. "How about tonight?"

The humming that had started to sound through my body from our exchange suddenly stopped. My smile drained away. "I can't. I wish I could, though."

"So change your plans."

"It's not that easy."

Handel's index finger glided lightly, almost imperceptibly, along the bare skin of my arm from shoulder to wrist. I wondered if anyone was watching the two of us standing here, witnessing this gesture. "What could be so important that you can't reschedule? Another night at Slovenska's with your friends?"

I decided to be honest. I suddenly wanted Handel to know

everything about me, even the painful parts. "I have to go to the O'Connors' for dinner with my mom. I haven't been there since the night of the break-in, and everyone seems to think it's important that I go back."

Handel was silent awhile. "Are you sure you want to do that?"

I shrugged. Didn't look at him. Just stared out at the water. "Maybe they're right."

"Who's they?"

"My mom and the O'Connors. The police. Maybe it *will* be good for me. Maybe it will help me remember."

"What *do* you remember from that night? You still haven't talked to me about it."

The ocean was calm today. Like fragile glass that might shatter. "Not enough. I remember voices, but even those are jumbled. Most of the time I couldn't see anything. And then, I didn't pass out exactly, but I hit my head, and it blurred everything."

Handel didn't respond, not at first. Then he turned to me, a flick of long hair swinging with the sharp movement. "I'm sorry you had to go through that. I wish I could make it all disappear."

I looked at him. Saw the sincerity on his face. The sorrow. And something else, something unidentifiable. I took his hand into mine, not caring who saw us. "It's okay."

He shook his head. His eyes were glassy. "No. It's not."

I closed the distance between us, and he pulled me to him, his strong arms around me, tightening around my back, his lips in my hair, kissing the top of my head. We stayed like that a long while before pulling apart. "I should probably go."

"Okay. Let's see each other tomorrow?"

The possibility brought a smile to my face, albeit a small one. "Definitely."

I was about to go when Handel stopped me. "Why were you asking me before about reading those Austen novels?"

"Oh," I said, remembering how this conversation started. "The first night we went out, before you told me how you got your name, you told me to ask my mother how I got mine, and I did. Turns out it's not an accident that Jane Austen and I share the same name." I smiled, thinking about what my mother told me earlier, even though it made me sad to think about it. "Apparently, naming a girl Jane is an auspicious way to send her out in the world."

Handel nodded in understanding. "Your mother was reading a lot of Austen before she had you."

"No—well, yes. But it was my father's idea. He was reading Austen because he wanted to impress my mother."

Handel winced a little. "Oh. I see." He turned around. Looked behind us. "It's me who should get going now. I've got to get to work."

"Okay. See you soon, then."

Handel seemed distracted. "Yeah. See you."

This time I did turn and began walking away. At first I didn't realize that we had an audience, but as my attention to my surroundings expanded beyond Handel, I saw that Handel's brother Colin was standing a little ways off, smoking a cigarette, eyes on me, his expression neutral. But next to him was someone else, one of the guys I'd seen with Handel that night when I'd run into him and Tammy and Seamus down on the wharf, one of those friends who made Handel want to keep things between us a secret. The skinny, mean-looking one. Between then and now I'd learned that his name was Cutter, and that he was probably as mean as he seemed, news that made me wonder why Handel would be hanging out with someone like that. It didn't seem to add up with the Handel I knew. And right now, this boy, Cutter, was watching me hard as I passed, the salty breeze mixing with the faint scent of cheap cologne, sour and sweet, an attempt to mask the smell of fish. Unlike Handel's brother, Cutter's face was full of expression.

Like he couldn't believe what he'd just witnessed.

There was malice, too. It was all over him. You couldn't miss it.

I hadn't felt that kind of violence coming at me since, well, since the night of the break-in. My skin prickled as I hurried away, his eyes cutting into my back the entire time, just like his name suggested, and I wondered if that was how he got it.

TWENTY-SIX

THE O'CONNORS' HOUSE, ALL pillars and brick and colonial features, loomed ahead. The back of my neck tingled, with anxiety maybe, or just plain old fear. Everything looked different in the summer sunlight, and I tried to hang on to this—the smiling flowers blooming throughout the garden, the grass the cheeriest of greens, potted plants overflowing with life and cascading leaves all the way to the front porch floor.

My mother turned around up ahead. "Jane?"

I stood, frozen, a few paces behind her. "Hmm."

She walked back and took my hand. "Come on. It's going to be all right."

But the way she said it, her voice flat, even uncertain, said that she was nervous, too. I let my fingers weave through hers and allowed her to lead me to the front door. We didn't even have to knock. The second our feet hit the stairs of the front porch, the door was opening.

Dr. O'Connor was standing there. "Jane!"

Her enthusiasm gave me some strength, I think, because I found myself bounding up the stairs and letting her fold me into a great big hug. "I'm glad to see you," I said, realizing that the first step of this evening had already been accomplished. I was over the threshold of the O'Connors' house, inside for the first time in months.

"We're so happy to see you." She released me. To my mother,

she said, "Molly, it's wonderful to see you, too. Thank you for bringing her."

My mother leaned in to give Dr. O'Connor a hug. "Martha," she said, then looked over at me. "We're happy to be here."

I nodded, remembering the other part of the evening. I couldn't manage to say I was happy about it, so I didn't.

"Come in, come in," Dr. O'Connor said, sweeping us toward the kitchen. "Sam's setting the table on the screened-in porch. We figured that since there was a nice breeze coming off the waterfront tonight, we could eat alfresco."

My mother followed after her. "That sounds lovely."

"We're just going to grill some fish," she went on, disappearing around the corner.

I paused next to the grand staircase that led to the second floor, studying the steps, noticing that the rug was gone. Pulled up. The sound of my father's shoes heavy against the steps—*thump, thump, thump*—was suddenly loud in my mind, like someone had turned up the volume in my memory. I grabbed the banister, trying to stave off the dizziness that came with all that noise.

My mother turned back. "Jane? Are you all right?"

I breathed deep, in and out. "I'm coming."

I took one more look at the stairs, this time prepared for the memory, then tore myself away from the banister and headed into the kitchen, wondering if these flashes were going to happen all night.

Dr. O'Connor was pouring my mother a glass of white wine. "Jane, would you like some soda? Lemonade? Seltzer?" Her tone was extra cheery. Maybe everyone was nervous about tonight.

"Lemonade, please," I said, taking a look around and realizing that something was different. The white cabinets were the same, the wooden island in the center of everything was still there, the floors were still the same old oak slats, little round knots dotted here and there.

"Sam will be happy," she said, opening the fridge. "He made it fresh today. He knows you like it." She poured the lemonade into a tall glass.

I took it from her. "Thanks." It was the light that had changed. The sun was streaming in over everything, unaffected by the stained glass that used to be set into the walls. "What happened to the windows?" I asked, before I could think better of it.

Dr. O'Connor's expression faltered. "Oh. Well. You know, the break-in."

My breath was released in a whoosh, like something had sucked it from my lungs.

"So, Martha," my mother started to say, wineglass in hand, shifting the subject. "Have you been down to the beach lately? I haven't seen you."

Just then Professor O'Connor peeked his head inside the screen door from the backyard. "Jane! So glad you're here. Come on outside and help me by the grill. I've got a nice surprise for you."

"What kind of surprise?" I crossed the kitchen, and he gave me a little side hug, patting my shoulder before releasing me. Tears prickled behind my eyes. Any sort of fatherly gesture seemed to do that to me now. He loped across the grass toward the patio, his strides long and sure, while I followed after him.

"You'll just have to see for yourself," he said.

We turned the corner. There was someone else there.

He looked up.

I halted. "Miles?"

Miles smiled sheepishly. "Hi, Jane."

"Um, what are you doing here?"

"My fault. It's my fault," said Professor O'Connor, putting his hand over his heart like he might be swearing the truth. "I know Miles's dad, and when I found out you two were friends, I thought you might like having someone else here your own age."

I was nodding, trying to agree. "It was nice of you to invite him," I said.

"So I did all right?" Professor O'Connor sounded so hopeful. So concerned. So genuine in his effort to make things as comfortable as possible.

"Yes," I said, giving him my best smile.

Miles's face lit up at this.

Professor O'Connor turned around to tend to the grill, and I gave Miles an annoyed look and shook my head. I didn't want him to get the wrong idea. "Let me help you," I said, approaching Professor O'Connor at the grill. I picked up a spatula and peeked underneath the edge of the fish. Striped bass, fresh from the wharf, I was certain.

Miles joined us. "I could use a lesson in cooking up the local catch."

This inspired Professor O'Connor to launch into a detailed explanation of how to pick out the freshest fish—look for the glassiest eyes at the market—how to salt it, among other step-by-step advice, while I looked on. As I listened to their exchange, I wondered if maybe Miles's presence would be a good distraction from the conversation turning to other things. Maybe he would save me from having to go upstairs and relive the worst night of my life.

But then, after Miles was directed inside to retrieve a platter from the kitchen, Professor O'Connor turned to me and said, "I think it's great that you're here, Jane. I know this is hard, but it will be good if you can remember something. And good to get it over with, too. We've missed you."

I just nodded. Apparently, no distraction would be big enough.

"Are you really sure about that guy?" Miles asked after the plates had been cleared and my mother, Professor O'Connor, and Dr. O'Connor had retreated to the patio for another glass of wine in the cool evening air. Miles and I were in the kitchen, rinsing off the dishes.

"And again," I said, watching the sink bubble up with suds. I turned off the faucet. "By 'that guy,' you mean Handel? My boyfriend?" Calling Handel my boyfriend out loud was a thrill. It made me feel brazen.

Miles sighed. "Yes."

"What would I have to be unsure about?" I handed Miles a dish to dry.

"I heard that his friends—" Miles paused, absently wiping the dish with a towel. He set it down on the stack of already dry plates. "Well, that they're not such good guys."

I handed him a bowl, still dripping with water. "That doesn't mean anything for Handel."

Miles's expression was skeptical. "But doesn't it?"

"Handel is good to me." I stared into the sink. I was so tired all of a sudden, and there was so much left to clean. I should have listened to the O'Connors and left it for them to do tomorrow. But I'd insisted. "That's all that matters."

Miles set the bowl on the counter. "His family has quite a reputation."

I walked to the other side of the kitchen island, away from the remaining mess. I was shaking my head, frustrated with Miles's line of questioning. I placed my hand on the woodblock to steady myself. "You're not my mother."

Miles followed after me, reached out and placed his hand over mine. "I'm not trying to be. I don't *want* to be."

I slipped it out from under his. Turned my back to him. "I'm sorry."

"For what?" he asked.

I crossed my arms. "That I can't give you what you want." I shifted uncomfortably. Turned my attention from Miles to the tall cabinets, the fridge, the blue-checked pot holder hanging on the wall. Everything looked so new. "I'm taken. That's not going to change anytime soon."

Miles shrugged. A bit of the gleam I was used to seeing in his eyes made an appearance, but his face remained serious. "You never know," he said. "It might."

Anger flared inside me. "I think I know better than you."

Miles's mouth was set into a straight line. "I don't trust that guy, Jane."

"Well, I do," I said.

"I can see that."

The way Miles looked at me in that moment was so intense,

so much that I wondered if he knew something I didn't. Before I could ask, the O'Connors and my mother came into the kitchen.

It was time for me to go upstairs and do what I came to do.

"I want to go alone," I said.

Before anyone could protest, I walked away, left the kitchen and went to the grand staircase that led up to the professor's library. I felt like a ghost moving through the rooms, hovering over the floor but not quite touching it, thin enough to pass through walls if I wanted to. I slipped off my flip-flops before going up the stairs, not wanting to make a sound, my bare feet against wooden slats slippery with the humidity of summer. There was a sharp creak, and I stopped.

"Jane?" My mother sounded so nervous. So worried.

Everyone gathered on the first floor in the foyer. They looked up at me. All anxious eyes.

"Let me do this," I said, and continued to the next stair and the next, until I'd reached the second-floor landing. I could already see into the library, the door ajar, a tiny sliver of light shining through it from the sun that was still high in the evening sky. I took another few steps, put my hand on the door, and gently pushed it open, the slow groan of it swinging wide the only sound other than my breath.

I closed my eyes to stop the next image.

The air was tingly with anticipation. I almost felt like I was tiptoeing through a fairy wood and not the professor's house, barefoot, exploring and peering about like there might be magic around the corner and not memories of horror and death.

I took another breath.

Opened my eyes again.

And the image I knew was coming, the inevitable one, well, there it was.

My father.

His body on the floor. Mangled and bloody.

I gasped. Shut my eyes to it.

"Jane?" My mother called up. "You don't have to do this by yourself."

"I'm okay," I called back.

But was I?

I tried to breathe. Gripped the wood around the doorway for support.

"There is nothing here that can hurt me now," I whispered, trying to reassure myself, trying to will my eyes to see. There was no one here but me, and a whole crowd of people who cared about me just downstairs. No robbers. No bad men.

But then, did those men, those boys, need to be here to hurt me? Hadn't they changed my life in a way that left me with a hurt that would last for all my days no matter where I was or what I was doing? An IV of hurt that fell into me, drop by drop, continuously?

Maybe.

Maybe not.

The O'Connors thought coming here not only might help my memory but might be healing. It might help me sort through what happened and begin to move on.

"Okay, Jane," I said, and forced my eyes open. "You can do this."

Suddenly the events of that night in February and today

mingled like two movie reels laid on top of each other and played at once, projected together onto the scene in front of me.

Everything was the same here and yet it was different.

There was my stack of books by the reading nook, piled high, like no one had ever touched them. Like no one had come in and brutally knocked them to the ground. The cushions were propped and inviting someone to sit, to gaze outside the wood-paned windows out toward the wharf. The professor's desk was righted again, scattered with papers and work and use. The shelves were packed with papers like always.

But the lamps were different. The vases were different. The little glass sculpture of two fish, intertwined, playful in the surf was gone. Gone, too, was the great crystal bowl the professor used to have on his desk, where he'd kept pennies and keys and other loose paraphernalia.

Then I noticed the spot on the floor. If I hadn't known where to look, if it hadn't been the last place I'd seen my father's body, I wouldn't have realized. The boards had been sanded down and re-stained to match the rich brown color of the rest. I could barely make out the faint outline of the work, but when I focused on that place, when I allowed the memory of my lifeless father to emerge from where I kept it buried, it floated up to the surface of my mind like a buoy, and his outline became as stark as police tape around a body. Whoever had restored this room had done their work well, and had almost erased the terrible memory from this house. But only almost.

It's strange, I thought now, how houses have memories just like people do. I wondered if this house was ready to share its memories with me.

I went and sat in the nook. In the same position as that night when they came for me. Feet curled up, book in my lap, my head bent over the words.

I waited for those movie reels to merge with each other.

I waited for the reel from that night to take precedence.

I didn't have to wait long.

The images came at me in great flashes. Everything was blurry, though, messy and out of order. The voices and the crashing, so much noise. The arm around my neck, the male body pressed against my back, taut and strong, the knife at my throat, the knife slicing across my skin. The second male body, new voices, so many male voices all at once amid the destruction. The surprise, the terrible surprise of the intruders at finding the house occupied.

Good girl. Good girl. Be a good girl.

This said to me so many times and by two different people.

My father's footsteps, his voice saying *Jane* and my voice saying *Daddy* as though from another girl who wasn't me.

But something else was niggling at my brain, trying to push its way up like an animal in the sea, trying to swim to the surface of my mind and fill all my senses, a memory, a new one, wanting air. Wanting me to help it rise, to remember it, to see it for what it was.

A smell. Faint. Ugly.

Sweet and rot. Sweet and rotten. R*otting*.

It returned to me, filling the space around me, wanting to enter my lungs, and I nearly had it, it was so close, *I* was so close—

"Jane!" my mother said from the doorway, rushing in.

The spell was broken.

The scent, the memory of it faded away.

Retracted itself from my senses.

"I couldn't wait any longer," she said. "Are you all right? Maybe this wasn't such a good idea."

I looked at her standing there, the dust in the air illuminated by the last rays of daylight. It gave her a strange halo, as though she were an angel.

I raised my head. "I'm okay." Swung my feet down to the floor. Tried not to be frustrated that my mother interrupted when I'd gotten so close to something, a new detail. A possible lead. Or something. "I really am." I stood. "But I didn't remember anything new." I sighed. "Not really."

"It doesn't matter," she said, pulling me into the halo with her arms. "One step at a time."

"I guess so," I said, trying to be proud of myself for taking this first step of coming here, wondering what I missed with that memory, my mind a fishing pole reaching down into its depths, trying to hook it and pull it up, but unable to find it. "Do you think we could go home? I'm tired."

"Of course we can. Of course. We'll go right now."

I followed her out of the room and back downstairs, once again a girl ghost floating just above the ground, a little numb, the air tingling with something more like relief this time instead of anticipation. The memory would come when it was ready, all of it, bright and clear as the ocean on a calm summer's day. I told myself this as my mother and I said our good-byes, as we made our way out the door and the last rays of sun disappeared from the sky.

TWENTY-SEVEN

WOULD YOU BELIEVE THAT Miles was there?" I said to the girls.

We were sitting on the seawall by the beach during the late afternoon. Legs dangling over the edge of it on the ocean side, barefoot. Bikini tops and jean shorts. People watching and neighbor watching and boy watching, of course.

"Miles must *really* like you," Bridget said.

Tammy snorted. "Or be totally stupid since he knows you're with Handel."

"I think he means well," I said, surprised to be defending him. But there was always something so sincere in Miles's eyes when he spoke to me. "Maybe if Handel wasn't in the picture, Miles and I would've gone out." This statement surprised me even more than the one before, though it was probably true.

"You've got to give the boy credit," Michaela said, twirling a lock of her long dark hair around her finger and then letting it go. "He's obviously not giving up, *and* he's a nice guy who's going places. Probably the same college-type places as you," she added, though her words were drowned out by the sizzle and crackle of fireworks.

The Fourth of July was tomorrow, and some members of the town were already setting off firecrackers, planting Roman candles in the sand before running away to watch the show. The snaps the children were crushing underfoot on the sidewalk provided a steady stream of *pops* amid the occasional loud *boom*.

I leaned forward to look past Bridget's place on the wall. "Well, he certainly doesn't think Handel and I are going to last," I answered Michaela.

"I like Miles more and more," Michaela said with a grin.

"Be nice," I said, leaning back. A big wave crashed onto the beach, and I was suddenly tempted to swim. It was really hot out.

Bridget put her head on my shoulder. "Oh, to have two hot boys, one rich and one bad, fighting over me."

I shrugged her off. "Are you joking? Aren't you the girl with three rich boys fighting over her?"

"Sadly, they are not," she said with a sigh.

"Liar," Michaela said, just as a little boy on the walk behind us threw a big handful of snaps onto the ground and we all flinched. Michaela turned to glare at him, and he hurried away.

"I'd be happy with just one boy fighting over me," Tammy said from Michaela's other side.

"If there's only one boy, there can't be any fighting," Michaela observed.

"How about fighting *for* me?" Tammy went on. "You know, to win me over."

"Well, you already have that in Seamus," I said, shaking my head. Wishing Tammy would just acknowledge what was going on with Seamus already. There was another loud *boom* from behind the wall, and the four of us jumped.

Michaela turned once more to see who'd set off the firecracker, but this time she didn't find the source. "Someday someone in this town is going to lose a hand."

Tammy nudged her. "Always the mother."

"I am not," she said. "I'm just prudent."

Bridget laughed. "Ooh, SAT word."

I shifted positions so I was sitting cross-legged on the wall, the sandy cement rough against the skin of my legs and feet. I zeroed in on Tammy. "Can we talk about Seamus and you?"

"*Yessss,* I suppose," Tammy said, like it was a lot of trouble to acquiesce to this request. But then she turned to me, the look on her face serious. "Though, shouldn't we talk about, you know, the rest of your night at the O'Connors' house first?"

"Was it difficult to be there?" Michaela asked before I could respond.

I sighed. I knew this was coming at some point, so I might as well get it over with. "Yes and no," I began, my eyes on the wall underneath me, my fingers pushing a tiny pebble around its surface. "I mean, yes, it was scary, and if I wasn't careful, you know, if I wasn't trying hard to control what was going on in my mind, I'd have these terrible flashbacks. Images of my dad. And the sounds of everything, like I could hear it happening all over again. Like I was *there*—"

Bridget put an arm around me. "Jane, that sounds awful."

I nodded. "But even though I hadn't wanted to go and I've been avoiding that house for months, it was good to get it over with. I'm kind of proud of myself for going."

"You should be," Tammy said.

I picked up the pebble and pressed it into my palm. "Thanks," I said.

"Did you remember anything new?" Michaela asked.

I laughed a little and looked at her. "Spoken like a cop's daughter."

She smiled sadly. "Takes one to know one." Her voice was soft.

"I didn't," I said. I rolled the tiny rock around the center of my hand. "Well, that's not true. I *almost* remembered something. It was weird. When I went up to the library, which is where, you know, it all happened, it was like there was this memory that wanted out, but I couldn't let it come back. My mind was almost reaching all around it, but then couldn't quite get at it."

"It'll happen," Bridget said. "You just need time."

I could feel her eyes on me, but I kept mine on the ocean. Opened my palm over the beach side of the wall and let the pebble fall into the sand. "I think it might have been a smell. Cologne," I whispered.

Michaela's eyebrows arched. "Cologne? Would you recognize it if you, like, went to the store and started testing them out?"

I thought about this. It was an interesting idea. But then I shook my head. "I don't know. It wasn't *just* cologne, though. It was kind of a combination of smells, but cologne might have been mixed in there." I sighed long and heavy. Pressed my hands into the side of my head. "I hate this," I groaned.

"Don't push yourself," Tammy said. "You're taking steps forward, and that's all that matters. And we're here for you."

Bridget gave me another squeeze. "Absolutely."

Michaela turned and hopped off the wall onto the sidewalk and came over to the place I was sitting, still staring out at the waves. "You should really see a therapist. You should have a long time ago. Right away after it happened."

"Maybe they could hypnotize you into remembering," Bridget said.

Michaela laughed. "I think that's only on the television shows, B."

"No, it's not! It's in real life, too."

I didn't have to turn to know that Michaela was giving Bridget a roll of her eyes. "All right, Ms. Expert," she said to Bridget. "But I meant that it might help you move forward," Michaela went on. "Not that it would help you remember. Though if that happened, too, it wouldn't be so bad."

I shifted my place on the wall so I was facing Michaela. "Maybe. I'll think about it. My mother wanted me to go, but I just, well, I just haven't."

Tammy hopped down and joined Michaela. "If and when you're ready, J," she said. "And only then."

I nodded. "We'll see. But back to you and Seamus . . ."

"Oh God," she said. "You don't give up, do you?"

"If we did, you'd continue in your severe denial of his interest," Bridget was saying, when my attention snagged on a group of guys hanging around at the far end of the seawall.

It caught on them because theirs seemed caught on me. Or maybe it was on the four of us. I had a feeling it was me, though, and I shifted my sunglasses from their place holding back my hair to cover my eyes so I could take in those boys without them knowing I was staring so directly. I recognized one of Handel's brothers, Colin, the one closest to him in age. The resemblance between them was startling when I let myself go there. They had the same build, that same dirty-blond hair and rough, suntanned complexion. They even had the same features, the shape of their lips and cheekbones, and those piercing eyes. Despite these similarities of face and body, I could tell that Colin was nothing like Handel. Handel might carry his brothers' bad boy reputation in his genes, but he had enough good in him to tip the scales in a favorable direction, whereas his brothers didn't. At least this one didn't. He was bad all the way through.

I had to admit, this frightened me a little.

It made me wonder if the bad was something that bubbled up higher with each passing year, to push out the good. If Handel might someday turn into his brothers, or if maybe he was already on that path. Colin was only older than Handel by a couple of years.

Worse still was one of the other boys with Colin. Handel's friend Cutter terrified me, and he seemed to be everywhere I went. A cigarette dangled from his mouth, and his eyes kept traveling to the place where the girls and I were sitting, like he didn't care if I noticed. I looked away, not trusting the cover of my sunglasses any longer. While I sat there, my back to those boys, unable to forget they were there, watching, a hot July gust of wind burst across everything, and quickly—so quickly I thought I might have imagined it—a scent wafted my way, filled my nostrils with something sweet and bitter and ugly. Just a trace of it.

Then it disappeared.

No.

Could it?

Was that?

Cutter? Colin?

Right then a loud, ominous *boom* broke through the air, followed by a series of sharp crackles. I gasped and jumped, almost so much that I fell from my place on the wall. Bridget grabbed my arm, steadying me.

"You okay?" she asked.

"Yeah, sure," I said, a shiver running up through my shoulders, as though I could physically shake off the attention of those boys. Pebbles of fear, of worry, of confusion had piled up underneath the bare skin of my legs on the wall, pressing into me. "Now what were you girls just saying about Tammy and Seamus?" I asked, returning to our conversation, deciding my focus was better served on my own friends as opposed to Handel's.

When I got home, I was glad to find my mother alone in her sewing room.

I stood in the open doorway, and before I could lose my nerve, I asked her, "How do you know when you're in love with someone?"

My mother put down her work, the gray spill of silk cascading off the side of her chair like a waterfall. "Are you thinking you might be in love with Handel?"

I nodded.

"That's a big deal, sweetie."

"I know." I leaned against the door frame for support. Talk of love and Handel almost made me feel faint. Then I asked something else, the thing that was really weighing on my mind. "What do you know about his family?"

My mother gestured for me to come sit on the chair reserved

for clients, so I did. "What does Handel's family have to do with whether you love him?"

I hesitated, not sure how to answer this myself. "I don't know that they matter really. No, that's not true," I backtracked. "I wonder how all those brothers affect Handel. His brothers have a reputation, Mom, and it's not good."

"That doesn't mean Handel is anything like his brothers."

"But how do I know that for sure?"

"Jane, why are you even asking this? Did something happen?"

"No," I said, maybe a little too quickly. "I just . . . see them around town. Well, one of them more than the others, and this friend of Handel's, too, and I don't like the look of them. And don't tell me you don't know anything about the Davies boys, because I won't believe it." I looked around my mother's office. "This sewing room has heard all the town's secrets and probably from multiple angles."

My mother ran a hand along the gray silk she was working on. "I don't like gossip."

"But do you have any?"

She sighed. "I haven't seen Handel's mother in a long while, and the last time she was here was for a funeral."

I nodded. "Handel's uncle. He told me."

Carefully, she set the delicate fabric aside on the table and looked at me intently. "All I'll say, sweetheart, is that she was sad about her family. About the business they were tied up in—that's what she called it—and sad not to see a way out of it. The only thing that seemed to give her hope was her youngest, and that would be Handel."

I tried to read my mother's expression. "Aren't you worried that I'm getting mixed up with a Davies? Everyone else is."

"I try not to judge someone I don't know," she said. She leaned forward, everything about her posture imploring. "And I trust *you*, sweetheart. I trust your judgment."

"But what if I'm wrong?"

"I hope that you're not," she said. "I don't want to see you get your heart broken on top of everything else."

"I don't want that, either," I said. "But Handel's not that guy. What he feels for me is real. I can tell."

"Then you should hang on to that. Doubt can ruin everything, especially when it's not warranted."

This consolation was running through my mind as I got up from the chair and left my mother to her work, even as I wondered whether my own judgment was as trustworthy as my mother believed. I knew she was right about one thing, though. I'd been through a lot, and I didn't want to get my heart broken on top of everything else.

But maybe I wouldn't.

Handel was too good to me to let that happen.

Later that evening, I stood facing the mirror. Tried to see the Jane I used to be, not just the one the boys were looking at today or the one before tragedy struck. But the Jane even before that, who had walked the world as though it was only and wholly good, as though nothing bad could ever happen as long as I did what I was told, as long as I always chose what was right. I was that Jane for so many years, almost the entirety of my life, yet I could barely see a trace of her in the dark circles under my eyes and the faint expression of distrust on my face.

Then I wondered what Handel saw when he looked at me, if he liked the long dark hair that fell past my shoulders, almost reaching the crook of my elbow, my limbs that Bridget always said were willowy, the swell of my chest underneath the tank top I wore. I tried studying my face like Handel might, its oval shape, the swollen arc of my lips, the fan of lashes framing wide-set eyes.

I wondered what other people saw in me now, not just Handel but everyone, not at all sure what *I* was seeing. I turned sideways, as though my profile might reveal that long-ago Jane, but instead all I noticed were the curves of my body, the ones that might be partly responsible for my appearance to Handel this summer, that somehow had called out to him, grabbing his attention without my having to try.

Then my mind went to the memory of his fingers tracing those curves, of his hands on my bare skin and how I'd wanted them to travel farther, lower, to that place just below the flat of my stomach that ached even now as I imagined the possibility. How touching his skin and him touching mine in the most intimate of places would make me feel changed yet again, a third Jane or maybe even a fourth one, a chameleon of a girl who morphed and shifted with each new significant experience, one of them tragic, certainly, but others surprising, even thrilling. I liked this thought, that I didn't have to be defined by tragedy, that though sadness and loss might be written onto my skin, there were other things that could be written over it, things dominated by joy and desire and pleasure. I wanted to be different again, to rewrite the Jane I was today so the tragic one would recede even further away.

I knew exactly how that would happen, too. How it could be done.

Tonight would be the night I'd sleep with Handel, I decided. I was in love with him after all, I reminded myself.

I took one last look at the Jane I saw in the mirror now, smiled at her, said good-bye, since tomorrow, I knew, there would be yet another Jane in her place.

TWENTY-EIGHT

I WENT STRAIGHT TO his house.

Handel was sitting on the front porch when I arrived, staring out at the water across the street, smoking a cigarette. It was like he'd been waiting for me.

"There's no one home," he said, like a warning.

"Is that a problem?" I asked with a laugh and some relief, too.

"No. I suppose not."

I stood in front of him, willing him to admire the Jane I'd just seen in the mirror, wanting him to think the same thoughts I'd had only a few minutes ago. He stubbed out the cigarette in the ashtray on the table, and when he looked up again, he smiled in that way that did me in.

"I'm glad you're here," he said, and I believed him.

I sat down on the wicker couch. Let my fingers dance on the cushions right near his leg, but not so close that we touched. "Me too."

"Is there anything you want to talk about?"

This question caught me off guard. Maybe Handel wanted to know about my dinner at the O'Connors' house, but I didn't feel like discussing it. "Not particularly," I said. My fingers stopped their dance. "I just needed to see you."

This made Handel smile again. "Needed?"

I nodded. Smiled back.

Then we talked for a long time as we sat there, the sky growing dark. We talked about all kinds of things. My relationship with my mother. His relationship with his father. My going to college. His going to college. What books we loved and which ones we didn't. Music. Movies. Hopes and dreams. Mine. His. The conversation went on and on, vibrant and lighthearted at points and full of feeling and sincerity in others.

I thought to myself on more than one occasion:

There are so many ways to love someone, sometimes just with words.

The moon came out, the stars were bright, and both soon provided the only light in our comfortable darkness on the porch. Handel got up, and I followed him around to the back of the house, down the steps into a lush garden I never would have dreamed was there, a beautiful secret thriving behind it. Flowers growing everywhere, vines winding around trellises, penned in by a tall fence that could barely hold it all back. It was something out of a book. Too magical to be real.

"What is this place?" I asked.

"It's my mother's," Handel said. "She calls it her haven."

"It's beautiful," I said, and thought about how Handel may be related to those brothers of his, but he's related to the woman who created this, too.

Handel looked at me, traced a finger down the side of my face and along the curve of my jaw. "I've never shown anyone before. I've never brought anyone here."

"No?" I asked, everything about me like petals opening to the sun.

He shook his head.

"Thank you for sharing it with me," I said.

"Jane, there are things I want to tell you," Handel began. "Things you need to know before we can—"

But I couldn't wait anymore, and I kissed him then, in the

cloak of the garden, kissed him in this way that was . . . suggestive. Pressed myself against him all the way to my knees. I felt delirious with love after all our talk, intoxicated with the sweet scent of flowers hovering in the air around us, freed by the darkness. I stopped being Jane altogether in this surreal place, alone with this beautiful, mysterious boy named Handel, and instead became some wild, confident nymph. Put his hand to my chest and made sure he found out quickly that I hadn't worn a bra. I wanted whatever came next.

I was ready.

"Jane," he said, lifting his lips from my neck, his voice hoarse.

But I pressed into him, my head thrown back, hair falling over the arms that held me, exposing neck and collarbone, handing myself over willingly. I wanted his touch on my skin, and I wanted it everywhere. "I'm all yours," I said, and I meant it.

I put my trust in him completely.

I wanted to try everything with Handel.

"Follow me," he said, taking my hand and leading me through an opening between two short, thick pines into a tiny, private space canopied with ivy. There was a bench in the center, and Handel sat down and waited for me to join him. Instead I went and stood in front of him, put my hand along the side of his face and leaned forward, stopping just short of his lips.

"This is fun," I said dreamily.

"You're driving me crazy." He sounded pained.

I smiled, eyes half closed. "Oh, am I?"

"Like you didn't know." His laugh was low.

But he hesitated to touch me. Something was stopping him.

"I won't break," I told him, and inched closer, and it's true, too, that in this place and time with Handel, in this secret garden behind his house, I felt unbreakable.

He slid his index finger along my collarbone and down until it hooked over the top button of my shirt. This time he didn't hesitate or ask. With one quick twist, he slid it open. His other hand went to my thigh, to the skin just below the hem of my skirt, and stopped. Rested there. We kissed a million times more, it seemed, exchanging whispered words and murmurs before his fingers traveled up along my leg until they grazed the edge of my underwear, and a million times more after that, it seemed, before they slipped underneath it, moving leisurely across my skin to what I thought must be the very center of my self.

"Oh." I sighed, with the surprise of his fingers. My eyes were closed, and I could feel the drunken smile on my face.

"Do you want me to stop?" Handel asked, his voice a mix of concern and desire.

"No," I said. "Definitely do not stop."

He laughed at this, and I melted into him like I might have become the ocean itself in this one moment, letting myself be changed by so much pleasure, so much attention that was all for me. I was definitely a new Jane by the time I opened my eyes and looked into Handel's, who watched me like he'd never seen me before.

And he hadn't, I suppose, not this Jane at least.

He blinked once. Again. Then, "I love you," he said to me amid this beautiful, moonlit garden, a world away from the town we lived in day to day.

"I know," I told him. "I do, too. Love you, I mean."

Then we lay down next to each other in the grass and didn't speak again.

TWENTY-NINE

B?" I WHISPERED THROUGH the screen. "Are you up?"

There was no answer. Not even a rustle of the sheets.

"Hey, B," I said, louder this time. "It's me."

I heard a sigh and some movement. "Jane?"

My hands pressed against the screen. "I'm outside your window."

"What are you doing there? What time is it?"

"It's early. I don't know, maybe seven a.m.?"

"Why aren't you at home in bed?"

"Um, I was, but now I'm here." I peered inside, but it was too dark to see anything. "I need you to let me in. Can you do that?"

"Sure," Bridget said, and there was more rustling.

"I have to talk to someone," I told her, trying to explain.

"Good or bad?"

"Good, I think," I said. "But I might have been a little bad."

This seemed to wake Bridget. "Meet me around the back of the house."

In the murky light of the very early morning, I slipped inside the porch door Bridget held open for me, and the two of us crept to her room. Her eyes were puffy from sleep, her long hair knotted and tangled. She fell into bed and twisted herself underneath the sheet. Lifting her head slightly from the pillow, she looked at me. "Well? Are you getting in or not?"

I nodded. Kicked off my flip-flops and curled into the quilt she'd tossed aside. "B, I did something."

She pushed a pillow my way. "What did you do?"

"I did . . . *the* something. Last night with Handel," I added.

There came a gasp. Bridget's head popped up from the pillow, and she propped herself with an elbow, the sleep gone from her eyes. They blinked wide. "Oh. My. God. You did not!"

I smiled dreamily at the ceiling. "I totally did."

"Am I the first person you've told?"

"You are. I couldn't sleep. I had to tell someone."

"I'm honored."

I turned to look at her. "It had to be you. You've been so supportive. Michaela would probably scold me and Tammy would make some sort of sarcastic remark and I . . . I just didn't want to ruin this moment."

"Okay," she said gently. "So . . . are you happy?"

"Very."

"Did you . . . like it?"

"I more than liked it."

"Did you . . . you know . . . *have one?*"

"I totally did."

"Tell me! Tell me!"

I closed my eyes. "It was . . . exciting and slow and wonderful and . . . sexy."

Bridget giggled. "Well, it was sex. Shouldn't it be sexy?"

"I guess. But I couldn't have imagined what that meant before Handel. He makes me . . . *do* things."

Bridget's mouth fell open. "What did he make you do?"

I opened my eyes again and turned to her. "I don't mean it *that* way. I meant that he brings something out in me that I didn't know was there."

"So, *good* things."

I let my attention wander back to the ceiling. A fan whirred softly above us, providing the room with a little breeze. "Definitely good. Great."

"Oh. My. God," she said again, admiringly.

"He told me he loves me. Just before we . . . you know."

Bridget clapped her hands together silently. "That is so romantic."

"It was."

"Did you say it, too?"

"I did. It's true. I do love him."

She gasped. "Hot, sexy, *and* you love him. What more could you want?"

I smiled. "More sex."

"Oh. My. God. You can't even wait to do it again."

"Not really."

"Oh. My. God."

"Stop saying that!"

Bridget smirked. "Why, does it bring back memories of last night?"

"B!"

"Sorry, sorry. I can't help it." There was a creak outside, the floorboards groaning in the living room. Maybe Bridget's parents were awake. "I'm trying to process this," she said, lowering her voice a little.

"Process?" I asked in a whisper. "You sound like a shrink."

She tried to stifle a laugh. "A shrink that says 'oh my God' all the time?"

I laughed, too. "Okay, maybe that's a stretch."

Bridget hopped up from the bed and turned the fan on high so the noise would drown out our conversation. Then she got back in. "So now is the time in our discussion when I have to act like a good friend," she warned.

I shifted so I could watch the blades blur as they turned. "I thought you were already acting like a good friend."

"Well, of course," she said. "But a good friend makes sure that her friend used protection."

I rolled my eyes. "I'm not dumb. I still plan on going to college after we graduate."

"Okay, all right. I just wanted to make sure."

"You have nothing to worry about," I reassured her.

"Good," she said with relief. "It sounds like it was perfect."

I turned to face her, hugging a pillow to prop myself up. "It was. Nearly," I added.

Bridget's blue eyes clouded a little. "Why nearly?"

"There's always this . . . hesitation about Handel," I admitted. "Like he's holding something back."

"Well, part of what makes Handel hot is the mystery," Bridget reminded me.

I moved aside the stray hairs that kept blowing into my eyes with the breeze from the fan. "This isn't about mystery," I said. "It's like he has a secret. I feel like we've gone right to the edge of him telling me and then he doesn't." I thought about Handel's brother. About Cutter. Then pushed these thoughts far into the next town, far away from Handel. That wasn't it. It couldn't be. I was being crazy.

Bridget shook her head. "I bet you're imagining things. Sex is a big deal, and it's normal to be nervous about it. But you didn't do anything wrong."

"I know I didn't. And you're probably right. It's just my imagination."

"Of course I am," she said with a grin. "So when are you going to do it again?"

"I don't know." I smiled then. I couldn't help it. "Tonight?"

Bridget brought the sheet over her to cover her squeal. "Fireworks amid the fireworks on the Fourth!"

"Could you be any cheesier?"

"I know. I'm practically a Dorito. I can't help it."

I sighed mockingly. "It's good that you admit it. But it's also why I love you, B."

"Love you, too, J."

I smiled. "Just because you said you love me doesn't mean I'll have sex with you."

Bridget groaned. "You're ridiculous," she said.

Then she hit me with a pillow.

"You left early this morning," my mother said when I walked in the door. She was swirling sugar into her iced coffee with a spoon, sitting at the kitchen counter. Her hair was in a ponytail, and she still had on her pajamas.

"I went to see Bridget." I gestured at her glass. "Is there any more?"

"In the fridge. I made a new batch at three a.m. I couldn't sleep."

"Oh," I said, turning away to retrieve some, hoping the blush spreading across my cheeks would fade by the time I turned back.

"Which is how I know you were out late," she went on.

I froze, my hand in the ice bin, took a deep breath, and regained my composure before managing to move again, retrieving a fistful of cubes that I plopped into the glass before pouring coffee over them. I topped it off with half-and-half and added a couple of spoons of sugar, this ritual giving me enough time to wipe the color from my face before joining my mother across the counter. I hoisted myself up onto the stool and took a sip. Swallowed it down. "I guess I was out late," I said.

"I'm not judging, just observing. I trust you, Jane."

"I know." A stab of guilt followed this recognition. Which was why I said what I did next. "There's something I should probably tell you."

"Oh?" Now it was my mother's turn to act casual. "You can tell me anything. I want you to be able to."

"You're sure about that?"

She nodded. "I am."

I didn't speak right away. I gathered my courage, stirring more sugar into my iced coffee. Probably too much and it would end up undrinkable, but I needed something to do.

"Is it something about our visit to the O'Connors' house?" she asked.

I shook my head. "No. Definitely not."

"Okay. You can talk about that, too. Whenever you're ready."

"I know."

"Good."

Another silence followed. I couldn't quite manage to get out what needed saying.

Then my mother asked, "Does this have anything to do with our conversation about love yesterday?"

"Yes," I admitted. Then I took a deep breath and just said it. "So I had sex with Handel."

My mother blinked rapidly, her eyelashes fluttering. "Oh!" They stopped, and she regained her composure. "That was fast."

"Please don't be mad."

She put a hand to the counter to steady herself. "I'm not mad."

I couldn't quite look at her, though. I could feel her eyes on me. My cheeks burned again. "You're not?"

"No. But before we take this conversation any further, you need to reassure me that you were smart and used protection."

"Mom," I huffed, allowing myself a glance at her. "Of course I did! You sound like Bridget. She asked me the same thing when I went to see her."

"Good for Bridget," she said with a smile. "I'm glad my smart daughter has smart friends looking out for her."

"I'll pass that along." I took a big gulp of my iced coffee and made a face. It was way too sweet.

My mother's eyebrows were raised. "I just want to make sure that you're taking care of yourself. After the year you've had, the last thing you need is . . . something else unfortunate to happen."

This was becoming torture. "Mom!"

"I'll stop. But only after I mention that we should go see a doctor so you can discuss all your options for birth control. You don't even have to go with me if you don't want to," she added quickly. "You can go with Bridget or one of the other girls if it makes you more comfortable."

"Okay, okay." I pushed my iced coffee to the side. I couldn't bring myself to take another sip.

"Good. Now, do you want to talk about how it went?"

I slid off the stool and began fixing myself a toasted peanut butter and jelly sandwich so I didn't have to look at her when I answered. "Do you mean, like, the details?"

I could almost hear her shrugging behind me, trying to act nonchalant. "If you want to share details, you certainly can. I'll listen."

I opened and closed cabinet doors looking for the strawberry jam and the peanut butter until I finally found them behind a box of pancake mix. I thought about how to answer. "I don't think I want to," I said. "It feels kind of private."

"Okay. Can you please tell me if you enjoyed it? I want you to enjoy it, Jane. Sex is something to be enjoyed."

When the toast popped, I almost jumped. "I did, Mom," I admitted, embarrassed. I put the bread on a plate and started spreading the peanut butter on one side and the jelly on the other. "Let's not discuss this anymore, okay? It's too weird."

She sighed. "Okay."

I turned around, plate in hand, and rejoined my mother at the counter, hoping she knew when to quit. "Promise it's okay?"

"Yes, I promise."

I munched on my sandwich and she drank her iced coffee in silence. When I finished, I was about to head into my room when she stopped me.

"Thank you for telling me."

I placed the empty plate in the sink. "I tell you everything."

"Do you? Really?"

Was my mother talking about my night with Handel? Or that night in February? Did she think I was holding something back? When I said what I did next, I looked at my mother straight on, with as much seriousness and honesty as I could conjure in my expression. "Really. I do," I said, because it was so close to the truth that it practically was the truth.

"Good. Let's keep it that way. I'll always be here for you. We can deal with anything together. *Anything,* Jane. I mean it."

"I know," I said. Somewhere deep down I did know this. I think I knew, too, that I would be glad of it, when the day came when I had to lean on my mother to help me through whatever difficult thing life brought next.

My mother grinned suddenly. "Now, do you want some pointers about sex from someone with a lifetime of experience?"

I screwed up my face. "Oh my God, no. Eww. Gross. Please stop there." I grabbed my iced coffee from the counter and dumped it out. "I have to get down to the beach soon, or we'll lose our spot for the Fourth. It's probably already crowded."

"Okay," my mother called after me with a laugh. "But I'm here whenever you have questions."

"Again, no, thanks! But I love you *despite* that offer," I added, shoving the various beach paraphernalia I needed into my bag and going through my drawers looking for the bathing suit I wanted, doing my best to block out the horrifically unsexy idea that my mother might have sex advice, a thought that made me shudder even as her effort to connect about it made me laugh.

THIRTY

ANDEL MADE IT TO the spot where I was hanging out with my girls a little after six.

"Heya," he called up to me where I sat, high on the lifeguard chair, like some queen of the town beach. I'd just come out of the water, and my hair and bathing suit were still wet.

"Hi," I called down to him, feeling shy. "You're earlier than I expected."

He grinned. "I was excited for the fireworks."

Every year on the Fourth of July, Michaela, Tammy, and I staked out one of the lifeguard chairs dotting the beach. At five o'clock, when they got off duty, we were in wait, ready with towels thrown over our arms, a cooler full of snacks and soda, some regular, some mixed with rum, armed with sweaters in our bags in case the air became chilly once the sun went down. Then we'd take turns occupying our chair until the fireworks started.

"So it was the show that enticed you?" I asked, flirty, taking in the way Handel's long hair framed his tanned skin, all rugged boy features, the memory of his muscled arms and legs under that T-shirt and jeans making me blush.

"Of course." Handel was smirking. He grabbed my ankle and held it. Stared up at me. Ran a finger along the ticklish, tender skin underneath the bone. "What else could it be?"

"Are you coming up or what?" I asked, the blush deepening.

"Now I am." He released his hand. "I was waiting for my official invitation."

I smiled and nodded. Bit my lip as I watched him grip one of the driftwood slats below, its white paint peeling off from the salty ocean air. He hoisted himself up quickly, and before I knew it, he was sitting next to me.

"So this is the place to be tonight," he said.

"It is, if I'm here," I said, confident even as I couldn't quite bring myself to look at Handel straight in the eyes.

"Oh really?"

"Mm-hmm."

"I'll have to agree with that."

I glanced over at him quickly. Grinned a little. "That's a smart decision."

Handel let his fingers come to rest on my bare knee, his touch light. Casual. "Did you enjoy your swim?"

"I did. The waves are great."

He looked me up and down. "I've seen that bathing suit before."

"Oh?" I acted like I was surprised. I had on the same bikini from the day when Handel first spoke to me. I'd worn it on purpose. I wanted to know if he might recognize it.

Handel let his fingers wander to the tie closest to him, the one at my left hip, and he traced the loops of the bow. "How could I forget?"

It was hard to breathe. "I didn't, either," I admitted. Looked at him directly.

"You did this to me on purpose, didn't you."

I smiled. Laughed. "Maybe."

Just then, a chorus of loud "Hello, Jane"s and "Hello, Handel"s came from down the beach. Tammy, Michaela, and Bridget were returning from their swim, warning us of their approach.

"Are we interrupting something, or is it safe to come closer?" Tammy called to us.

I rolled my eyes. "Just get over here."

"Hi, Handel," Bridget dripped, all knowing.

"Hi, Bridget," he said back casually.

I hoped he missed the meaning in her tone. I didn't want Handel to think I ran straight to my friends to tell them all the details of our night together, even though that's exactly what happened. At least with Bridget. Today, during our long afternoon at the beach, I filled in Michaela about the evening's events, though with more restraint than with Bridget so as to better withstand her disapproval. With Tammy I could barely get a word in edgewise, she was so full of opinions she simply had to share once she'd heard the news.

"Miles and company will be here any minute," Michaela said, looking from me to Handel and back to me again from where she stood below us on the sand.

I glared at her. "Thanks for the heads-up, Michaela."

Bridget put her hand on one of the wooden slats of the chair, right by my foot. "I can take a shift now, if you guys want to, I don't know, go for another swim or take a walk?"

"Thanks, B." I smiled at her gratefully. Whether she knew I wanted to have alone time with Handel or to avoid Miles's arrival or a bit of both, I wasn't sure, but I appreciated the opportunity for all of the above and for the easy exit. To Handel, I said,

"Do you feel like going in the water? I could definitely go for another swim."

He shrugged. "Sure. It's got to be about ninety degrees out."

Handel jumped down from the lifeguard chair first, and then I followed. I hit the sand hard and almost lost my balance, but he put an arm out and caught me around the waist before I could fall. The touch of his skin on mine, even casually, even in front of all my friends, made my body feel like it might burn up. His arm dropped away quickly once I recovered, but I was left standing there, longing for it back. Between my friends next to us and Miles and his friends on their way, the sun glaring down over everything, the children everywhere, playing and shouting in the sand, parents trying to catch the last rays of the day, shading themselves under colorful umbrellas, munching on sandwiches between gulps of beer and cheap wine, it seemed impossible Handel and I would ever be alone again.

Bridget made her way to the top of the lifeguard chair. She took the spot we vacated, and I handed up her towel and bag. She plopped it next to her on the bench. When I glanced back at Handel, I caught him staring at me, and when he turned away, he was smiling. I wondered if he was thinking the same things as me, about how here we were in broad daylight, surrounded by half the town, acting as though he hadn't had his hands all over me less than twenty-four hours ago and in all those places good girls aren't supposed to let the bad boys go.

"Oh, please get a room, you two," Tammy said, eyeing us.

"Here comes Miles," Michaela said, giving me a look.

"And James and Logan and Hugh," Bridget called down, her hand cupped over her eyes to block the sun.

"Which one shall I pick? I just like them all!" Michaela called back up to her, laughing.

Bridget nudged her with a toe. "Shut up."

Handel looked at me. Eyebrows arched. "Ready?"

"Okay," I said, a little torn between the duty I felt to be nice to Miles and the desire to be alone with Handel.

He leaned in and gave me a quick peck on the lips. "Jane?"

My name, from Handel's mouth, just like that first day. A question, a statement, an invitation.

Hearing it made the world shimmer.

That woozy feeling halted me long enough that Miles caught up.

"Jane?"

My name a second time, this time from Miles.

He walked straight over to us and planted himself next to me. "How are you doing? You know, after the other night." He didn't acknowledge Handel. Didn't even look his way.

But Handel was looking at Miles. Staring hard.

I turned to Miles. "Let's not talk about that now," I told him. Squinted into the glare of the sun going down. "It's sweet of you to worry, but I'm fine. More than fine," I added, my eyes on Handel as I said this.

Miles wasn't ready to quit. "Jane," he said, leaning toward me, whispering in my ear. "Stay with me. Swim with me."

Pick me. This went unspoken, but I could hear it all the same.

I glared at him. "Stop it," I said, my voice low.

"No," Miles said, his tone less sure than his answer.

I looked at Handel. His eyes had hardened. I could tell he didn't like what was happening, didn't trust Miles, and my heart

298

sank. Maybe this meant that Handel didn't trust me, wasn't sure if I'd stay with him if I had the choice to be with Miles. He was waiting for me to do just this, to choose him, but before I could, he shrugged and said, "We'll swim another time, Jane. It's okay. Really."

Then Handel walked off. Down toward the water without me.

I came to, remembering my voice. Called out, "Wait!" and he stopped, his back still to us.

"Jane—" Miles started.

"I have somewhere to be," I told him. "I have to be with Handel," I added, as if this wasn't clear.

I started toward Handel then, couldn't wait to reach him.

"Jane, I'm sorry," Miles called out from behind me.

I didn't turn around—there was nothing left to say. I didn't stop, either, not until I reached Handel's outstretched hand and wove my fingers through his. Together we headed down to the place where the water met the beach. By the time our toes touched the water, we were so close I couldn't tell where my skin ended and Handel's began. I didn't care if Miles was watching—I didn't care who else was, either. Not Miles, not my friends, and not Handel's. Not even his brothers. All there was in the world in that moment was Handel and me, the two of us, together.

Alone in the sea.

By the time I made my way back to the lifeguard chair later on, the sun had almost set, the center of the sky a bright sapphire blue and ringed all around with fiery pink. I'd walked the entire length of beach twice on my own, my bathing suit now dry. After our swim, Handel went up on the boardwalk to change his clothes. I thought he'd only be a few minutes, but he'd been gone for over an hour.

I didn't think much about it.

Only wished that he'd be back soon.

I craved him constantly. His presence. Nearness. All that possibility.

There was a crowd around our lifeguard chair now. Bridget was high up in the seat, with James to her left, and Hugh to her right. While she talked mostly to James, Michaela was halfway up the slats, hand along the wood to hold her steady, deep in conversation with Hugh, who leaned so far forward trying to get close that if he wasn't careful, he might fall. To the far side of all this were Tammy and Seamus, talking and laughing. They turned toward each other in a way that said *this is a private conversation*. This made me happy to see.

But Miles was gone. This made me relieved.

I grabbed my clothes. Slipped on my jean skirt. Buttoned it. "Hey, B?" I called up to her. "Have you seen Handel?" I asked.

"I thought he was with you," she said.

"He was. Whatever, it's not a big deal," I said, wondering where Handel could have possibly gone. Just when I was starting to feel a little abandoned, I saw him making his way up the beach, but not from the place where he told me he'd be. From the other end entirely.

"Where'd you go?" I asked him when he reached me, trying to sound nonchalant.

He immediately leaned toward me for a kiss. The second his mouth touched mine, my lips parted. I reached up and wove my fingers through his hair, rose high on my toes. I couldn't help wanting him closer—wanting him in a million different ways I hadn't known existed before we met. His hands went to the small of my back, light against my skin. Tammy and Bridget started clapping and whistling. Michaela yelled, "This is a family beach, J."

Handel was laughing, all low and sexy, when he pulled away. "You missed me," he said.

"Yeah," I said, smiling, blushing like crazy—it was impossible not to. "But where were you?" I asked, unable to stop the question a second time.

Handel's smile faltered. He looked off into the distance. "I ran into some friends."

My stomach grew queasy. "Friends like that Cutter guy?"

His head snapped toward me. "Why do you ask that?"

"I don't know," I said—when of course I did. Of course. That smell, that cocktail of rot and sweet, suddenly filled my senses. "His name popped into my head."

"Cutter's not really a friend of mine," Handel said. "More of a colleague of my brother."

The smell disappeared, replaced by relief. I shrugged. "I saw them hanging out yesterday down by the sea wall. Cutter and Colin."

"You did," Handel said absently. He grabbed my hand and grinned. Planted another slow kiss on my lips that brought me back to the present. To him.

I was all for him.

Handel's mouth made its way toward my ear. "Let's oust your friend Bridget from her throne," he whispered. "The fireworks are going to start."

My laughter returned. My joy, too. So fast and so easy.

"She's not coming down from there," I said as we pulled apart once again, my breath stolen by that kiss. "I think we're better off trying for Hugh. He's already halfway down, anyway, busy with hitting on Michaela." I collected myself a moment. Then marched up to them. "Hey, Hugh, you want to trade places?"

"Sure." He jumped to the sand, continuing his conversation with Michaela like we weren't even there.

I turned to Handel. "See how easy that was? Come on," I beckoned, starting my climb. James and Bridget were all too happy to squish together to make room for Handel and me up in the chair. Soon the four of us were enjoying the evening as it settled upon us and the sky became dark enough for the first fireworks to light up the night.

"You were right about this being the best seat on the beach," Handel said at one point, squeezing my hand.

"I'm right about a lot of things," I said. "I'm right about you," I added, giving him a quick peck on the cheek. "And I was definitely right about *them*." I pointed a little ways off down the beach, where Tammy and Seamus stood, their bodies pressed close together, hands clasped. Then I turned my attention back to the fireworks bursting overhead.

After the last one broke across the blackened sky, leaving a trail of sparks that bloomed like a willow tree, Handel and I left the lifeguard chair and everyone else behind us. We walked, arm in arm, through the spaces between the blankets people had set up to watch the fireworks. Some of the smaller children somehow slept through all the noise and flashes of light and were curled up under a towel or in the base of a shallow beach chair, while others had their eyes and mouths open wide, staring above us like they'd just seen some heavenly show. Families were enjoying pizza and snacking on cheese and crackers from paper plates they'd set on top of their coolers.

"This is nice," I murmured into Handel's neck, just below his ear.

"It is," he said, his grip on my waist tightening a little, the finger he had hooked through the belt loop of my skirt grazing the skin at my waist. Handel maneuvered us left so we avoided stepping onto a blue-and-white-checkered blanket where a grandma and grandpa sat sipping wine in plastic cups.

When we reached the boardwalk, we climbed the ramp and headed down the center of the pavilion toward the exit where a million cars were probably already fighting their way out of the parking lot. The snack bar to our left was packed with patrons buying food. Not a table and chair in sight was unoccupied. But to our right was the quiet labyrinth of old, rickety bathhouses where the townspeople who lived too far from the beach to lug their stuff down every day locked up their umbrellas and chairs. Handel steered us into the maze, then made a left down one of the aisles that was darker than the rest. The lightbulb at the end had burned out, and no one had bothered to replace it.

"Where do you think you're taking me?" I asked, laughing.

"What, are you scared?"

"Terrified."

"That's too bad," Handel said, even as he led me further into darkness. "We can go back down to the beach if you're worried about being alone with me."

"Maybe it's you who should be worried about being alone with me," I said with a swish and a sway of my voice.

"Now *that* I might believe. Especially after you took advantage of me last night."

"I did not," I protested, giving him a little shove.

He stopped, resting his back against the wall at the end of the aisle. "Oh, so *now* you're pushing me away."

I leaned against the wall directly opposite. Tried for some flirty distance, though the space was narrow. "Only because you deserve it."

"What can I do to make it up to you?" Handel asked.

His gaze set my skin alight. I lifted my knee and pressed into his thigh with my toes. His jeans were rough against the bottom of my bare feet. "I can think of a few things."

"Oh?" His fingers wandered up to my calf.

I nodded. "Mm-hmm." Watched as they traveled higher, all the way to the center of my thigh, then stopped.

Gently, Handel lowered my leg to the ground. He pushed off the wall so he was standing close. His eyes were so serious. "You don't have any regrets? I mean, you're okay with what happened last night?"

I looked back up at him with all the honesty I had in me. "I'm more than okay with it. It's what I wanted. And I want it again," I added in a whisper.

"I'm glad," he said.

This made me laugh. "You're glad that I want it again?"

He laughed now. "That, too. But I'm just glad you're okay with everything. I want you to be okay—no, *more* than okay, like you said. I want you to be happy. I want to make you happy, Jane. It's what I want, too. All I want."

"You do make me happy," I told him. I leaned in to kiss the

triangle of skin where his shirt was open at the neck. "And right now, I could think of a few things you could do that would make me even happier."

"What—*now*?"

I kissed just below his jawline. "You sound surprised. That isn't why you brought me here, down this long, dark, empty corridor?"

"I thought it would be a good place for making out."

I pulled away and gave Handel a surprised look. "Oh wait! You thought I meant *sex*. I was only talking about making out, too. Just like you."

Handel groaned. "Have I told you how much you drive me crazy?"

"Maybe once or twice."

"That's because you do. All the time," he said. He looked at me, his eyes wide open with emotion, his face lit up by a smile. "I love you, Jane Calvetti. You change me."

"I love you, Handel Davies," I told him back. "You change me, too."

"I do?" He sounded surprised. A little worried about what that might mean.

I nodded. "Now let's make out. I can't take it any longer."

"You want me that bad, huh?"

"Don't flatter yourself," I said, even as I rose on my toes and pressed my mouth against his, letting the night and everything around us fall away. And somewhere in the middle of all of it I thought to myself: I couldn't be happier than I am right now.

It was a happiness that felt like it would last forever.

THIRTY-ONE

FOR DAYS, THERE WAS no room for anything else in my head other than Handel. Handel and I kissing. Handel and I gazing at each other. The sound of Handel's voice. His voice saying, *I love you, Jane*. Those eyes that could level me and make me swoon. The silky feel of his hair in my hands.

And a million other things.

Thoughts about my past melted away. So did thoughts about all that might happen in the future. There was only now, and now was about Handel and being in love and being loved. Cloud nine became the bed where I slept.

I walked around in a perpetual, dreamy haze.

Everyone knew why, too. Handel and I became a big source of gossip again.

I was too happy to care.

Then one afternoon I was headed down to the beach, flip-flops dangling in my left hand, bag bumping against my hip. I was even humming. Out of nowhere someone stepped onto the sidewalk in front of me, and I was forced to look up.

Joey McCallen, all six-foot-square ugly of him, was blocking my path.

Maybe if I'd paid more attention, I could have avoided running into the oldest McCallen brother. I would have seen him sitting out on his stoop drinking a beer and turned left at the previous corner instead of walking straight on by. But I was too busy thinking about what Handel and I did out on his boat last night with the moon shining down on us and only the waves as our audience.

"Jane, we need to talk," Joey said, the freckles on his face darker than ever after so much time in the summer sun.

I forced myself not to look away. "I thought we said all that needed saying last time. Your brother Patrick found those boots. I heard you. What more is there to discuss?"

He took a long swig of his beer, draining it. Then he crushed the can and tossed it onto a burned patch of lawn. "You hanging around all over town with Handel Davies."

"Why is that any of your business?" I asked, trying to keep my tone smooth, even as my heart sputtered a little.

His eyes were hard on me. "It's a bad idea."

I dropped my flip-flops to the ground to give myself an excuse to focus on something else. I slipped my feet into them, one by one. "Is there something you know that I don't?"

When I looked up at Joey again, there was a flash of panic on his face. Like he hadn't thought through where this conversation might go and, now that we were having it, he regretted starting it. How strange, I thought, to see someone like Joey McCallen get nervous.

"The Davies family isn't good for you," he said.

"Oh yeah? Tell that to Mrs. Davies." I was getting defensive. "She's good to me and so is her son." Handel had been bringing me around to his house when either no one was home or if only his mother was. To say that she was happy about me hanging out with her son was an understatement. But Handel kept me far away from his brothers.

Joey stared at me, unblinking, despite the fact that the sun was at my back. "I'm giving you some sound advice."

I tilted my head. Narrowed my eyes. "So the Davies boys aren't good for me and the McCallens are?"

Joey took a step back, like he'd been hit. If it was possible to hurt the feelings of a McCallen boy, it seemed like I might have just done it. "Don't listen to me, then. I'm only trying to protect you. I've always—*only*—wanted to protect you."

I took a step forward, feeling bolder now. "And why would it be *your* job to protect me?"

"Your father was a good man," he said, the emotion in his voice unexpected. "He helped me out once. And now that he isn't around to look out for you, I thought somebody else should."

I let out a big breath, my body deflated. "Oh," I said, unsure where to go next. I shifted my bag to my other shoulder, trying to find something to do, my nervous trick. "I didn't know you knew my father that well," I went on, gaining a little confidence. "I really appreciate the gesture and you wanting to help me out, but I'm a big girl and I know what I'm doing."

"I don't think you do," Joey said, but his attention was already on the front stoop, where another beer was sweating in the sun, waiting for him.

"It's nice to see you, Joey, but I've got to go," I said, and got up the nerve to walk past him, swerving to avoid the place where he stood on the sidewalk. I assumed he'd immediately go back to his beer and his people watching, or whatever it was that Joey McCallen did on a hot July afternoon. But when I turned around for one last look, he was still watching me. He raised a hand to wave good-bye.

It was this image—of Joey McCallen waving on the sidewalk, seeming so helpless—that somehow knocked away thoughts of Handel for the first time in what felt like forever.

"What's wrong?" Bridget asked when I reached the girls' spot on the beach. "I haven't seen that look on your face in, well, you know . . . since . . . um . . ." She trailed off.

"I get it," I said. "I'm fine. I guess. I just had a weird encounter with Joey McCallen," I added, but as soon as this was out, I wanted to stuff it back in. I didn't really want to talk about what he'd told me.

But Michaela was going to try and make me, of course. She looked up from her magazine. "What kind of weird encounter?"

"Forget it." I plopped down on my towel and immediately lay on my back. I pulled my shirt over my face to block out the sun.

Michaela tugged it away. "Spill."

"It was nothing." I felt around for my sunglasses and put them on, then set the shirt aside again. "Where's Tammy?"

"Off somewhere making out with Seamus," Bridget said with a laugh.

"Really?" I asked, a bit of happiness returning. Those two were finally acting like the couple they were meant to be. I looked over at Michaela for confirmation.

Her eyes were on her magazine again. "We don't know that for sure."

Now I looked at Bridget on my other side.

"But we have our suspicions," Bridget said.

"Where's James?" I asked her.

"He's with his family today. *Golfing*." She rolled her eyes.

I smirked at her. "Who knew that you would date a *golfer* this summer."

"Oh yeah?" She took her sunglasses off and smirked back. "Who knew that you'd be *sleeping with* Handel Davies every chance you got this summer."

My skin flushed hot. "Not *every* chance."

"Right," Michaela said, trying to sound bored about it.

"Like you should talk," I said to her. "Ms. I'd-rather-be-kissing-Hugh."

She turned a page of her magazine. "Maybe. But at least I'm not sleeping with him."

"Now you're judging me for having sex?"

This time, when Michaela went to turn another page, she snapped it so hard it tore in half. "Shit," she said under her breath. Then she looked at me. "I'm not judging you for having sex. That's really not it. I'm judging you for having sex with *Handel*."

I sat up. "Handel loves me."

"So he says."

Bridget gasped. "Michaela!"

Now I got up, grabbing my bag and stuffing my shirt inside. "I don't need this today. Or any other day. You've had a problem with me and Handel from the very beginning, Michaela, and now it's turning into a problem I have with you." I grabbed my towel from the sand so quickly the sand flew up into the air and landed all over Michaela.

"Hey," she protested, turning over, brushing it off the side of her face, and shaking it from her hair.

It was so satisfying I almost smiled. "I'm leaving. See you, B."

Bridget's mouth was hanging open. She closed it. "Jane. Don't go."

"If it was just you, I'd stay. But certain people are making me feel unwelcome," I added, turning my back on Michaela to wave at Bridget before stalking off. To where, I wasn't sure. Definitely not toward Joey McCallen's stoop, though. I'd had enough unpleasant encounters for one day.

Or not.

I hadn't thought much about the direction I was taking when I left the beach, but for some reason my feet headed over to the rich side of town. I was there before I thought about it. I found myself entering that fancy coffee shop, the one where I'd met up with Handel when we were still hiding from his friends. It was empty except for that same girl who pronounced her syllables totally and completely working behind the counter.

And Logan—Miles's friend Logan. The one who hadn't taken an interest in any of us girls this summer. Or if he'd had an interest in Bridget, he'd lost that fight.

Logan glanced up from the table where he was eating a bagel. "Jane?"

"Hey," I said, going over to him. "I haven't seen you in a while. Or Miles," I added.

He took a sip of his iced coffee, then set it down again. Shrugged. "I'm the odd one out among you and your friends," he said, but not in a way that sounded bitter or angry. Just like he was stating the truth.

"But Miles isn't, either—"

Logan stopped me from finishing with a look that said *really,*

Jane? "He may not be dating one of you, but we all know he'd like to. And *who* he'd like to. As do you."

I studied the floor. "Yeah. I guess so."

Logan's eyes were on me. I could feel them. "He's a really great guy."

There was something about this big confident boy advocating for his friend that made me want to cry. "I know he is."

"You shouldn't have led him on. Miles would treat you like a queen if you went out with him."

I sighed. Guilty. "I know that, too."

"Then why don't you?"

My toes were nudging the leg of the table. I still couldn't bring myself to meet Logan's eyes. "Because I'm with someone else."

"Miles is better than that other guy."

"Not for me," I said, finally looking up at him. "I care about Miles. I do. But not in that way."

For the first time Logan lost his composure a bit, and scoffed. He was shaking his head, like I'd disgusted him. "You never gave Miles a chance."

Anger flared in me, as it had all day. I tried to tamp it down, but at this point I'd had too much of it. Too much anger and too much judgment from the people around me. "That's because he never had one. Miles is no match for Handel, and Miles knows it. *Logan.*" Logan sighed long and disapproving. I turned around and stalked out of the coffee shop without buying a thing. I could feel his disapproval hit my back and stay there, hovering around me, following me everywhere I went.

I couldn't shake it.

THIRTY-TWO

THAT EVENING, I WAITED for Handel to come in on his father's boat. I watched Mr. Johansen and his sons dealing with their catch for the day. Mr. Lorry and Old Man Boyd. I watched one of the Sweeney boys, the oldest one, chain-smoking cigarettes and looking out over the ocean like he had a lot to think about, and for a while I wondered what. Then I watched a few of my father's former colleagues doing their rounds along the wharf and to the docks and back, making sure they didn't see me. I watched Mrs. Lorry, too, shuffling along the boardwalk toward her husband with a paper bag of something that made his eyes light up when it and she arrived, then he bent down and kissed her sweetly.

But no Handel.

I thought he was working today.

He told me he was.

Had his plans simply changed like plans do sometimes?

Or worse: Had he lied?

The image of all that worry on Joey McCallen's face entered my mind without permission, and the judgment and scolding of everyone else tugged at the purity of all my happiness with Handel, tugged at it in this way that threatened to unravel it.

I took a deep breath, got ahold of myself, and shooed it away.

When the sun had drained entirely from the sky, I had to accept that Handel wasn't coming, at least not on a boat. I gave up waiting and started through town, first along the wharf, and then down Chestnut, thinking I'd take the long way home. It was a nice night. Or maybe I was thinking that if I went this route it would take me past all the street corners where Handel stood around with his friends and right near his house, too, close enough that I'd be able to see it at the other end of the block.

It wasn't long before my efforts were rewarded.

I heard voices and loud laughter a ways down the street. My head snapped in its direction and my heart leapt when I saw that familiar long dirty-blond hair, tangling like it always did in the summer breeze. Without hesitation I headed in Handel's direction. Relief and excitement mingled with a dash of doubt, my confusion about finding him here and not where he said he'd be pressing in on the certainty I'd come to have about him. These feelings and others stormed through me as I got closer, and with my new proximity I realized I was wrong, that the person with the long blond hair was slightly shorter than Handel, that I'd mistaken his older brother Colin for him. Out of the shadows emerged Cutter and Mac.

I halted in the middle of the street, right while I was crossing it.

Then I saw another head of long blond hair, a second one. Handel was with them. There came the raised voices, but this time I understood that it hadn't been laughter I was hearing, but fighting words and anger, shouting that those boys were trying to hold down. It was getting the best of them, though, and ringing through the streets.

I didn't know what to do. I didn't know what I was witnessing, but it left me cold. I stood there frozen, unsure if I should go forward or turn and go the other way.

They hadn't seen me. Not yet.

But then Cutter's eyes shifted, just a little. They didn't have to go far to land on me. His mouth moved, forming words I could not hear, and the rest of them turned around.

Handel, too.

And the scent, that scent of something rotten and sweet, wafted toward me in the breeze.

I thought I might collapse right there in front of all of them.

Could it be coming from Handel?

I was going to be sick.

"Jane," he called to me, and came jogging over.

The smell—it disappeared.

It wasn't Handel.

Of *course* it wasn't him.

"What are you doing here?" he asked me.

Everyone was staring at us.

"I'm walking through town," I said, not entirely friendly. Not entirely recovered. "What does it look like I'm doing?"

"Yeah. Of course." His eyes darted all over the place, like he was worried someone was watching, even though of course he knew more than a few someones were already doing just that.

"I waited for you down at the docks for over an hour," I told him.

"You did?" he asked, in this way that tried for nonchalance, like it was no big deal he'd told me he'd be one place and then I'd found him in another.

That's when I knew he was lying. "You obviously weren't there because you were here. I thought you were working today on the boat. I guess not?"

Handel sighed. Then he finally looked at me straight on. "My plans changed."

"I see that."

He glanced at his friends and his brother again. "Let's get out of here. Do you want to get out of here?"

I shrugged.

"Come on," he said, grabbing my hand and leading me away.

The pull of him was too strong for me to resist.

The second his fingers laced through mine, I nearly melted.

Handel led me right past Cutter and Colin and Mac, who weren't saying a single word, just eyeing us in that disbelieving way I'd seen from them on other days. I held my breath as long as I could. I didn't want to collapse beneath that smell again.

It wasn't long before Handel's house came into view. Handel was two steps ahead of me the whole time, my arm stretched taut. Just before we reached the edge of his front yard, I stopped short, as though I was about to go over the edge of a cliff. Handel tugged me forward at first, but I didn't budge, and then he came to a halt, too. Turned and looked at me. "What's wrong, Jane?"

My heart was hammering and not in a good way. "I don't know. You tell me."

He let go of my hand, went searching around his pocket, hovering over his pack of cigarettes. He was dying to smoke. He was nervous. "There's nothing to tell."

"I think you're lying. Don't lie to me, Handel."

He pulled out a cigarette and lit it. So he didn't have to look at me, I thought. He took a long drag. Blew out the smoke. "It's just family stuff."

"That wasn't just your family back there. Your friends, too."

"I was arguing with my brother."

"What about?"

"I can't say."

"Why not?"

He looked at me finally. He had that darkness in his eyes again. I hadn't seen it in a long time. "It's complicated."

"I can handle complicated. We've already gotten through complicated. Remember?"

"Jane, don't press me. I can't talk about this right now. It's long past talking about," he added. He was pleading.

"You can tell me anything," I said, my heart hammering harder. I was a little afraid of what Handel might say next. "I'm not going anywhere."

"You don't know that. You don't know what you're asking to hear."

"There's nothing you can say that would push me away. Not now." I took a step forward, stepped right off the cliff. Forced myself to look into Handel's eyes without fear or worry or doubt. "I love you."

Handel opened his mouth. He opened it, and I thought he was going to tell me whatever was on his mind, whatever it was that weighed him down, made him feel desperate and maybe even afraid. But then he closed it, without a word.

That's when I noticed his eyes were glassy.

There were tears pooling along their rims.

My heart just about broke.

Handel Davies, crying?

I couldn't let it happen. Just couldn't watch it happen.

So I went to him. I went to him and put my arms around

his waist and pressed my cheek into his chest. I did this until he bent his chin low and it came to rest on the top of my head and his arms wrapped around my back. We stayed there a long time. When he finally released me, without a word, we went into his empty house, empty of his mother and father and brothers, climbing the stairs to his room and locking the door behind us.

I didn't go home that night.

THIRTY-THREE

IT WAS EIGHT A.M. when I tiptoed through the porch door in the backyard. I was hoping and praying my mother was sleeping in.

Luck was not on my side.

"Jane!"

My mother's shout met me the second I entered the kitchen.

"Oh, Jane," she said again and got up from where she was sitting at the counter, pulling me into a hug, her arms tight around me.

Her cheeks were wet.

I leaned away, panicked. "Mom? What's wrong? Why are you crying?"

"Because I didn't know where you were!"

"Calm down," I said. "I'm right here, and I'm fine."

She took a step back from me. "Don't tell me to calm down." The relief that flooded her eyes when I walked through the door turned to anger. "I've been frantic! I've been up since three a.m. waiting for you to come home, telling myself you were probably fine, but honestly, Jane, you had me terrified. From now on you need to tell me where you go at all times!"

"I was at Handel's," I mumbled. Then I walked past her and went into the fridge. There was barely enough iced coffee to fill half a glass. "You drank it all? You could have left me some."

"Keep me informed and maybe they'll be some left," she snapped.

I looked at her. "What has gotten into you?"

"Sit. Sit down and I'll tell you."

There was something about her tone that scared me. I did what I was told and took my usual place on one side of the counter.

She took her place on the other. "The police called. Officer Connolly."

I swallowed. He'd finally gotten tired of trying me and went to my mother directly. "Yeah?"

My mother nodded. "That's why I've been up, Jane. He called wanting to make sure you were all right." She laid her hands flat on the counter and studied them a moment. Her nails were extra short, their polish chipped and worn away, casualties of her work. She looked up again. Took a deep breath to continue. "There was another break-in last night. The first once since . . ." She didn't finish. She didn't need to.

I gasped. It came out of me like a shriek. "Where?"

"Just over the border in Smallton. No one we know. Rich family. Big summer house."

I was nodding as she talked like this all made sense. "Was anybody . . ."

"There were no witnesses."

Still nodding. "Okay, okay."

"Officer Connolly wanted to make sure we found out from him before we saw it in the news." She eyed me. "He said he's been trying to reach you for weeks."

I blinked. Ignored that last bit. "So they have no idea who . . . ?"

My mother shook her head. She reached over and put a hand over mine. "Sweetie, what is going on? What are you thinking about? Tell me."

"That's why you were so worried when I came in," I stated.

"Yes."

"I was with Handel. I was safe with Handel."

"I know, honey. You said that. I just wish I'd known earlier so I didn't have to be so scared."

"Handel was with me," I said under my breath, taking in this fact. This reality. "All night."

"Jane?"

But I couldn't answer. Not just yet. I was trying to figure out for myself what was going on inside me, why a sense of relief so total and complete was washing through me, washing away all the doubt and insecurity and the tiny sneaking suspicion that had been rooting around in my heart. At the same time, my brain was telling me I should feel angry and upset and maybe even a little scared that the break-ins had started up again. That I'd get pulled into this mess of having to talk to the police and having to relive what happened just when I felt like I'd been moving on. Moving forward. Leaving it behind, little by little. The relief was bigger, though. Big like the waves during a storm, the kind that come in and take everything with them. Sand, shells, seaweed, leaving the beach clean of debris.

My mother squeezed my hand. "Jane?" she repeated.

I smiled. I felt exhilarated. Airy. Like I could do anything I wanted. Anything at all was possible.

"Why are you smiling?"

"I don't know," I said, but the thing is, I did. "Just nerves, I guess. My body not knowing how to react."

"You should give yourself some time to process this today, okay? We can talk more later. I'm just so relieved to see you. I'm so relieved you're all right."

"Hmmm," was all I responded.

My mind was elsewhere.

My mind was on Handel.

Handel, who'd been with me during the break-in.

That's when I knew. Somewhere deep and unspoken inside me, I'd been worried that maybe, just maybe, there was a connection between Handel and those break-ins, a connection between Handel and all the chaos and grief I'd been through. That the source of the darkness that would come into his eyes, that would wedge itself between us and hold us apart sometimes, was related to it. This tiny seed of suspicion had sprouted last night when I found out Handel had lied to me and when I saw him with his brother and those friends, arguing. Fighting. Sprouted and tangled itself around my insides, squeezing them until I almost couldn't breathe.

But now I knew the truth.

It couldn't have been him.

I laughed giddily. "I think I'm going to head to the beach," I told my mother, ignoring her confusion at my cheery reaction. I got up from the place where I'd been sitting. Twirled a lock of hair around my finger, distracted, skipping off to my room.

"I don't want you alone today," she said while I was changing clothes and gathering my beach things into my bag. I pulled my hair up into a ponytail and then headed back out, through our tiny kitchen–living room combo, well aware that my mother was watching me like I was acting stranger than ever. And maybe I was.

But I practically danced all the way down to the beach that morning.

I practically danced.

"I thought you'd be more upset, Jane," Bridget said when she showed up, bag resting at her side. She was the first one to arrive for the day.

I smiled at her, relaxed and basking in the sun. Baking like some bikini-clad girl-cake. "Maybe I will be later. But right now I feel fine."

"Well, that's . . . great," she said. "Weird but great. When I saw the news, my heart just fell through my body. I couldn't stop thinking about what you must be feeling, but here you are, perfectly okay."

"I am perfectly okay," I echoed.

Bridget set out her towel and sat down next to me. Gave me a wry look. "Does your mood have anything to do with Handel?"

My smile got bigger. "Maybe."

"You two are like rabbits."

"What about you and James?"

Bridget laughed. "Right. Not going to happen. Not anytime soon at least."

"No?"

"I'm not in love."

"You don't have to be."

"But I'd like to be. Besides, right now I'm just enjoying all the makeout sessions."

I rolled over onto my side and propped myself up on my elbow. "I think it's about time you spilled some details on that front."

Bridget lit up at this request. "I'd be more than happy to discuss James's unexpected, yet surprisingly appealing kissing techniques," she began, and we went on talking about this and a dozen other particulars, about all that had happened between her and James, analyzing it until we were satisfied to have looked at it from every possible angle.

Later on, when Michaela and Tammy arrived, at first they wanted to tiptoe around me, concerned I might be shattered from the events of last night. But all that relief from earlier was still buoying me, bobbing me around like I was floating on a little raft, allowing me to drift away from the darkness pressing in on me ever since February. I was more than willing to let it recede into the background.

Instead of break-ins and burglaries, we focused on boys.

Seamus and James and Hugh and Handel.

Just the way it should be when you're four girls sitting on the beach in the middle of a perfectly beautiful summer day. Just the way we'd always imagined it would be in our future, after the boys finally discovered we were worthy of their attention.

A dream come true.

THIRTY-FOUR

S THE AFTERNOON HEAT settled over us, I went home to change out of my bathing suit for once. Then I snuck off to Handel's house. I knew he was around today, and I couldn't wait until tonight to see him. I marched up to his front porch with all the confidence in the world, hips swaying in my short skirt, freed by the serendipitous coincidence of the night we spent together. I went straight inside the front door and up the stairs to his room.

"What's the matter?" I asked when I found him there, head in his hands, looking like the weight of the world was on him. I couldn't tell if he was staring into space or studying something on the desk where he sat.

He startled and turned around in his chair. "Jane," he said. Mustered a smile.

"Is anyone home? I didn't see your mother on my way up here."

"No," he said, reaching out his hand. "We're alone."

"Good," I said, taking it and pulling him to his feet. I led him over to the bed. Pressed my hands on his shoulders, signaling he should sit. "I bet I can make you forget whatever you're worried about." Now I pushed at his chest, tipping him backward.

He lay down and rested his head on a pillow. Eyes on me. "You always can."

I lay down next to him, and we watched each other a moment. I ran my fingers through his long hair. "That makes me happy," I said. "I'm so happy, Handel," I went on, and then drew him toward me until he was close enough to kiss.

There was a moment when he paused, when he pulled away, blinked, long pale lashes fluttering up toward the ceiling like he had something on his mind. Like he was hesitating. But then it passed, and he turned to me, turned back with a big grin, reached out and tickled me in that place on my stomach he knew would make me laugh and scream—laugh and scream in a way that would make everything light again. Playful and fun like it should be between us. Like it always should be between a guy and a girl who are in love like Handel and me. Eventually things cycled from playful to passionate and from passionate to romantic, which was right where I'd wanted them to go.

One by one, Handel popped open the buttons on my white eyelet blouse. I'd worn it on purpose, thought about Handel doing exactly this. Earlier, when I was getting dressed, I'd dug down deep into my drawer and pulled up the flimsy, lacy white bra and matching underwear that Bridget made me buy in the fall just in case I ever met someone special. After so much waiting I finally had; today was the day. I'd picked this bra and underwear since I knew Handel would see them, finally cutting the tags that still dangled from their delicate hems, trading my bathing suit for something that would tell Handel what I wanted, beyond any doubt.

Handel undid the last of the buttons and, gently, slid the two halves of my shirt aside, looking at me. Watching the slow rise and fall of my chest.

I was shaking.

I don't know why. We'd done this before. Many times.

All you could hear was our breathing.

"Pretty," he said, running a finger across all that lace. Then underneath it. "Did you wear this for me?"

A shiver ran through me. Even though my cheeks burned red, I laughed like he was being ridiculous and said, "You wish."

He smiled. Kissed a trail to my stomach, then back up to my neck.

And I sighed.

Today was turning out to be the best day.

I wanted more from Handel, just like always. It felt like my reward, to have *this*.

To have *him*.

I sat up a little, enough to slide my blouse over my shoulders and down my arms until I could pull it all the way off. Then it was Handel's turn to pull his shirt over his head and toss it aside, until it was my turn again, and Handel was reaching around my back, unhooking the clasp of my bra, and it was falling away. Next was my skirt, and I was naked except for my underwear, lying on top of Handel's sheets, pressed up against him, our legs intertwined. We'd spent a few weeks practicing these steps, this slow undressing, until it was a regular part of the time we were alone and kissing, whether it was down on the beach at night, or on his boat by the docks, or here at his house in his room when no one else was home.

Like now.

One thing I'd learned this summer: There was nothing like lying in bed, making out, clothes coming off piece by piece, unhurried and unworried about the time, with the boy you love.

And I loved Handel Davies.

Without a doubt, I loved him.

"I love you, Jane," Handel whispered in my ear as though he'd heard my thoughts, his fingers light on my bare skin.

Giving me chills.

We spent the next hour resisting, wanting, whispering, kissing, waiting for that moment when Handel would hook his fingers into the elastic of my underwear, slowly sliding it down over my thighs, my knees, my ankles, until it slipped over the tips of my toes. Until all I wore was the tiny heart on a chain around my neck. Then it was Handel's jeans and everything else getting tossed to the floor, the two of us panting, trying to catch our breath. We both knew these steps would happen, too; we knew it the second I walked into his room.

We pressed ourselves against each other.

When the moment finally arrived, my heart sped up, and everything seemed lit from the inside, him and me, so much skin touching and hands everywhere, gently but urgently. Each time we did this, it got better, if you could believe it. It really did.

There was nothing like being with Handel.

Nothing.

My cheeks flared a little afterward, when we were lying there in the quiet, catching our breath.

I turned to him. Took in the way the sunlight sent rays of light across his hair. Tried to suppress a smile. "Bridget said we're like rabbits."

Handel propped his head on his hand, studying me, a mock-serious expression on his face. "You do look a bit like a rabbit now that I think about it."

"Shut up. You know what she meant."

"My Jane rabbit," he went on, playful.

"You're making me bad, and I like it," I told him, sitting up a bit, my eyes seeking the pile of clothes all over his floor. The sheet slid to the middle of my stomach, but I didn't care. I liked having Handel's eyes on me, on my body, all over me. I relished it. I wanted him to look. To see me. See the way the tiny blue heart hovered against the skin of my neck.

"Bad?" he murmured with a smile. "You could never be bad, Jane. Not all the way through."

I rolled my eyes. "I'm always stuck playing the role of good girl," I said with a pout, even though I knew this was no longer true. The break-in had changed me. No—Handel had changed me. "I can't seem to get away from it," I went on, all flirty and forward. I pulled him on top of me again. Smiled. "Not even with you."

Handel laughed. Dipped his head until his lips were on my skin. Hands along my curves.

I closed my eyes, smiling.

When his mouth reached my ear, he spoke. "I wouldn't exactly call you that," he whispered softly. "The good girl?" he added with another laugh, while something clicked inside me, finally fell into place after all this time.

Two words, *good girl,* lifting up a memory from the darkest recesses of my mind, fishing it out from the place it was hidden, the worst memory of all.

And my eyes flew open.

THIRTY-FIVE

I DIDN'T SAY ANYTHING.

Not right then. I couldn't.

It was *impossible*. I was wrong.

All the blood in my body went cold.

Handel lifted his head. "I'm going to get a glass of water." He smiled at me, eyes full of tenderness. "Do you want any?"

I shook my head no. I couldn't speak.

Even then I didn't believe it.

It wasn't until Handel got up and left his room that I jolted myself out of the horror that held me frozen, tangled in his sheets. And it wasn't until I got out of his bed, unsure what to do, looking around frantically, at the drawers and the closet, the pile of clothes draped over a chair, at the small mirror hanging on the wall, all the while my lungs unable to get air, that I saw it.

My necklace.

The other one—the original. My seventeenth-birthday present from my mother. Broken. *Sliced*. Lost the night of the break-in. Carefully curled up in a little jar on Handel's desk. Like some keepsake.

My boyfriend, the one I was in love with, *Handel Davies,* was holding on to memories from the worst night of my life. He had them. Held them. All along he'd been doing this. All summer long.

The necklace was right there, staring up at me, the tiny heart in so many shades of blue—similar to the one I wore now, but different all the same. It was almost in plain sight, so obvious that

I wondered if it was left there—if Handel had left it there—on purpose. Because he'd wanted me to find it. Because he'd wanted me to know, to *finally* know the truth.

He wanted me to see him for who he really was.

And I knew, I knew right then, I mean, how could I not? It had been Handel that night, whispering in my ear, telling me to be a good girl, trying to keep me calm, after his friend Cutter sliced that knife across my neck, his friend that smelled of sweet mixed with rot. It had been Handel witnessing those moments in which the Jane I'd once been was shattered for good, the same boy who would kiss me so tenderly, with so much love and passion and desire that I'd believed he could put the pieces back together and make me whole again.

I picked up the broken necklace.

Watched as it dangled from my fingers, swaying so gently through the air.

Looked from one mosaic blue heart to the other that rested against my chest.

There were footsteps on the stairs. *Thump, thump, thump.*

Coming toward me.

It was in this moment that Handel returned, that he walked into his room and saw me standing there, hypnotized by the seemingly innocent swing of the necklace in my hands, of the heart at the end of it. My heart. The one that told a story I didn't want to believe.

"Jane," he stated.

Just like that.

Nothing else. Only my name.

My name for the first time now that everything would be

different, now that there was no going back to the time of be-fore—there would *never* be a going back to that before. My name, because, really, what else could Handel say?

"It was you," I said to him, and I could feel the heart inside my chest breaking apart as we looked at each other, stared at each other with new eyes. Falling to pieces and disintegrating into a pile of dry heart dust. "It was you all along. You and Cutter, and if I had to guess who else, your brother."

Tears ran down Handel's face. "Jane, please. I can explain."

But I was already hardening myself. Turning myself to stone. "No," I said. "No, you can't." I grabbed my clothes from the floor, stepping into my skirt and throwing on my blouse. Fum-bling and stumbling as I buttoned everything up. "It's too late for that," I said.

Then I walked out of Handel's room. I walked right by him, careful not to let any part of me touch any part of him. Slowly, carefully, I made my way down the stairs.

"Jane," I heard him say from above, just as my shaking hand was reaching for the knob on the door to the outside.

My name from his lips for the last time, I thought to myself then.

I would make sure of it.

I ran from the house. I ran and ran and then I ran some more.

When I finally slowed, I saw that I'd made it all the way to the next town. Somehow this was soothing. A relief to be out of *my* town. The town where I was no longer safe. The place where I thought people took care of one another, where I thought peo-ple looked out for one another. Where everyone knew everyone else, where kids still played hide-and-seek at night, and where we all held the beach so sacred in our hearts.

Idyllic. As though from another era.

I laughed out loud, a hysterical sort of laugh.

Who had I been kidding all this time?

A man out walking his dog took one look at me and then crossed to the other side of the street.

This only made me laugh harder.

Was I too frightening to see?

I went straight to the center of this town, this town that was not mine. I didn't have my purse because I'd left my bag at Handel's, and I didn't have any money in my pockets, either, but that didn't stop me from going in and out of stores.

I stole something.

I stole it from the drugstore. A bottle of dark blue nail polish. I studied it while I sat on a bench down the block.

Now I've got something in common with Handel.

I'm a thief.

I started to cry.

It was the crying that finally sent me headed home. I couldn't seem to stop once I started. All day I'd been blindly going about, laughing and talking to myself like some crazy girl, like nothing bad had happened. Nothing horrible and awful and utterly unspeakable. I hadn't shed a tear.

But when the tears came, they came with the force of a storm.

Sobs choked my throat when I arrived at my destination. By then it was getting dark. I don't know how many hours had passed between leaving Handel's and coming back here. It wasn't my house where I went, either, or Bridget's or even Tammy's. I surprised even myself when I realized where I was headed, but when I did, I knew it was the right place to go.

Michaela was sitting on her front steps when I got there.

Sitting in the dark, her long dark hair falling all around her. She looked up.

"Jane," she said, a mixture of relief and expectation, like somehow she'd already known I was on my way.

I sat down next to her on the stoop and curled into a ball.

She put her arms around me.

When I finally caught my breath, when the sobs slowed enough that I could speak, I said, "I have something to tell you, Michaela. You were right. You were right about him all along." I held out my hand, my fingers balled tight into a fist. Opened it to reveal the necklace I'd found in Handel's room.

She stared at the broken heart chain lying along my skin. Then looked up at me. There wasn't triumph or smugness in her eyes. Just sadness. Sadness and I think some shock. "I know, Jane."

I inhaled sharply. Closed my hand, pushing the necklace deep into the pocket of my skirt. "You know? What do you know?"

She shifted her gaze. Watched as an ant carried a crumb three times its size along the cement toward the grass. "Handel went to the police."

This, I wasn't expecting. I straightened up, my back like a rod. "He what?"

"He told them everything. The police have been looking for you. Everyone has been out looking for you. My dad. The O'Connors. Seamus and Bridget and Tammy. Your mother is worried sick. We've all been worried. My father wants to speak to you."

"Your father?"

She nodded. "He wants to make sure you're all right. He wants to take your statement."

All the air deflated out of me. My body caved into a C, my shoulders meeting my knees.

"Come on," she said. "We'll go together. Bridget and Tammy and Seamus and your mother and anyone else you want will go with you. You're not alone, Jane. You never were."

"I am, though," I whispered, my throat hoarse. It hurt to speak. It hurt to breathe. Everything about me hurt and Handel was responsible. It seemed impossible, but I knew it was the truth. "It's my fault that I'm alone. I did this to myself. You warned me so many times."

"But, Jane, I didn't know. No one did."

I laughed, the taste sour in my mouth. "Obviously. Me, least of all."

"Don't blame yourself." Her eyes flickered away, somewhere off in the distance, before settling on me again. Michaela seemed like she was hesitating. She took a deep breath. "There's something else you should know. About Handel."

I nodded. Braced myself for more terrible news. A bird flew over our heads. A sparrow. It landed in the small plot of grass in front of Michaela's house, and my eyes went to it. Stayed and watched it prance around in all that lush green.

"Handel was there that night," Michaela said carefully. "But he wasn't there originally. He wasn't part of the plan for the break-in."

A tiny sliver of hope pierced my heart. I tore my eyes from the sparrow. "No?"

Michaela shook her head. "That's what he said."

The sliver in my heart grew and expanded, the hope painful and sharp, like it was prying me apart. "What else did he say?"

Michaela reached out and plucked one of the daisies from the pot brimming with them on the porch. She stared at its delicate white petals. "He said he only went to the house to try to keep you safe from his brother and his friends, that he went because he wanted to save you, that he tried to save your father. That it all went wrong, that you and he were both in the wrong place at the wrong time, and your father most of all."

Michaela offered me the flower then, and I took it. "Do you think he was telling the truth?" I asked.

"I don't know, Jane. I think that question you'll need to ask him."

The hope left me then, vacating my heart, the thought of facing Handel after he'd lied all summer long, keeping everything he knew from me, seemed impossible. No amount of him being in the wrong place at the wrong time could surmount this. Nothing would change what he failed to say all those days and nights we spent together. He'd wasted that chance.

Wasted our chance.

"Jane?" Michaela's voice brought me back from my thoughts. Her eyes were on the daisy.

Its stem was twisted around my fingers, threaded through them, crushed. I untangled it and set it aside on the wooden slats of the porch. It lay there, limp and dying. "I don't want to ask Handel anything right now. I don't know if I ever want to see him again," I added, though I knew this wasn't true.

I wiped my face with the back of my hand. Found the strength to stand. Michaela got up, and she held out her arm for me to take. I leaned on her because I needed to. I leaned on her because I could. But I leaned on her, too, because she was my friend and I could trust her all the way through, and this I needed most of all. Michaela was good all the way through, even if I no longer was. We walked down to the wharf, to the place where my father once worked, to the place where everyone was waiting for me, together.

ONE MONTH LATER

I SAW HIM BEFORE he saw me.

Handel sat at a long brown table, the kind they have in the school cafeteria for lunchtime. His eyes were downcast, and there were dark circles underneath. He'd cut his hair. Gone was the long mane that was always twisting in the breeze, that he was always brushing away from his face and that I'd loved to run my fingers through. It was so short now, he looked younger than before, almost boyish.

Almost innocent.

The guard led me into the empty gray room, the light dull except for a small window high up in the back corner. He left me there. Turned around and went to stand by the door.

Right then Handel looked up and saw me. His eyes went wide.

"Jane," he said quietly, but the pain in his voice was clear.

I went to him.

I sat down on the other side of the table, facing him for the first time since I'd fled his room on that awful day that had at first been wonderful. By the time I looked into those familiar dark eyes, the ones I knew could hold me like no other boy in this world, I'd turned my heart totally and fully to stone.

What else could I have done?

Handel pressed his hands flat into the table's surface, pale skin against all that ugly brown. "I've come here every single day," he said. "Hoping that one time I'd see you walk through that door, wanting to talk to me."

I blinked. I couldn't speak.

It was probably better this way. For now.

"I've missed you," he whispered, his voice hoarse. "You're all I can think about."

I wondered if he might cry. He *should* cry.

I certainly wanted to.

The guard shifted behind us, the faint step of one shoe, the hard rustle of stiff fabric.

Handel glanced at him over my shoulder. "It's almost killed me not to see you, not to have the chance to explain."

"Explain?" I said, the word like a punch coming out of me. It filled the dim gray room, exploding through the stuffy air. "How could you ever explain?" I asked, but even through the anger I could hear the pleading in my words. I wanted Handel to convince me I wasn't wrong about him—that I'd never been wrong about him. More than this, that I hadn't been wrong about us.

Handel stayed steady. His eyes didn't leave me. "You don't know the whole story."

I drank in his stare, though I tried not to. I'd missed how he looked at me, like I was the only thing in life that mattered. "I know enough," I told him. "I know the important parts. I know that you lied. You lied all summer," I added, as if he didn't know this already—as if it needed to be repeated. "You had all summer to explain to me, and you chose not to."

"I wasn't supposed to be there that night, Jane. I wasn't going to be."

I looked away then. Stared at the only ray of light cutting across the room, tiny particles of dust floating in it, glowing like phosphorescence in dark waters. "So I heard." I kept my voice even. "If it wasn't supposed to be you, then why are you in here?" I asked, my eyes darting all around this dank visiting room. Everywhere but Handel.

"Because I should have gone to the police earlier. Because I knew the whole time and didn't say anything. Because I deserve to be punished," he added, his voice thick with remorse.

"You do," I said quietly, my eyes on the wall.

"Jane," Handel said. My name again, but I didn't turn back to him. "I only went when I was called and only then to try and keep you safe."

This made me laugh. I could taste the bitterness in it. "A lot of good that did my father."

"Jane—"

"What, Handel?" I asked, my eyes on him now. It was all I could do not to stand over him and scream. "What could you possibly say to make this right? Maybe it's true what you claim, and you went to the O'Connors' that night to try to fix a break-in gone wrong, but it doesn't change what you did afterward. Was I just some sick game to you and your friends? To you and that Cutter? For you and your *brothers*? Some fucked-up fantasy you needed to fulfill? Get the girl you held hostage to fall in love with you? To sleep with you, too? Did you report to them what I was like in bed?" It was there that I stopped.

"No."

"That's all? Just 'no'?"

The way Handel watched me now, with more love in his eyes

than I had ever seen—love and vulnerability and strength, too—
it radiated out from him, a light in the fog of this room. I had
to turn away. My heart, it was softening. Despite everything,
it was. I could feel it. Handel could still do that to me. Take my
heart and mold it however he'd like. I could make him into a
lying monster if I didn't see him, but now that he was here before
me, the monster disappeared, and all that was left was the boy
I loved who obviously still loved me back. Who—somewhere
deep inside—I knew had never meant to hurt me.

"I didn't plan to fall in love with you," Handel said, as though
he'd read my mind, like always, like nothing had changed and
instead of this visit happening in a detention center, we were in
his room in his bed, lying across his sheets.

"You want to talk about love," I said. "Here?"

"I do love you."

This made me wince.

"I didn't plan any of this," he went on.

I kept my eyes lowered; I wanted my heart to solidify, a tiny
iceberg drifting at my center. But I made the mistake of staring
at Handel's hands, and all I could think about then were his fingertips on my skin. "Well, what did you plan, then?" I managed.
"How was it that you ended up dating the girl you held hostage?"

"I just . . . I needed to find out what you knew. If you knew
anything at all. If you could identify them. Us," he corrected.
"They were afraid you would figure out who they were and go
to the police. They were going to kill you before you could. I
told them I would take care of . . . the situation. I wanted to keep
you safe."

My gaze rose to his face—I couldn't help it. "Right. So that's why you talked to me that first day on the beach. It wasn't because you thought I was beautiful or because I caught your attention. You planned our encounter. You wanted to know if I'd recognize your voice."

He didn't say anything. He didn't say yes, but he didn't say no, either.

I didn't, either.

Then all he said was, "Can you ever forgive me?"

My knuckles were white from the way they'd balled so tight into fists. It hurt to breathe. "No," I whispered. "Never," I said, even though this was a lie. With time I could forgive him. With time I might.

Handel inhaled sharply. The room was so still. So silent.

"You broke my heart," I said, realizing that even now, even after finding out the truth, Handel still had the power to undo me, to see right through everything, my clothes, my skin, my heart, leaving me exposed and raw and vulnerable. I was sure, too, certain beyond a shadow of a doubt, that even now the only thing Handel wanted was to love me fiercely and gently until I was whole again. That in loving me this summer, he'd handed over so much power to me, freely and openly, in such a way that I was stronger now, stronger and more confident, despite everything else.

True love will do that to you.

And this part, the love we'd shared that was truer than anything I'd ever known—that I couldn't regret. I could never. And I wouldn't.

Handel placed his palms flat against the table, his fingers spread wide. "You said before that the first time I spoke to you wasn't because I thought you were beautiful or because you'd just caught my attention—but you're wrong," he said. "I'd seen you at school and had always thought you were beautiful. There was something about you that made me look twice, that made me want to talk to you, Jane." He turned away a moment, his profile sharp. Then he went on. "I loved you from the moment I saw you in that window at the professor's house, even before I went inside. I loved you even if I didn't know it then. I think I've loved you all along." Handel's eyes were glassy with tears, the second time I'd seen them this way. "I probably always will."

"I don't care," I said, the words choking me.

I said this, but it wasn't true.

I'd probably always love Handel, too, no matter how hard I tried not to. But this I didn't say to him. How could I?

Instead, I said: "I hate you."

Because this was true, too.

Sometimes love and hate can be so closely intertwined that you can't tell them apart. So close they can even become one and the same. "Please don't hate me. Please. Jane?"

I looked at him one last time. "What, Handel?"

"Even if you hate me, I won't stop loving you."

As he hung his head, waiting for some sign of hope from me, any sign that I might someday forgive him, that our love was powerful enough to overcome all of this—I realized something so clearly.

It was my turn to break Handel's heart.

Maybe not forever.

But, at the very least, for now.

Sometimes love was like that, too. It was violent and it was reckless, and it was tender and soulful. And there were times when love didn't play fair, not at all, not even a little, and this was one of them.

"I have to go now," I told Handel, and then the two of us looked away from each other and didn't look back.

I didn't at least.

Not me.

Bridget looked up. "Jane?"

Tammy and Michaela turned to me.

My girls were waiting there on the steps of the detention center. Waiting for me to come out after my visit.

Miles had offered to be here, too, just like he'd been offering all sorts of things over this last month of summer. To take me to the movies, to dinner, to get ice cream, to meet his family for a barbecue, to take a drive in his mother's Mercedes that purred so softly you almost forgot you were in a car. I hadn't said yes to any of it, not at first, but then I started to.

But not today.

"Jane?" Michaela said this time, her arm outstretched.

I went to them—my girls. They folded me into a hug.

We stood there for a long while, the four of us. Together.

When we pulled back, Bridget took my hand. Squeezed it. "Do you think you'll ever forgive him?"

I was silent for a long time. My girls seemed to stop breathing as they waited for my answer. "I don't know," I said. "But some-day I might want to. I still love him," I added, these last three words lodged tight in my throat like stones.

"No one is going to judge you for it," Bridget said, squeezing my hand harder. "Not us, at least."

"Not even me," Michaela said softly.

"Did you tell Handel you feel that way?" Tammy asked.

I shook my head. "No," I said. "It's not the right time. Not yet. Maybe someday."

Bridget's eyes were glassy with tears. "There's no rush. None at all."

I sighed long and heavy, as though by letting out this rush of air I might be letting go of all the heaviness I'd been carrying around these last months.

"Let's go down to the beach," I said eventually.

Tammy's smile was sad. "It's the perfect day for a swim."

We started to walk, the four of us, straight into the sun, to-ward that place I always went when I needed comfort, when I needed to feel better. When I needed to think, and when I needed to stop thinking, too.

Today it was all of the above.

On our way there, as the sounds of the surf got closer, the waves crashing in that uneven yet familiar rhythm, I thought about the Jane I'd become these last few months, the many dif-ferent Janes I'd been this past year. And the Jane I was right now, too, this very minute, which was a different Jane still.

I was no longer the good girl I used to be. Definitely not her. That girl was gone. I wasn't sure what Jane I was becoming at this moment, though, as we walked along the sea wall to the wooden stairwell that led down to the beach. Maybe a mixture of all the others, or maybe an entirely new one, a girl who would surprise me. One that was strong enough to handle anything. One that was good, too, but a different kind of good this time, a kind I'd yet to discover and appreciate.

Or maybe that's the girl I was already.

Either way, it was okay. I was willing to wait for that Jane. I knew she was there. I was sure of it. I could feel her stirring, even as I took my flip-flops off, letting them dangle in my hand, and made my way, slowly and carefully, down the steps, one by one, my toes curling around their edges. Hanging on. Making sure I didn't fall or stumble.

I reached the bottom, whole and upright and strong.

I took a deep breath, inhaling the salty tang in the air. Looked into the eyes of my girls. Bridget, Tammy, Michaela. Knowing with my whole heart that, boys or no, with them in my life, I would always be loved.

Then I set my bare feet onto the sand.

ACKNOWLEDGMENTS

JILL SANTOPOLO, wonderful editor and friend, believer in this novel's possibilities and future, I thank you for your guidance, your gentle prodding, and your talent for knowing how to shape this story into what it needed to be. I am grateful to have you as an editor and also just overall in my life! To everyone at Philomel for welcoming me into their publishing home, especially Michael Green and Talia Benamy. To all those at Penguin who have been involved in the production of this book, thank you for the care you've taken with it as you send it out into the world.

Carlene Bauer, Marie Rutkoski, and Daphne Grab all read drafts of this story at different points in its life. I am grateful to you for your feedback, ideas, and, most of all, your continued encouragement and friendship, especially over the last several years.

I feel confident in saying that Miriam Altshuler is the best agent in the whole wide world. I am so lucky to have you in my corner, Miriam. I think we just passed our tin anniversary. Thank you for your continued encouragement, feedback, and tireless cheerleading of my career, and your friendship most of all. I am grateful, too, to Reiko Davis at MA Literary for her support of this novel, willingness to read, offer feedback, and meet for brunch.

To Daniel Matus, for everything you are in my life.

Whenever I start a new novel, I realize that my heart seems to permanently reside along the beaches and towns of Rhode Island, where I grew up. I am grateful to this place and all those people who've inspired the various stories I've set there.